Weird Horror Tales

WRITTEN BY MICHAEL VANCE
ILLUSTRATED BY EARL GEIER

AIRSHIP 27 PRODUCTIONS

An Airship 27 Production
www.airship27.com
www.airship27hangar.com

Interior illustrations © 2010 Earl Geier
Cover illustration © 2010 Christophe Dessaigne

Editor: Ron Fortier
Associate Editor: John C. Bruening
Production and design by Rob Davis
Marketing & promotion by Michael Vance

ISBN-13: 978-0615889047
ISBN-10: 0615889042

Printed in the United States of America

10 9 8 7 6 5 4 3 2 1

Weird Horror Tales
The Feasting

Contents

In the Beginning

Lyrics by Schlomo Nantier

In the beginning, before the light
Before the burning, borning sight
Before the bursting of the fleshy ball
I had it all

God save this child, spare the bubble
Turn back your hand, save the trouble
God save this child, set him free
God spare the child, please kill me

In the beginning, before the pain
Before the murky, spreading stain
Before the bursting of the final wall
I had it all

God save this child, spare the bubble
Turn back your hand, save the trouble
God save this child, set him free
God spare the child, please kill me

Down In The Mouth

The bleached, white bones lay scattered in the dust, the evidence of sudden and seemingly random violence and death. The priest frowned at the damning, irrefutable and canny evidence of his own mortality, and then ignored them in passive defiance. He walked on with the determined stride of a man with a mission down in the mouth of an almost indiscernible valley under a sky of cerulean blue. The air was fresh and alive with the subtle smells of spring, of blueberry, whorled pogonia, and fringed orchids, and of red and white spruce, balsam fir, white and red pine, and eastern hemlock. It was the first day of the celebration of liberation, the Feast of Unleavened Bread, in 1698.

Father Louis Maske walked briskly along the northeast edge of an isolated, small field of stunted, diseased maize, singing the canticle "Te Deum" to glorify the Lord of all physical and metaphysical Creation, more from routine than from faith, life experience, or long, theological study. It was thirty-nine years after Caleb Elliott and Ezekiel Azreal were eaten by the great white worm with teeth by the nearby bay on the coast of what would become Maine, and seven years since Maske's first nagging doubt.

Tall and lean and filled with the same athletic vitality that seemed to infuse the summer day, he had traveled from the abbey in Ndakinna, the land of the maritime Abenakis Indians that lay between the St. Croix and St. John's River valleys, the eventual border between Maine and New Brunswick. As he walked, he unconsciously stroked the small wooden cross on a leather thong that hung around his neck.

Singing in his native French, the clear sound of Maske's exuberant

2

"Holy, Holy, Holy, Lord God of Hosts!" carried far in the cool air as an unseen mourning dove cooed forlornly like a muffled sigh. Behind the Jesuit priest, the yellow sun hung on the edge of the sky, one-fourth below the somber trees on the west side of the Memphremagog forest. The ancient stand of trees skirted the field of maize except where it was interrupted by the Gihon river to the north, where Maske had earlier stripped off his wool robe, a vest of interior pockets, and cotton breechclout, to ford its chilly waters. Above those trees, a thin line of sullen clouds stretched from horizon to horizon.

Fifteen summers had come and fourteen gone for the round faced Abenakis Indian named Quamis who stood at the southeast edge of the field who was rubbing an ear of maize in the heel of the palm of his left hand with his right. He wore the common dress of his people, a belt of bark supporting a breech cloth concealing his groin. When he saw the priest approach, the half-eaten ear was dropped, forgotten. He raised his muscular arms and began waving both above his bare head, and broke into a halting trot towards the priest that became a full gallop.

"My son! My son!" Father Maske called out in Quamis' tongue, and raised his own arms as he quickened his pace.

But the priest's arms, now lowered in anticipated embrace, were met with Quamis' hard palms on his chest, pushing him unintentionally and momentarily back on the heels of his worn sandals.

"It is not 'your son'; it is Quamis," hissed the Indian from a nut brown face alive with fear and confusion. "Don't you remember? I am the son of Metacom called Azreal, and of Yellow Dove, now the whore of Metacom's twin, Hiram Azreal, who shames and dishonors my father."

"But Quamis, I didn't mean you are literally my–" The priest's thought was broken as he saw no glimmer of comprehension of simile or metaphor or even synonym, or of anything outside of the grinding, mundane reality of his life, in the brown eyes of the Indian.

"Hush hush" said Quamis, glancing furtively about. "Lower your voice, Father. I have come to warn you. You must turn and flee, now, right now!"

"Why? I've always been welcomed by your people, and I sent a message I was coming through Hiram Azreal's trading post."

"Father Maske," hissed Quamis, "you must listen to me. Odzihozo, the White Worm with spider's legs and gnashing teeth has taken the form of man and waits, hungry for blood."

"But, my brother," Maske answered with patient disbelief, and ran a hand through the brown fringe of hair that circled his tonsure. "I thought you believed."

The Jesuit priest smelled the tang of fear on the only member of the shameful, ostracized tribe who had accepted his Lord.

"Oh, Father, I do believe. But my people lay our finest furs and eagle feathers at the westus where Odzihozo swallows people whole, starting at the head like a snake. He breaks their bones as he eats them, Father Maske, and Sachem Madockawando is going to sacrifice you to him! You must run now, now, now!"

"How do you know this?" asked Maske, shaking his head in frustration because he knew Quamis believed in one God, Jehovah, and Odzihozo as if the two contradictory beliefs were not incongruous; as if one added to one equaled three.

"When I was passing his teepee, I overheard Madockawando say to the tribe's elders that the 'Christian fool' would be sacrificed to Odzihozo."

"Have you seen this Odzihozo with your own eyes?"

"No, Father; I have only heard."

"You have heard, Quamis?" asked Maske, with a sparkle in his hazel eyes. "What did you hear?"

"I overheard Madockawando say to the Old Men that the 'Christian fool' would be fed to Odzihozo tomorrow," repeated the young boy, frantically pushing against Maske's chest with short, powerful jabs of his calloused palms. As he spoke, the priest watched five Abenakis rise behind the boy and whisper out from the stunted corn. One in a ruined headdress scowled from a face of cracked, dry parchment, poached eyes, and a frown that seemed to touch the edges of his jaw

"Bind the useless dreamer," he commanded.

Quamis startled at the sound of the barked order and turned his head, but too late; both of his forearms had been jerked behind his back by two of the five Indians, one carrying leather thongs in a hand.

"What is the meaning of this?" demanded the priest. "Sachem!"

Madockawando ignored Maske, his jaw moving up and down like a cow chewing its cud. The pungent, fetid smell of Asafoetida hung around him in an invisible cloud. He pointed to an Abenakis with his head lowered in submission or fear or simply indifference to life, and said, "Go, run, and tell the others to prepare the feasting; the sacrifice is found. Tell them to go to the westus and prepare for us there.'"

"S-so I am the Christian fool," stuttered Quamis in an incredulous whisper. "F-Father Maske, don't l-let them kill me."

"Don't despair, Quamis. Trust in God. I will find your father. Surely he will help you."

"That," said Quamis, his eyes welling with tears and nodding his head to indicate the man nearest the Sachem, "is my father."

"I demand you release him," barked Maske. "Now! This is an outrage."

"So it seems," said Madockawando, touching the canker sore on his upper lip. "But the asquutasquash is not your concern. Your business is pond scum and frog's warts, godman."

"What means 'asquutasquash'?" asked Maske of the boy as one of the Indians pushed Quamis into a stumbling trot.

"It is f-from the Narragansett, F-father. It means 'that which is eaten raw'."

The horizon was muffled by sullen clouds and the air was disturbed with a drowsy, deep-throated rumbling as two of the Sachem's men with Maske and Quamis came down from the maize to the Abenakis hovel of two dozen or so squalid, bark-covered wigwams on the south bank of the Gihon river. They entered the encampment just as the last yellow sliver of sun sank beneath the horizon, and Macdockawando and one other could still be seen behind them in the distance.

The Indians who called themselves Alnanbal, or "men," but were named by the Algonquin Indians as Abenakis, or "the people of the dawn," came down in silence to the shameful hovel of conical shaped wigwams like bottoms-up wooden bowls. Maske knew before he'd even traveled to the New World that they had not always lived so.

Soon after explorer Sebastian Cabot's voyage in 1497, European ships had traveled to America's eastern seaboard, drawn by the story of a fabulous Indian kingdom of gold. Although never found, their search led to profitable fur trading and English and French outposts.

The first British exposure to the Abenakis was in 1607 when the Plymouth Company tried and failed to establish themselves on the Kennebec River. Maske had learned as a boy how his people had discovered a higher quality fur in the St. Lawrence Valley, and abandoned their first outposts to escape costly English raids. By 1616, only Port Royal and a tiny trading post on the Penobscot River remained where Abenakis could trade their furs. By 1621, the Abenakis could still visit the Plymouth colony and greet an Englishman, but the relationship had already become strained because the Abenakis were trading furs with the French.

Then for a half-century, the central body of Abenakis watched, dumbfounded, as the English and French fought over who owned their land.

By 1649, a nasty cancer had grown among the Abenakis, a twenty-one year old bastard possessed by "the spirit of depravity" named Macdockawando. Because of his unspeakable, dirty perversions, blatant theft, adultery, and drunken and bizarre rituals, a dozen of his aberrant followers had been murdered in two years. Then Macdockawando and his tiny clan of devil worshippers had been banished by his own people to an uninhabited and forbidden part of the coast.

Maske mulled over Macdockawando as he, the Sachem's men, and Quamis arrived at the north prong of a horseshoe of befouled, twelve-foot circular wigwams covered with bark, animal skins and mats woven of corn stalks. The subtle, unclean smell of refuse and human waste hung in the air.

As the guards argued over their orders, Maske watched two bloated, middle-aged women in patched and frayed animal skins decorated with shells, bones, and beads. Their black hair, braided into pigtails behind each ear, was dirty and matted. They cooked at small fires under clay pots at the mouths of their wigwams with an implacable surrender to the inextricable, grinding, repetitive acts of life.

Above them, half of the western sky was now a slow moil of sullen, gray clouds; below their bare feet, the hard-packed earth, beaten naked of grass and weeds, was littered with the unclean refuse of a people for whom life had lost any meaning other than of continuance accomplished by the unremitting, mundane acts of hunting, gathering and preparing that which sustained them.

In the center of the horseshoe of filthy wigwams behind the bloated women stood a newly built westus: two elongated, connected domes that looked like an abscessed mound of earth upturned over a septic grave.

One of the gaunt Indians pushed Maske to their left to the mouth of a wigwam. Maske opened its flap and stood in the entrance as his eyes adjusted to the gloom. Inside, he could discern the ashes of a dead fire whose smoke was meant to rise through a hole in the center of the roof, and the wooden benches covered by woven grass mats and animal skins set like couches against its circular walls. He genuflected, entered the half-light of the wigwam, and fell to his knees in fervent prayer for Quamis' release, for an epiphany for damned Madockawando and his blasphemous tribe, and for his own wavering faith.

"I believe," he said out loud. "Forgive my unbelief. Amen." With this, he rose, removed his vest, lay it carefully on the wigwam's bench, and then sat down by it. He placed his elbows on his thighs and hid his face in the palms of his hands, suddenly overwhelmed by a heartbreaking sadness and longing to gather into his arms this dirty, selfish, blind people, to whisper that they were loved, and that life was more than fear and pain and isolation, and his eyes welled with tears as his hands shook.

When he looked up, the Sachem stood backlit in the mouth of the wigwam, a leather bag in his hands, his jaw moving slowly up and down like a cow chewing its cud. The smell of Asafoetida preceded him.

Holding the end corners of the bag, Madockawando flung its contents onto the floor at Maske's feet. The bones lay scattered on the packed earth, the evidence of seemingly random death and violence.

"These are the bones of Odzihozo's sacrifices and they say that death will visit soon. They say that something terrible waits for the priest of the false god."

Maske studied the bones on the floor.

"They say that they are the bones of deer, squirrel and possibly a beaver," he said without inflection. "You have forgotten that I am a medicine man, Madockawando, and not easily fooled like your ignorant people. Please. Come in."

"So," said the old man with restrained, cold violence as he stepped inside, "what herb or powder have you brought to ease the suffering of my people today?"

"I will show you," said the priest as he unconsciously stroked the small cross on a thong that hung around his neck, "after you tell me the name of your confederate who pretends to be Odzihozo so that you can filch what little your people have to enrich your own miserable lives."

"Odzihozo is no man. He came out of the bowels of the mountain when I was preparing a blood sacrifice," said the Sachem, touching the canker sore on his upper lip, "He came out, a loathsome mockery of man."

"Ah. A blasted Englishman," said Maske.

"You are a fool," said Madockawando without heat. His poached eyes did not narrow or his slashed mouth twitch as he moved to the bench opposite the priest and laboriously sat down.

"Why so down in the mouth, Sachem?" asked Maske. "Did you really think this merchant of 'pond scum and frog's warts' was blind to your lies these many years?"

"Odzihozo was a man of dust without legs," said the Sachem, ignoring the priest's accusations. A distant peal of thunder broke and then slowly rumbled into silence outside of the wigwam. "Before the Alnanbal remember time, he pushed up mountains and gouged out valleys and lakes in his wake where he crawled."

"Strange how such a great god could fit in a westus."

"I have seen your 'churches' in the big camps where your little god lives."

"God does not live in churches, Sachem, but in the heart of each believer."

"Then he is even smaller than I thought. Odzihozo," the sachem continued, "turned himself into a stone in a lake. This made the sky gods angry, and Odzihozo was made a god unable to die who must shed his flesh and eat a human spirit once every hundred years to put on youth again."

Maske waved a hand indicating the bones scattered on the floor. "Is it not a weak god who needs blood to live? Or furs to warm himself in winter?"

"He requires a human body without blemish," said Madockawando, still ignorning Maske. "His ruined face was mottled by the deep shadows of the wigwam.

"Enough of this. Neither of us will convince the other. I have brought something special," said the priest, and picked up his vest from the rough-hewn bench and laid it across his lap. "It will ease the pains in your old bones and bring sleep to you again. It is yours for Quamis' freedom."

"It is mine at any time, if I kill you," said the crippled, foul, old man.

"There are no more like me at the abbey, Madockawando. My death would mean the end of the medicines I bring your tribe."

"To fail to sacrifice to Odzihozo," said Madockawando as he slowly and painfully rose from the bench, "would mean the death of my people."

"Is there nothing I can do to set Quamis free?"

"Nothing." Thunder rolled and broke as the fey old Indian stood in silence and studied the anxious face of the priest.

"Sachem, surely you'd agree that no man should die alone. Let me at least attend the feasting and say the last prayers of my god for Quamis."

"For the powder that brings sleep," said the Sachem as he moved to the open mouth of the wigwam, "and eats the fire in my joints, let your prayer be the last words Quamis hears. But you will not enter the sacred inner chamber of my god, Maske."

"So be it," Maske said. He rose from his bench as the Indian leader turned, paused, and then stepped out of the wigwam. "So be it," he repeated in a whisper as a salve for the turmoil in his heart. He stepped to the entrance as well and paused, watching the receding back of the Sachem as a fat drop of rain struck his face. He extended his hand, palm up, and felt another and then another big drop of rain spatter on his palm.

The rain storm broke with a cool gust of wind and a peal of thunder as a little Indian boy less than three years old ran out from behind the flap of his wigwam next to Maske's. The priest watched as the little boy greeted the gentle rain with an open mouthed and beautiful smile, his tongue eager for the cool drops, his eyes squinted against their sting, and his arms spread with palms upturned and open in pure, unadulterated happiness. The boy giggled and began to slowly turn in the shower with his head thrown back and his mouth open to catch the rain.

The child lowered his head, spat the rain out, and squealed with shameless joy as the clouds suddenly opened and the sun cast a sparking wave dancing through the rain.

An electric tingle thrilled through the priest, and Maske was overwhelmed by the unapologetic love of a God for his foolish children who, deadened by the sick and fallen world they had created, settle for fleeting physical pleasure when eternal bliss is theirs to claim, and Father Maske wept in his longing for Eden for Quamis and the lewd Abenakis and the French and the world as he watched Jesus dance in the little brown boy dancing with complete innocence and abandon and joy in the rain.

That night in the otherwise empty, silent wigwam, as a guard stood motionless at its mouth, Maske was seized by a vision as he slept beneath his vest on his bench.

He stood naked in the half-light of a narrow cave. The air was warm and smarmy, and he was filled with overwhelming shame because he lacked the courage to give his life for Quamis because the priest was dirty with doubt that there was a Jehovah or any god or anything outside of the material universe.

His naked feet cold and damp on its hoary cave floor, the priest padded to a slimy wall and a door where a small keg of gunpowder and ball were stored. He picked up and loaded the flintlock that had appeared in his hand as a deep sobbing, like a woman whose lover has been swallowed by the ocean, rose faintly from behind the door. Maske opened the door slowly, the loaded flintlock leveled at his waist.

The preternatural chamber inside was cool, no more than fifteen yards deep, and cluttered with materials salvaged from wrecked ships. Against its far wall, a crude, low, semicircular well of un-mortared stone skirted a large crevice that ran from the wall to the floor. Around the gaping crevice, stones had toppled to the floor as if pushed out from the inside.

Bones picked clean of flesh littered the floor.

Maske yelled, "Hello?" There was no echo and no answer, except an eerie scratching and the deep sobbing like a woman and a chittering rising from the well. And, abhorrent and reeking, in a dance of foaming, rising bubbles, Odzihozo rose up to the lip of the well, out of the well's womb, and spit Quamis' bloody, tattered body, eaten away from the waist down, out onto the floor.

The teeth. The blood. The screaming, laughing horror from which Maske turned and fled, dropping his flintlock to the floor, was a monstrous obscenity of spider's legs writhing around the bloated head and gnashing razor teeth of a gigantic, pustulant maggot.

Startled awake and gasping, Maske fell from the bench onto the hard-packed, dirt floor and, all that remaining night, wrestled with the Lord. At first light, weary from lack of sleep and heavy with fear, he spread his vest of many pockets on a bench, committed his soul to God, and prepared himself to die.

In the half-darkness and utter silence of Odzihozo's westus, the rank air heavy with smoke from ritual pipes already exhausted, Maske let the gray powder slide from the gutter of a tiny folded paper into the wooden cup of an Old Man. Dust drifted in the miasma of yellow light that filtered through the hole cut in the center of the roof.

"Soon, you'll sing," said Maske in broken Abenakis, "and dance and hunt for deer like a lustful young man again."

The moribund Indian nodded his head, lifted the dirty cup, and drank deeply as the priest let the empty paper fall to the dirt floor next to a now silent fetish drum still smelling faintly of tanned, dead skin. Maske crossed himself and straightened as he had done with the eleven other elders.

The twelve old men sat, indifferent and sluggish, in ceremonial garb on the benches around the outer wall of the westus with Madockawando, his chin cupped in the palms of his hands and his elbows on his knees, by the closed entrance to the inner chamber of the cannibal god. The Sachem's poached eyes were narrowed to red slits as he sat in his ratty leather tunic and cape, and an ill-fitting but elaborate headdress of decaying feathers, porcupine quills and hair, fox tails and rattlesnake skins.

Feckless, Quamis stood naked in the center of the westus in a pool of his own clothing, chin hung on his chest, eyes closed, shoulders slumped, and his hands tied with leather straps behind his back. He began to tremble and sob as Maske reverently sang "Holy, holy, holy, Lord God Almighty;

Early in the morning, our song shall rise to thee." And as the priest sang, the grotesque heads of two elders began to sink upon their chests, and one Abenakis, struggling to rise, slumped to the floor.

"Violence only begets violence, Madockawando," said the priest as he moved behind Quamis. "Death begets death. Only love brings joy and life."

"You...talk...like...squak," said the Sachem in English, realizing he'd mispronounced squaw even as he spoke it. "Skaw," he said, miserably failing again, and "Skak" followed as the heavy lids of his puffed eyes closed.

"Holy, holy, holy," sang Mask as he placed his hands over Quamis' raw, bound hands. "Merciful and mighty! God in three Persons, blessed Trinity!"

Slowly and one by one, each of the remaining elders fell over on another's shoulder or chest or lap, or simply slid onto the hard-packed dirt floor into deep sleep as Maske began to untie the leather straps that bound Quamis.

"What is happening, Father Maske?" whispered Quamis. "Have you killed them?"

"They are not dead, but will be unable to follow where you run for at least three or four hours, my son." The straps fell onto Quamis' pooled clothing.

"We will run to your abbey, Father, to the north."

"No, Quamis. God says that nothing is more important than love, and that there is no greater love than a man lay down his life for another. Hurry. Dress."

"Father..." Quamis objected as he squatted to pick up his clothing.

The priest raised his hand, palm forward, to stop the Abenakis's words. "I love you, my little brother in Christ, but I am commanded to love all. I cannot allow whatever obscenity lies in that room to hurt anyone else. I am not coming with you."

"But, Father Maske...!" the Indian boy began as he wrapped his breechcloth around his loins; the resolution on the priest's face quashed his objection.

"Before you go, tie my hands loosely with the straps that bound you," said the priest, his voice breaking with suppressed emotion as he shrugged out of his robe. "D-don't ask why. H-hurry.

"Now go, Quamis. Run and don't look back!"

Naked except for the undergarment around his loins, the mortified priest turned away from the boy, raised his right arm, covered his mouth with his hand, and sobbed quietly.

Quamis stumbled away backward from the priest towards the open mouth of the westus, glancing first left and then right at the sleeping Old Men. At the entrance, he turned to see Maske pull back the filthy leather flap that led to the lair of the hellish cannibal god, step inside, and let the flap fall behind him. Quamis stooped and gently removed a rusted knife from the belt of a snoring elder, then let the leather cover for the entrance fall closed.

He stopped in midstep and surveyed the desolate encampment that, normally buzzing with preparations for another day, lay seemingly deserted and utterly silent in the haze of the morning sun. He thought of his tribe huddled and sweating in fear inside the wigwams, and glanced east to the unseen field of maize, then behind him at the westus. He stroked the blade of the knife in his hands, then turned on his heels. Quamis skirted the westus to the east until, reaching its back, he squatted and began to quietly dig a hole in the packed dirt and maize husks and grass of the outside wall.

The unclean stink of urine and feces hung in the close air.

"You are not Abenakis," burbled the putrid horror from a cut of a mouth in its swollen face. "No matter. The Abenakis call me Odzihozo and God. I have had many names." The morbidly obese, hideous mockery of a man slumped naked on a mound of packed earth, his skin cascading in obscene folds of tallowed, diseased flesh hanging from an otherwise skeletal body. Odzihozo blinked fevered eyes and waved a mottled, fat ham of a hand in dismissal of the priest.

Maske said nothing as he stood in the miasma of yellow light filtering through the hole in the roof, his hands clasped at his chest and his head lowered as if in prayer. The evidence of death, bones lay randomly scattered in the debris before the blasphemy of human flesh on the mound.

Ignoring the priest's silence, the squamous monstrosity clasped his own rancid hands, shifted his weight, and sneered, baring crooked yellow teeth.

"Ah, a Christian? They sacrifice," he wheezed, "a fool for Jesus. He began to laugh, a low, painful laugh that convulsed his putrid stomach and made red slits of his eyes as he began to painfully rise.

"Terror, tears and trembling," the lewd god gurgled. "You are...afraid. Fear is my favorite condiment. Kneel. Kneel before me, stupid child of 'God'."

His head still lowered, the priest knelt obediently on the unholy ground as Odzihozo limped to him in waves of putrid, gelatinous flesh.

"Madockawando told you I eat the souls and flesh of men," Odzihozo gurgled, breathing heavily with a funny smile like a cut, and began to move his jaw from one side to the other. "The legion of souls you will soon join inside me bear witness to this; it is true.

"And I hunger." The god cupped the priest's chin with its oily left hand, lifted Maske's head, brought his face nose to nose with the priest, and, reaching up with his flabby right hand, dislocated his own stubbled jaw with a muffled thup.

He opened the lurid cut of a mouth wide, wider, and unnaturally wider still, and slowly placed his hideously gaping mouth over the lower half of Maske's face.

And down in the mouth of Odzihozo, the priest found the tiny pig's bladder with his tongue that he'd hidden in his right cheek when he'd turned his back on Quamis, pushed it to his parted lips, and bit down, squirting a stream of clear liquid into the back of the monster's goitered throat.

Odzihozo startled back off of Maske's face and fell back and down on his putrid haunches, his bloodshot, bulging eyes showing the confusion and disbelief that distorted his suddenly pale, flaccid face and its grotesque, dangling, disjointed jaw.

Then his hideous, burbled screams began.

His right eye against the hole in the outer wall of Odzihozo's hoary slaughterhouse, Quamis jerked back on his callused heels, his face a sudden mask of surprise and horror, and fell hard backward onto the ground, then scrambled crab-like back from the wall as the inexplicable nightmarish thing inside screamed and screamed.

"F-Father," he whispered once. Then, gasping for air, the Abenakis rose, turned, and fled with the unsustainable speed borne of terror away from the westus and out of the settlement where his people crouched in fear and deep shadows in their teepees. He fled into the ancient woods that skirted the encampment, then north up the bank of the sluggish Gihon river, falling into a measured lope sustainable over long distances, and out of the history of the repulsive, syphilitic Abenakis forever.

On the third day of Unleavened Bread, while the putrid thing lay writhing and screaming on the dirt floor of the long westus, Father

Maske, pale and shaken, walked out of Odzihozo's chamber, and dressed himself in the clothes he had discarded. He walked carefully through the circle of thirteen bodies immersed in profound sleep, knowing that the powerful sleeping powder he'd sprinkled in each of their drinks would keep them immobile for at least another five hours. Then the priest walked to and through the door, out of the westus, then through and out of the seemingly abandoned and eerily silent settlement without hurry, but with determination, because he knew that he would be well beyond Abenakis pursuit before the elders woke and the overdose of powerful laxative laced with the sleeping powder knocked them to their knees and guaranteed his escape from Madockawando's perverse and ostracized tribe.

Father Maske walked briskly along the east side of the already forded Gihon river, now singing "Te Deum" not to glorify his God because of experience and study, but because he no longer had faith in the unseen.

The air was again fresh and alive outside the horseshoe of decaying teepees with the subtle smells of spring, of blueberry, pogonia, and orchids, and of spruce, balsam fir, pine, and hemlock, all the good work of God's hand. As he walked, Maske consciously stroked the cross on the thong that hung around his neck.

When he came upon the bones still scattered in the dust, Maske stopped and methodically kicked dust over the damning evidence of mortality until he had buried them, then he turned, smiled, and walked out the mouth of the valley of death.

He smiled because the thing, whatever it was, that writhed and screamed and screamed and screamed on the floor of the westus should have died from enough poison to kill ten men in ten minutes, and yet did not die.

He smiled because he knew that the Abenaki would no longer fear a god who could scream with pain, and that it would not eat at the Abenakis table again.

And he smiled because he had seen the face of Hell and, therefore, the promise of Heaven, and knew what he had before only believed by faith.

And as he walked, filled with unspeakable joy, Father Maske and Jesus danced with the boy dancing in the rain.

WHERE BRIGHT ANGEL FEET HAVE TROD

It fell out of the sun.

"And I looked, and behold..."

Heavy with age, it fell through space like a whisper on deaf ears.

"A whirlwind came out of the north, a great cloud...and a fire infolding itself..."

It fell like a burning cinder across the night sky, across the broken, bleached old stones of the lighthouse, across the barren, decaying wharves. Erasing a thin line of stars, it fell where the village of Light's End crouched like a wounded beast against the rocky, isolated coast of Maine.

Burned to the color of ash, the space ship fell where the seeds of death were gathering.

***

"And I saw another mighty angel come down from heaven...," she continued in clear, modulated tones as she sat on a white stone veined with moss. "Clothed with a cloud and a rainbow was upon his head, and his face was as it were the sun, and his feet as pillars of fire..."

Her words carried in the chill air of autumn above the gurgle of the river Pishon that flowed to the bay of Light's End. At her small feet, the horror watched her, then the reflection of trees on the river's banks shimmering in the water. The horror watched the space ship, like crumpled aluminum tangled in the tree tops, wink in the cold waters.

Her thin, small hand fell to the yellowed pages of the open Bible on her lap.

"This is from ancient times," she said, smiling. "I have found these

16

words in other places, in different verses."

She smoothed the wrinkles in the skirt of her white shift with a hand, carefully closed the book, and lay it on the crisp, pale grass at her feet next to a tattered hymnal. She straightened on her rock.

"God's presence is felt here, where we sit, and there," she said, pointing with an alabaster finger as the horror watched the gesture. "In the heavens."

Her white hair shone in the sun. Her blue eyes sparkled.

"All things, my friend, are gathered into two hands." She held her hands out, palms up. "One restrains chaos, the other declares harmony. Only we can twist peace into evil. But someday, even as we have set aside our differences, all things living shall put away blind fear and prejudice, and our two worlds shall be one. I feel it."

"The promise is there," she said, pointing to the Bible on the ground, "in the book, and elsewhere. Hold fast. Believe. Our love is living proof that this promise will be fulfilled," she said, picking up the hymnal. Turning to a dog-eared page, she closed her eyes and sang softly.

"Shall we gather at the river...Where bright angel feet have trod?

"With its crystal tide forever...Flowing by the throne of God."

A festering sore, the horror's finger brushed the scar that erased the perfection of her face as softly, slowly as fallen dust, the unseen rifle's trigger was cocked.

It took stone mason Jeroboam Azreal and the castaways of Light's End eleven years to cut and set the tortured, white stone of the lighthouse. Its wooden beams had been scavenged from the ribs from a ship wrecked in broad daylight on the treacherous shoals of their harbor. Rumors of the devil's dirty hands and worse on the ship's bow stopped Jeroboam's hand until the captain admitted himself a drunken sot and himself the wreck of the vessel. The captain's confession cost Jeroboam three bottles of rum.

For eleven years, Jeroboam met each sunrise chanting from the leather bound Bible given to him by his father, and secretly writing strange geometrical symbols in chalk on each stone. When he was seventy-two years old, Jeroboam cut an inscription on the cornerstone with bloodied, crippled hands and a wooden mallet whose head had been pounded into mush. His twelve year old son, John, held the chisel. The inscription read: *As above, so below.* Jeroboam set the cornerstone in its niche, the inscription hidden by the face of another stone, and mortared it into place.

And Jeroboam died.

The tower stood for forty years after his death as a warning of pain and destruction. In five minutes, God shook it into rubble.

For five years after the shaking, the village choked on the dust of the ebon tower that God had shook into ruin, burying an ancient horror and killing John Azreal. The grief of the village's widows and orphans was thrown like stones from the tower into still water. It rippled out into nightmares that rippled out into whispered heresy, and spread into the ocean. It took fifty-seven years from the setting of its cornerstone for Light's End to become a curse. Even whalers dreamed it in night sweats, and Light's End became blasphemy.

And as trade sagged and the great, creaking merchant and whaling ships abandoned the village, the dirty people, the sick, the demented, and John's son, Issac, were thrown inland. As year crumbled into year, the villagers scattered away after the ships, and Issac scattered away inward. He took his grandfather's and father's Bible and the Shaking God with him.

Issac was tall and straight with a face like beaten meat. His thick, black hair, deep set eyes and hawkish nose had never endeared him to Light's End. So when Issac was twenty-seven years old, he built a house of sod and stone in the wilderness outside of soiled Light's End, and sunk a stolen stone from the lighthouse rubble in its dirt floor. He lived and wandered north of the river Pishon where he trapped, butchered and skinned animals that fed him and clothed the villagers, and Issac's thick, black beard grew. He slowly abandoned the village as it had abandoned him, and Issac sank into desperate loneliness.

On rare trips into Light's End to sell skins to buy salt, sugar and coffee, he traded a skunk pelt for a mongrel pup of scabs, bone and hair, and named him Ebenezar. He and Ebenezar became wild and dirty and stank, and the pariahs of Light's End endured their visits in the same way they endured the bleached sepulcher of the lighthouse. It and Issac served them as a reminder of God's wrath.

And as year crumbled into year, Issac continually read aloud from his grandfather's and father's Bible by the dying light of his fireplace every night. A sword and his grandfather's and father's names were burned into its white leather cover, and foreign words and arcane symbols were written in red in the margins of many pages. Issac marked out the words *mercy, forgiveness, love* and *Jesus* with ash from his fire and circled the words *Retribution, Justice, Wrath* and *Judgment*. These were the words of the Shaking God. And as Issac turned the yellowed pages, he whispered these words and muttered of the Law. On bad days, he shouted of the thing buried under the lighthouse and of vengeance and a righteous God, and slowly, his ranting grew into prayers and curses that became heresy and clenched fists and screaming in the dead silence of his sod house. Ebenezar whimpered and cowered in shadows.

He could not erase the foreign words and geometrical symbols, and tore their pages from the book, and Jeroboam's and John's became Issac's Bible. And over the long years, Issac and Ebenezar became one madness.

He yelled at himself and Ebenezar and the Shaking God for seven years before finding Sarah. Sometimes he shook and Ebenezar whimpered, and he forgot he was thirty-four years old, and Issac dreamed of the thing buried under the lighthouse in night sweats until Sarah.

Sarah was tall and straight with a face like smooth almonds. But her thick, red hair, green eyes and even nose had never endeared her to Light's End. Sarah was young, educated, foreign and fearless, so she was hated and ignored by the uneducated, sullen villagers. In turn, she ignored the whispered stories of the madman of the Pishon and the weakness of virgins, and wandered deeper and deeper by the river and into the wilderness. She believed in neither gods nor demons but in One God, and choked back her fear when the madman found her bathing in the river.

Sarah understood loneliness and the frightened man beneath the heresy, the ranting and dirt. She saw the boy buried in Issac, sobbing and shaking with grief, who stood among the jumble of broken stone that buried his father. She held that boy and shook with Issac until the shaking stopped. Sarah brought her books to Issac's mud and stone house and read to him from pages without coal smears, gibberish and odd stars in the margins, and told Issac that only man can twist truth into lies.

Issac bathed and shaved his strong, black beard, and his clenched fists relaxed under her cool touch. He traded pelts in Light's End for woolen breeches, a long coat, a wide brimmed hat, and muslin that Sarah sewed into dresses. He covered his laughter with his hand at the village stories he had started of Sarah's rape and death at the hands of monsters. He beat the sod house into mud and raised a log cabin for her in its place. His ranting faded into a stoic irritability and then a clean silence. And Issac talked to Sarah instead of the Shaking God, and put the white leather Bible on a shelf. And Sarah told Issac that only man can twist love into hate.

When he was thirty-seven years old, Issac fell to his knees on the bank of the Pishon and wept, alone, into the silence of the wilderness. His deep sobs racked his body and wet his clean-shaven cheeks and rose in diminishing waves above the trees and across the river and echoed. He collapsed on the ground. When he rose, Issac felt clean.

Then Issac and Sarah did the unspeakable.

And the Shaking God shook Sarah.

"Sarah. What must I do?"

Young Issac leaned against the rough hewn doorjamb to his bedroom, the light from the dying flames of its fireplace reflected in his fevered eyes. Sweat glistened on the hard ridge of muscle at his naked jaw. Ignored, Ebenezar jumped around his legs, excited by the smell of fear and Sarah's guttural moans. The bedroom's wild shadows danced with Sarah in bed, danced as she twisted in the pain of childbirth, as she danced in the throes of death. The bedroom's wild shadows danced with the crib.

"Sarah. What must I do? There is no...midwife."

"Oh. Oh. Oh. Oh."

"The seed you bore...tainted, marked," Issac whispered as he knelt beside her bed, clutching her sweating hands and pushing the matted red hair out of her eyes.

"The child," Sarah choked, "...Issac. A...part of us. We...all born in sin. Love...our child. Raise in fear of..."

Like a whispered prayer, Sarah's trembling finger brushed the wrinkles that painted the anguish of Issac's face. "If...I die..."

"I cannot bear this, Sarah."

"You...you must love...Shelley, our baby, as...as you love me. Only," she gurgled as a line of blood trickled down her chin, "Only man can twist love. Pray for...forgiveness, and....forgive. Forgive....Issac..............."

"Sarah. Sarah? Sarah! Don't leave me! I have no strength! Oh, God! If Thou are just, punish me! *ME!*"

The Shaking God answered and Ebenezar buried his head between his paws.

"*NO!*" Issac screamed at the Shaking God, and, weeping, buried his face in Sarah's damp, cold, still sheets. And the Shaking God's answer rose again out of the crib and broke the silence, and fell where the seeds of death were gathering.

As Shelley Azreal wailed.

Issac scratched Sarah's name on the stone dug from the floor of their cabin and sunk it as her tombstone on a clearing circled with trees by the river. He cleaned the mound of grass, twigs and leaves, and outlined the grave with small, white stones from the Pishon. In the fourth year of her death, Issac trimmed his ragged beard, put on his woolen trousers, coat and hat, and took Ebenezar with him to the grave to build a crude, whitewashed wooden fence around her grave.

In the fifteenth year after her murder by the Shaking God, Issac trimmed his dirty beard, peppered with gray, put on his tattered woolen trousers, coat and hat, and found Sarah's Bible. Issac took the Shaking God and a rifle with him to the grave even as Shelley whored at the river.

"'Whatsoever a man soweth, that shall he also reap,'" he read in a murky voice. "'For he that soweth to his flesh shall of the flesh reap corruption.' This is the truth."

His hands trembled with the weight of his emotions and Sarah's Bible, and a spasm in his left leg made Issac involuntarily kick the rifle lying in the grass. He thought of Ebenezar, long dead, and frowned.

"Sarah, I am greatly troubled. I turn my head away from our child. It burns me. I see the unholy lust in Shelley's eyes. The shyness and silence of shame mark the child as surely as..."

Issac threw Sarah's Bible to the ground in a nest of fanned pages.

"Oh, Sarah! Their tongues rattle behind my back in Light's End! Against our child! What they say! Their voices stop as I enter the room! They whisper! They titter! Their voices bile me! 'Where is this child we have never seen?' They chide me! 'Is it true Shelley sleeps with pigs and howls at the moon? Are the feet really cloven?!'"

Issac picked up his rifle.

"Holy God! It is Issac! Your servant!" he screamed, shaking the rifle at the sky. "Unstop your ears! Hear me! I stand naked and ashamed before Thy Holy Wrath—filthy with sin! But I cannot bear these words! I cannot stand silent forever!"

Issac fell to his knees in the soft earth of Sarah's grave and wept, alone, into the silence of the wilderness. His deep sobs racked his body and wet his bearded cheeks and rose in diminishing waves above the trees and across the river and echoed. He collapsed on the ground.

When he rose, Issac was dirty.

"The house stands dark, Ebenezar. Come," he whispered hoarsely to the dead dog, his chin hung on his chest in shame.

"Shelley prowls like a cat in heat."

Issac raised his head, and he and dead Ebenezar became one madness.

"Shelley!" he demanded of the empty clearing circled by tortured trees. "It grows late and I hunger! Shelley!! Shelley! Put aside your work. Come greet your old father!

"Sarah, I have found Shelley's footprints; I know where they lead," he said to the stone dug from the floor of his cabin that he'd sunk at the head of her grave. The tombstone read:

As above, so below. Sarah Sullivan.

"At the riverbank, they are muddied with other tracks...oh, God. For all things living, God has given a helpmate, but not for our Shelley...marked in the flesh because of our sin."

Issac leaned against the trunk of a tree and tore at the dry bark, the light of madness in his eyes.

"Sarah. What must I do?"

Issac leaned against the clean, smooth skin beneath the dry bark he'd torn from the tree, the dying light of memory in his fevered eyes. Sweat glistened on the hard ridge of muscle beneath his graying beard. Panting with exertion, long dead Ebenezar slunk at his legs, excited. The wild shadows of early twilight danced with Issac and Ebenezar, danced as Issac twisted in the pain of shame, danced at the river with Shelley and Satan.

"The wages of sin is death," Issac hissed between his yellowed, clenched teeth. He straightened away from the trunk of the tree. "The wages of sin is death.

"An eye for an eye, sayeth the Lord! I shall NOT be mocked in the streets!" he muttered, wracked with emotion, as he balled a hand into a fist.

"My God! My child...!!!" he cried, and slammed his fist into the tree.

"A whore...a......whore," he screamed and collapsed, face pressed against the blood smeared bark, crying.

"Slut," he hissed. "Dirty. Burn!!!" he swore to the Shaking God.

Issac's words fell like a whisper on deaf ears.

Issac licked his thumb and ran it along the cold bore of his rifle. Her song carried to his hiding place through the chill air of autumn above the gurgle of the river. At her feet, the horror watched the river and the crumpled aluminum winking in the cold waters. Squatting in the bushes, Issac fingered its trigger as her image fell out of the sun and into the rifle's sights.

"And I looked, and behold..." she said again, "a whirlwind came out of the north, a great cloud...and a fire infolding itself...

"My whirlwind," she said, and began to sing.

"Shall we gather at the river...Where bright angel feet have trod?

"With its crystal tide forever...Flowing by the throne of God.

"On the margin of the river," she sang.

"...washed in blood," Issac hissed, and squeezed the trigger.

KAPOW!!!

The first bullet fell through space like a whisper on deaf ears and bit the stone where the horror sat at her feet.

"Washing up its silver spra....."

KAPOW!!!

The crack of the second ate her last word as she heard the first bullet.

KAPOW!!!

The third bullet ate her.

KAPOW Oow oow

The echo shocked birds from the trees in a flurry of wings and fear as she fell like a whisper into the cool autumn grass, like a cinder burned to ash.

Issac leaned back in his rough-hewn rocking chair, closed his old eyes and smiled. Its creak in the still air was a relief from the silence of isolation as the wild shadows of early twilight danced on the porch of his log cabin. He pushed at the hard ridge of muscle beneath his graying beard on a face like beaten meat.

"Hush, child. Stop your tears," he said quietly. "HIS will is beyond understanding. HIS justice is hard. We obey. We obey!"

He knew the waves would bring new people to Light's End, hunched against the massive, clammy piles driven into the sea. Clapboard shanties would totter crazily against the barren, empty coast. And Issac knew he would find friends in the derelicts who would not mutter. He would find other strong arms to pull down the great, silver-ash abomination in the trees and erase the evidence of other feet.

"I love you, son," he said.

A festering sore, Shelley's finger brushed the scar that erased the perfection of his father's face. And softly, slowly as fallen dust, the unseen seeds of chaos were gathered.

THE END

Home Invasion

Mao "Rodney" Wong simply did not know that the sharp crack like a firecracker that disrupted the otherwise calm morning wasn't a gunshot. He had just jogged under a telephone pole topped by a siren used to sound an alarm at the approach of severe storms, daemon hurricanes, or an atomic attack by Russia, and had nothing on his mind but a Doris Day tune that he was humming.

It was 7:11 a.m., and the day was chilly; the sky was a clear, cerulean blue. There was nothing to hamper the off-duty policeman's hearing or response as he trotted down Goodwin Street in the rundown Stonebreaker Heights district as part of his rigid exercise routine. The only other sounds were the beating of Wong's heart, the rhythm of his labored breathing, the pad-pad-pad of his sneakered feet punched out on the sidewalk, the tinny sound of the "The Yellow Rose of Texas" on an unseen radio, and the remote clang of a trash can being emptied into a big, unclean sanitation truck.

Wong was a cop who played strictly "by the book," so he noted all of this as he veered from the sidewalk to the black iron fence that circled the modest brick house at 1427 Goodwin. The house's back door was slightly ajar, an anomaly for early morning.

A short, athletic man with Asian characteristics, he wore loose, dark blue, cotton sweatpants, and a sweatshirt stained with dark half-moons under both arms. Wong easily vaulted the fence by using his right arm as leverage, landed squarely on his feet, and reached for his service revolver on his right hip as he jogged to the back porch of the house. There was neither holster nor weapon to draw. But at that unexpected moment frozen forever in time, neither death, nor life, neither time nor distance, god nor daemon, no law of man or nature, nor any other thing could stop the sure, measured execution of Wong's sworn duty.

As his foot hit the porch's first step, with one silent, graceful movement, a cat swept fearlessly, like a whisper of cool air, down the stairs, pausing once in mid-flight to glance disdainfully over her midnight black shoulder at Wong before she finished her descent and was gone.

Although startled, he did not cry out; silence helped conceal an accent that might reveal he was an alien withoug legal documentation. Wong had been employed as a policeman for less than five months after completing his academy work, and had lived in smarmy, long decaying Stonebreaker Heights for three weeks. Unmarried and childless, he knew few people outside of the police department, and no one in the neighborhood.

Wong pushed the door open without hesitation and moved rapidly through a well-organized and clean utility room with a clothes washer and dryer, a folding table for clean clothes, a hot water heater, storage shelves, and water and food dishes for a cat. Above the folding table hung a small, framed poem with a photograph of two infant girls. Wong stepped through an open door next to the washer into a hall.

"Police!!" he barked, and moved cautiously down the empty, lit hallway. There was no response or sounds.

Wong passed what his cursory glances identified as framed diplomas, certificates, and family pictures on the right wall as he approached an open doorway on the same side eight feet away. The left wall of the hallway was covered with bookshelves and books. The hall emptied several feet beyond the doorway through an open arch into a living room.

His heart was beating rapidly as he flattened his body against the wall next to the right doorjamb, stepped inside, then out of the doorway to flatten against the wall by the left doorjamb. In those seconds, he memorized an unmade bed, two end tables with lamps on either side of the bed's headboard, and a chest of drawers to his left. The drawers of the chest were open and the clothes within were in chaos. On top of the chest were framed photographs of children next to an inexpensive jewelry box with its contents spilling over its sides, and an opened package of Camel cigarettes. Wong stepped through the door into the otherwise demure room.

The off-duty policeman looked at a book of Christian devotionals, an empty glass, and an ashtray half-filled with cigarette butts on the end table on the left side of the bed. The room also held two tall dressers on the wall to his right, and a blonde, wooden trunk at the foot of the bed. An elaborate, metal doll house sat on the hardwood floor next to the chest of drawers, and a toy motorcycle straddled by Dick Tracy lay on its side next to it. At the foot of the truck lay fluffy pink house shoes in a neat parallel row, and a woman who watched Wong with complete indifference. She wore modest, yellow pajamas decorated with flowers, and her red hair in a poodle cut lay soaking in a spreading pool of ichor.

Wong stepped to her side, knelt on his left knee as he carefully avoided the pool of blood, and placed two fingers on her neck in search of a pulse. The woman was forever in her early thirties.

"Poor skirt. Forever punched out of life," Wong whispered in imitation of the slang in the cheap paperback detective novels he enjoyed.

He deduced from the toys that her children were probably in the house and in danger. Wong glanced over his right shoulder at a large print on the wall next to the door of a painting of a bookshelf built under a window. In that painting, two cats with their backs to the policeman ineffably sat between potted plants on the bookshelf looking onto a yard. Next to the print, a man trembling slightly, his face flushed with fear and rage, swayed in the doorway. In his right hand hung the revolver that surely was used to kill the woman.

The burglar looked at the murdered woman and Wong and began to raise the revolver.

Wong estimated the trajectory of a shot as he saw the suspect adjust the angle of the gun to leave a bloody hole in Wong's forehead. He lunged, knowing that to do nothing meant death, but to attack did not substantially raise his odds for survival.

The impact of Wong's body slammed the suspect's right hand against the doorjamb, and, as the burglar cried out, hurled both men back and out of the doorway into the hall. The revolver clattered across the floor and under the left end table.

Wong rose as the suspect pushed himself up from the floor, his back against the bookcases. He memorized the man's clean black sneakers, creased tan dungarees, long-sleeved white shirt, an owlish nose and eyes set in a waspish, face tapering into a rounded, clean-shaven chin. Wong named him Joe to humanize him.

Slight but wiry in build, Joe's brown hair was prematurely thinning for a man surely thirty-five to thirty-eight years old. There was no blood evident on his person; he must have shot his victim at a distance, indicating luck or expertise with a firearm.

The instant the thug straightened, Wong shoved him backward in an attempt to disorient the dour burglar and subdue him with the least physical damage. Joe stumbled hard against books that exploded in a hail of hard edges that fell to the floor with him. Joe scrambled to his feet, slipped on a book, and stumbled backwards out of the hall into the living room. He quickly found his footing and Wong realized that purpose and reason now tinged Joe's fierce rage.

Wong shoved him again with greater force, and Joe stumbled back, fell, and tumbled two times before coming to rest on the floor next to a Davy Crockett coonskin cap. To his left Wong saw a dining table and chairs, an open arch into another hall, an overstuffed chair, a television with rabbit ears antenna on an aluminum stand, and the front door in the wall opposite Joe. On the dining table was a paint-by-numbers canvas, little paint cups, and a paintbrush. Nearest Joe was a half-empty coffee cup by an open Bible, likely forgotten when the murdered woman rose to investigate the sounds from her bedroom.

To Wong's right were a closed closet door, a curio cabinet filled with cat figurines and trophies, an overstuffed chair and couch, and an upright piano and bench next to the front door. The piano was covered with framed photographs, a telephone, and a Bakelite radio playing "You're the Apple of My Eye."

Wong stepped into the living room.

Joe viciously punched out at Wong's left knee with his left leg. With a yelp of pain, the policeman collapsed backwards, striking a glancing blow with the back of his head on the doorjamb as he fell. He instinctively rolled away from Joe and up on his feet, wincing from the hellish needles of pain.

He faced an opponent already on his feet, his arms and balled fists raised in the defensive posture of a boxer, and weaving slightly from side to side. Resolve and calculation had replaced the fear on his face, and Wong realized the murderer had had training, possibly during military service, although a sedentary lifestyle may have robbed him of much of his previous strength.

The thug struck out viciously with his right fist, and Wong ducked to his left. Joe struck out with his left fist, and Wong ducked to his right, strategically determined to let the waspish man wear himself out before countering his attack. With lightening speed, Joe struck with his right fist and hit Wong thuck hard on his nose.

Wong staggered back in surprise and pain onto an unseen cat's toy on the floor that squeaked under his foot. He felt blood at his nose with his left hand. A snarl twisted his face as he stepped back into Joe's striking field.

Joe jabbed with his left fist and Wong blocked with his right forearm, striking Joe with his left fist below his ear. The burglar snatched the coffee mug from the dining table and hurled it. Wong dodged and the cup struck thud the wall behind him as the murderer turned his back to the policeman.

Wong tasted blood in his mouth before he could shout stop. He put the first two index fingers of his right hand to his mouth; they came away with a smear of vicious red.

He lunged as the burglar fled, catching Joe around his waist with both arms, and both men fell squirming to the floor in the middle of the living room. Fighting like an enraged animal, the thug threw him off and staggered to his feet. His face was flushed, his breathing labored, and his face was glazed with sweat. Wong knew as he rose that the only way to subdue Joe now was to beat him into submission.

Wong stepped close to Joe and struck him in the stomach. When Joe doubled over, clutching his midsection, Wong raised his left arm and jabbed a crippling blow down on Joe's left cheek, spinning Joe half-around to drape his sagging body on the top of the television. Wong made a fist with both hands and struck Joe in the left kidney, sending him to his knees but still clutching the television.

Wong stepped back; his intention was to subdue, not kill. Certain of success, he watched as Joe, breathing heavily, struggled to his feet, his head lowered, still clutching his stomach. Wong willed himself to slow his own breathing as Joe straightened, huffing with the effort, his face flushed and hoary with blood, his eyes as cold as steel. Joe raised his hand at chest level, palm forward, indicating surrender. Then faster than Wong thought possible and with terrific force, Joe kicked him in the crotch, lifting him slightly off of the floor. Joe waited for Wong to double over in pain, clutching his groin, but Wong smiled and, taking advantage of his opponent's bewilderment, struck Joe in the face.

The man staggered back and hit the television, knocking it off its stand and sending it with a crash to the floor. Panting, Joe's snarling face flushed red with animal rage.

He shoved Wong back hard against the piano. The framed pictures rose, violently, in a sudden, frantic cloud of hard edges that, with the telephone, fell with Wong, then struck the brown and tan hardwood floor like a string of firecrackers, and the floodgate of volcanic repressed rage cracked inside Rodney Wong.

Rising from the chaos of photographs in blind fury, he violently struck Joe's face, forcefully pushing him backward so that Joe fell painfully onto the floor near the front door. Wong pounced on Joe's stomach, and continued to beat Joe's already raw face.

"Stop it!!" Joe screamed and tore at Wong's face with his fingers.

The Bakelite plastic radio whispered muffled music as Joe tore Wong's right cheek ragged and a piece of faux flesh and the squamous green skin beneath it fell off.

Joe stared at the slobber of green flesh, slaughtered.

Wong hit Joe in the face with all his strength, then pinned Joe's right hand against the floor with a knee. The thug could not protect his face with his right hand; his left struck out, again and again, uselessly.

Wong pulled Joe's fish-eyed and rigid head off the floor and threw it down on the hardwood floor with terrible force. Wong huffed and cupped Joe's head in his right hand as he pinned Joe's left hand behind his frantic, arching back.

At that frenzied moment, frozen forever in time, neither death, nor life, neither time nor distance, god nor demon, no law of man or nature, nor any other thing could stop the vicious, frenzied attack of Wong's right hand.

Wong's wrath was everywhere evident on Joe's face, hard on his bruised right temple, on the thug's twisted mouth and his lips and teeth, weeping blood and gore, brutal on his broken, gray nose until Joe's face was pressed like a dead flower against his left hand that was thrown between it and the hardwood floor in a startled, futile defense against death.

Joe shook with deep throated sobs. Wong struck.

"Joe?" Wong hissed.

"Oh, Jesus," Joe bleated.

Wong rose, breathing heavily, the rage slowly bleeding away. He looked down at Joe and then at the chaos of framed photographs on the checkerboard floor.

Joe blubbered.

Wong shoved his right hand down the front of his pants to his crotch to remove his repair kit and fix his damaged face. He looked at the telephone on the floor that he would use to call headquarters and at a photograph next to the telephone.

Wong knelt, laying his forgotten repair kit next to the telephone, and picked up the photograph with his right hand, then straightened. With his left, he unconsciously tried to tamp the faux flesh hanging from his cheek back into place.

Behind him, the closet door next to the curio cabinet exploded open and, with one silent, graceful movement, the blur of a man swept fearfully, like a whisper of hot air, past the policeman, pausing once in mid-flight to glance disdainfully over his midnight black shoulder at Wong before he opened the front door and was gone.

Wong's heavily redacted report sent to the police department in response to their internal investigation recorded everything he could remember of an event that lasted no more than ten minutes. He stated that he understood an investigation was standard procedure, that his actions were a violation of orders, and the allegations seemed reasonable, but maintained that he deserved no reprimand, demotion or dismissal.

Wong admitted that despite extensive training, he still didn't understand many human motivations, and that his actions were defensive. He asked how he could be accountable for what he didn't know, and that every action taken was right; that the consequences were wrong was due to ignorance.

Wong wrote that he knelt and picked up the photograph. He was looking at it as, behind him, the closet door exploded open and a man raced past him, wrenched the front door open, and disappeared.

Wong wrote that he looked back at the photograph of the dead woman seated on a sofa next to a girl in white lace who was no more than two or three years old. Across the bottom of the photograph was written "With love, Schlomo."

On the dead woman's left was a man in a pin-striped suit cradling a four or five year old boy in an ill-fitting suit. Everyone in the photograph was smiling.

He wrote that shock and disbelief must have washed over his face as he realized that the man in the picture–the man that he'd punched out and sent to the hospital, the man who'd thought Wong was the murderer–was the dead woman's husband.

THE End

X: Effervescent #3
(We are Brass)

Lyrics by Michael Vance

Though I speak with poet's or angel's
tongue and lung, yet have not love
I become sounding brass
I become tinkling cymbal

All the children cry
to see the dragons die
stumble from the sky
smash their wings against the tree
sputter, gasp, wheeze, and pass
into the past, darkly

He sat beside his hat and coat, the poet,
and wrote: "There is nothing quite so sorrowful
As the cry of a wounded dragon." Then he
left his flagon and pen and flapped on
home to shed his shark skin suit, and
faint before an open fire. Yet, as the flames

hypnotize, in his eyes a fire dies (though
wood still burns to ashes) and lies cold
against his brow.

As the natural consequences of his day
 drops dew upon his lashes, down his cheeks,
 this poet softly speaks: How?
"The seconds melted into days
"The days have blurred into weeks,
"The weeks have drained away my years
"and left me more than tears
"all has gone to tears."

All the children cry
to see the dragons die
stumble from the sky
smash their wings against my knees
sputter, gasp, wheeze, and pass
into the past, darkly

The poet wrote:
We are brass
All are tarnished
We are cymbals clashed

Jesus was a soldier when he ran the dragons through,
Slew the lizards in our heads, left
a lamb to reign instead; broke
our illusion's horny back, pinned
veiny wings to the cross, to writhe
as the scaly butterfly did gag and toss and hack

Ah, our childhood cries
to see the dragons die
stumble from the sky
smash their wings against our knees

sputter, gasp, wheeze, and pass
into the past, darkly

When we was child, we spoke as child,
thought and understood as child.
But when we became man, we
put away childish things...
      dragon wings.

A Change of Heart

Softly, slowly as fallen dust, the seeds of chaos were gathering.

"It's all right, it's all right," whispered Randall Stubbins as he pragmatically patted both of his shirt pockets and the inside pockets of his jacket as he wondered, mildly irritated, how a man could misplace his glasses. The newspaper rolled up and tucked under his left arm fell loose and open on the pavement as he checked the top of his head. When he bent to retrieve it, an unforgiving rigidity in the left pocket of his slacks solved his mystery. Stubbins removed the austere black-framed glasses and put them on the bridge of his nose.

He stood on the bleak corner of Chesham and Wells by a black, cast-iron lamp post topped by an opaque onion bulb. A sign on the lamp post read: *The Best Little Town Around.*

"Well, it's better to look like the truth," he brooded, "than to be the truth."

That was the philosophy of Townsend Advertising, and as one of its burned-out former advertising copywriters, Stubbins had looked askance at everything as "near truth," which had made him wildly successful. At the peak of his career, he no longer wished to sell his creative soul to toothpaste and corn flakes. When he demanded a much higher price, they fired him.

He looked up and squinted into the sun at the queer "Ultimate Building."

Corpulent and feminine, The Crawford Hotel rose from its foundation like a huge, uneaten, three-layered cherry cake that had been heavily lacquered to preserve it for wedding anniversaries. A smear of yellow on a blue slate, the sun hung low on the edge of its enigmatic roof as

Stubbins thought of fairy-tale gumdrop houses, naughty German children and cannibalistic witches.

He felt trivialized by the massive anomaly that rose in sedate, ethereal Victorian beauty before him. It was rectangular, perfectly symmetrical and alive with an impossible static movement. It's east face of brick was one-third the width of its west, and the corner facing Chesham and Wells had been replaced with a round turret capped with an inverted ice cream cone cosmetically painted sky blue. On the first floor, a door with a burgundy colored cloth awning opened onto a restaurant. A small, wooden sign over the door read The Old Van Buren Inn.

Smaller turrets rose on its remaining corners and on the west face on either side of double doors on the ground floor. These turrets were decorated with columns of horizontal rungs or with rising curls like blush licorice. The east windows between the turrets on the first and second floor rose into arches; the windows on the third were circles flattened at their base, and large lush plants hung like pupils in each. Overlapping bluish-pink, slate shingles covered the face of the top floor, and every story was adorned by cornices of burnt cherry.

Stubbins looked at The Crawford's dots and doughnuts, flowers and runic details and decided the wedding cake couldn't be worth the advertised $50.50 a week room rental. He took off his glasses, cleaned them with his tie, dropped his paper again, put his glasses back on his nose, and walked across the intersection. The forgotten newspaper blew away as he neared the blue double doors of The Crawford's west face. He stopped before these oak doors, took off his glasses, put them in his left pant pocket, and raised his clenched fist to knock.

"It's all right," he declared like a talisman against the evil spirits of change. "Damned!" he cursed as he missed the door and skinned his knuckles on brick, leaving a smear of blood as his sacrifice on the altar of The Crawford.

"I lived in New York City before I accepted the job of manager for your Chamber of Commerce," he bragged. Stubbins watched the young woman fearlessly ascend the narrow, almost vertical, rich brown steps ahead of him in a melancholy, diffuse light. She was in her mid-twenties with the saturnine face of a fashion model, and she moved in perfect symmetry. Her eyes were cerulean blue, her hair jet black, and her pink legs were bare and hard-muscled below her polka dot shorts. She wore stained, white linen gloves.

"You attended the Tenebrae church there, Mr. Stubbins?" she asked, ascending without touching the dark, hardwood rail on the wall. "This will be quite an adjustment for you, moving from The Big Apple to our frightening little town."

"Word gets around in these little burgs, doesn't it? I was a member, and The Big Apple has little worms." He was impressed with her blunt honesty, and, bluntly, her lithe body. He paused at one of many esoteric pictures on the pale lavender walls of the stairwell. It was slightly askance. He straightened it. "I'm looking forward to living in a quiet little town without traffic jams or political corruption."

"The only jams we have are spread on bread," she said from the small landing at the top of the stars, neither expecting nor pausing for a response. "But if you don't like political squabbles, then you'll need to stay away from the Phillips and Moran families."

A large, old railroad trunk stood open behind her, full of pockets and shelves needed for long travel, and a distant memory of the clip-clap, clip-clap, clip-clap of iron wheels on iron rails. A brass urn sat next to it, and a very large, glass sphere like a fortune teller's ball rested on an ornate, blue-iron stand on the left corner of the landing.

"The Crawford was built in 1889 as a bank." said the young woman. "She is made of marble from the Tennessee Valley, wainscot and hardwood trims from around the world and custom designed ornate tin work. But 'The Ultimate Building,' as it was known, didn't survive the Great Depression as a bank. She was purchased and run by the local gas company until '52. Her third floor was a speakeasy during Prohibition, and the original door still has a peek hole in it." She paused in her memorized speech.

"You might appreciate the fact, Mr. Stubbins," she said, brushing a strand of her jet black hair from her face, "that the Azrealites worshiped at The Crawford for many years after the first church was destroyed and until the second building was constructed only a few years ago."

"Excuse me," said Stubbins, wrinkling his nose, "but, do you smell something?"

"Her second floor," she continued, ignoring his remark, "this floor, was remodeled into rooms for boarders. I chose the furnishings from my favorite era, the Victorian. Full of hushed-up nastiness and all kinds of repressed desires, you know."

"You must be quite the historian since you can't be more than twenty-five years old yourself," he flattered her as he looked at an outre painting over the trunk. He pushed the left corner of the painting up in an unconscious, reflexive and completely useless effort to straighten it on the wall where it hung.

"Flattery will always turn a lady's head," she said with a demure smile, "but, luckily, I am no lady. I am the landlady." She paused for a chuckle that did not happen. "Oh, well. Just to the left is her small water-closet. Next to it is a small room where you may eat supper, and next to that, a bathroom that you'll share with the other roomer on this floor. Not at the same time, of course." Ageless and sedate, she opened the door to the water-closet.

Inside was a porcelain toilet with its tank decorated by an ivory, lace doily stained yellow at its edges, and a faded print of two nineteenth-century women in diaphanous gowns above it. The sink had wooden water handles and in it was a smear of black with white paws and luminous yellow eyes. It looked up with the utter disdain of complete ownership and unequivocal, occult power, then leapt soundlessly to the faded, fringed rug on the dark hardwood floor.

"Oh," she said as the cat slunk between Stubbins' legs and paused on the landing, "that's Oreo. She actually owns The Crawford, so I guess we all rent from her."

In one silent, graceful movement, Oreo swept fearlessly, like a whisper of cool air, down the stairs, pausing once in mid-flight to glance disdainfully over her midnight black shoulder at Stubbins before she finished her descent and was gone.

"I don't mean to be rude," he said, "but what is that...raw smell?"

The young woman closed the door with an impalpably feminine movement. "You have discovered the black secret of The Crawford. And so soon. Are you ready to see the available room, Mr. Stubbins? Just follow me," she added, already moving east of the stairwell down the narrow hall.

"Have you ever felt you were being followed, yet no one was there?"

"Well, no one important."

"That's very funny. They'll like that at the Chamber." She stopped before a door inset with an opaque glass panel. There was an old-fashioned transom above it. She pushed it open with a sigh of wood on cloth and gestured at the room inside. "This was a lawyer's office before it was remodeled, and it's really large enough for a small family. But we don't get many new families, small or otherwise. This is where you'd bunk."

The turn-of-the-century furnishings of lace curtains and table cloths, ornate beds and flowered comforters, hurricane lamps, gilded clocks and crystal were nestled in rich, burgundy walls. The woods were heavy and dark and softened by shadows. Dust motes hung, somber and timeless, in diffused shafts of pale, yellow sunlight seeping through the curtains. The room was sultry, hungry and carnal, yearning for that lover's embrace that brings wholeness and satiation.

"I-it is an amazing room, but I don't think it's a, well, a man's room," Stubbins said with the profundity of a thirty-seven-year-old confirmed bachelor.

"It is her room, Mr. Stubbins. I don't mean to dissuade you, but there is an unseen presence inhabiting The Crawford."

"A presence?"

"Yes. She turns lights on and off sometimes, and whispers in the dead of night like a sound of rushing wind from a great distance. She turns the water heater on and off indiscriminately, and shows herself as a face in mirrors or as a ghost in midair standing on a balcony that was removed years ago. She is that faint smell of fish you noticed."

"Bet she attracts gullible, superstitious tourists to The Crawford like moths to a flame," he said, decidedly neither superstitious nor a tourist. "I couldn't help noticing you call this building 'her' and 'she'."

"The presence is female, sort of sullen and agitated like an unfaithful woman awaiting her lover. In fact, a man was murdered by her lover here, Mr. Stubbins, and she was found cradling his bloody head in her arms, whispering 'it's all right, it's all right.' But the emanation isn't a ghost."

"Blluhhh," he said satirically, faking a shudder. "Don't you ever think of moving?"

"Oh, dear, no. 'Love me, love my Crawford.' I'm used to her pranks, and, in many ways, I think of us as two of a kind. Azrealite sisters."

"There's that word again. Azrealite. You seem deeply committed to your church."

"The chief purpose of life is to glorify The One."

"Hmmmm. Well, the ghost thing. That isn't a bad angle, actually, for a town in desperate need of something more profitable than retired government employees on pensions. Sort of like 'safe fear.' Any other local malignant ghosts and monsters about?"

"You don't believe in the supernatural, Mr. Stubbins?"

"Of course I do. It's one of our tenants. 'As the collective consciousness of humanity is greater than any individual mind, there is an immeasurable supernatural realm greater than the material world.'"

"How convenient. You must be of the reformed church."

"I'm of the denomination that thinks angels," said Stubbins, "fallen or otherwise, are just symbolic of human psychological glitches."

"And I'm a fundamentalist who thinks that reducing The One to a symbol of human 'glitches' is disheartening and... dangerous. But enough 'ology. 'Time and the inexplicable surprises in life' have a way of affecting a change of heart, anyway, don't they Mr. Stubbins?"

She stepped out of the room, corpulent and feminine, closing the door. Stubbins pointed at another door on the north wall of the hall not five feet away. "And this is...?" He pragmatically patted both of his shirt pockets, and the inside pockets of his jacket. He checked the left pocket of his slacks. "That's odd," he said, puzzled. "My glasses. I could have sworn..."

"To whom?" she interrupted. "I'm sorry. It's my room, Mr. Stubbins."

"Your room, Mrs. Horne? But I thought...?!?"

"Oh, dear, I'm not Barbara Horne. I'm Cynthia Wells, her sister. Barbara and her husband, Jake, live on the third floor, and I manage The Crawford for them. She's at a Daughters of the Star meeting, and asked me to show you around. I'm so embarrassed.

"So," she said as she peeled off the white glove of her right hand with her left, and brushed a strand of jet black hair from her face. "Will you take her?"

And without disturbing the flesh, she reached in and changed his mind.

"Great tea," Randall said, sitting the delicate cup on a solitary antique trunk next to his bed. Its muffled thud drew his eyes to where it lay, the tea spilled on the tasseled rug on the floor. "But I know I put it...!"

"Maybe the presence is sticking its tongue out at an unbeliever," said Cynthia with a twinkle in her eye as she knelt and began moping tea with a cloth. She wore a light, yellow dress of intricate flowers. Her jet black hair was pulled back in a severe bun.

"I'm really, really sorry. Listen," he said, kneeling next to her, "maybe I could make it up to you with a movie and supper at The Old Van Buren Inn?" He put his hand on hers, and their eyes met in an uneasy, carnal anticipation.

They ate baked potatoes, salads and lobster. They walked together in the chill of early dusk to the theater, chatting about The Crawford, about Barbara and Jake Horne, and about Cynthia. The lobby of the theater was pitch black, full with the timeless smells of candy, salt, popcorn, pop and human sweat The air was warm and smarmy. Randall bought buttered popcorn, soft drinks and Sugar Babies. He found his black-framed glasses in his pocket and put them on the bridge of his nose. They sat in the middle of the dark theater, and he uncharacteristically put his arm around her shoulders. The movie was Alfred Hitchcock's "Psycho."

"Oh lord," she shuddered, "I'll never take a shower again."

They showered together.

As days died and fell away like autumn leaves, their eyes and hands met again and again. They took long, leisurely walks around the town at dusk and picnicked at the haunted lake with its dead, spectral trees. Cynthia told him of a number of ghosts and gargoyles around her moribund town, and on its grassy bank, they kissed passionately.

She wore pink, and Randall talked of his obsession for old pulp writers like Lovecraft, Bradbury, Robert E. Howard and Maxwell Grant. He told her how an unexpected epiphany at The Crawford had became a fully realized plan that he had presented a week earlier to the board of the Chamber of Commerce. He would exaggerate the aberrant legends of the town until people would flock to see the ghosts. Haunted lakes and the lighthouse restaurant he proposed to build over the town's most infamous ruins.

"After all, the best place to hide nasty secrets is out in the open," he crowed with the ancient and universal dance of a young cock impressing his hen. "They liked that."

"Have you seen the ruins?" asked Cynthia, hiding with feminine coyness her joy that he wore his heart on his sleeve, and wore it for her.

At dusk on the Friday of their fourth week, they walked from The Crawford and to the abysmal old ruins, hand in hand, happy and quietly talking, sharing the intimate, delicate double entendres, innuendoes and mundane details of the life of new lovers.

"Great site," Randall said, beginning to sit on one of the stones that lay half buried and moss covered in an odd, chaotic circle. The muffled thud drew Cynthia's eyes to where he lay on the ground, livid with disgust and embarrassment.

"Hell hath no fury like a presence scorned." Cynthia stood above him in a perfect symmetry of static movement with one hand over her mouth. She wagged a finger at Randall with fained petulance.

"Go ahead and laugh," he bleated, humiliated as he struggled to his feet and meticulously dusted off his pants. "I'd expect that from a blasted orthodox Azrealite."

"No," she said, trying to suppress her giggling. "No, I-I shouldn't, considering what is buried in this place."

"Oh, God damn it, not that again."

"Randall!?" cried Cynthia in surprise and outrage as she glanced quickly about to see if another had heard him blaspheme. "How could you say that!?"

"Just natural talent, I guess," he said, grinning broadly and inviting her to share the brilliance of his dark wit.

"For thousands of years we have been hated, hunted, persecuted and slaughtered in defense of the freedom you seem to take for granted. Even when the time was ripe and the first church was openly built where we stand, it was ravaged by fanatics. How can you not believe?"

"Hey, I believe you believe it. But I must admit that I wish you could lighten up sometimes. I'm tolerant of your opinions. Is there any chance you could stop being so narrow minded and fundamentalist and bigoted and respect mine?!"

"Not without trivializing what I believe!" she spat, her voice powerful and female. "Bigoted? How very convenient. How pat. If I disagree with you, I'm bigoted and narrow minded and you win. But we are the chosen people. The Azrealites will make the events happen that will trigger the Second Incarnation! Do you think you can keep denying and betraying 'The Three' and 'The Three Sixes' with immunity forever?"

"'The Three'? The three what?"

"'The One,' perfect, beautiful and full of power, who bought free will for us and paid for it with his life, and the Mother and Son of Tenebrae."

"With all of the perverse horrors we do to each other already, I think we don't need a flesh and blood Satan. Listen, that's all just ancient poetry to get across complex ideas to simple-minded, stupid people."

"Like me?" asked Cynthia with a gathering storm behind her cerulean blue eyes.

"No, not like you, but like the savages thousands of years ago who didn't even know the earth is round or how babies are made. Complicated philosophical ideas had to be simplified using symbolic flesh and blood characters and stories so that they could understand. That doesn't mean the ideas aren't powerful. And as for 'The Three Sixes,' don't you think deifying our church fathers and some prophesied messianic leader goes against our own tenants? I'm sure they were or will be terrific guys, but 'The Three Sixes'? Come on, Cynthia, they were or will be just men. Our first Admonition is all creatures are equal and there are no gods."

The storm exploded with profane, feminine power.

On Monday, Randall reluctantly attended worship with Cynthia at the First Church of Tenebrae on the corner of Ash and Ebaugh, although he would not sing "Come Quickly, Mighty Prince of Light" or participate in the communal chants.

They fought with redoubled intensity on All Hallow's Eve as they returned to The Crawford from Mass. Randall had stubbornly and publicly refused to partake of the closed communion of the "goat with no horns," the ancient and nascent celebration of First Incarnation.

They reconciled with profane, carnal power.

He pushed the left corner of a painting up in a reflexive and completely useless effort to straighten it on the wall. "I want you," Randall whispered, burning with the ancient, restless, animal lust and primal fear of mortality that drives man to perpetuate himself in flesh and cheat the insufferably undeniable finality of death.

"You'd better," she whispered, her voluptuous mouth on his, hot, female and uninhibited, her flesh voracious in its utter surrender to the inevitable fertility and mortality that woman instinctively understands: that to give is to begin to die, that to withhold is to never live.

"It's all right," she whispered, pulling his head down to the French silk of her neck and cradling it as she rocked back and forth in a timeless and universal female dance.

She had already named the child inside her who would father the Great DemiUrge of the Third Sixes and wed science and the supernatural and breathe new life into the dry bones that would destroy three billion human beings and shake the world to its knees.

She giggled.

And at that moment, in a clandestine and illegal meeting in a home, Jake Horne and the board of directors of the Chamber of Commerce rejected Randall Stubbins' new ideas. "Why buy the cow," said Jake with a lurid smile like a cut on his face, "when you can get the milk free. Even if it's an Azrealite cow?"

They would eventually implement less than half of them.

"Everything!!" Randall raved, throwing his notebook on a table. Its muffled thud drew his eyes to where it lay, fanned open on the tasseled rug on the floor. "The lighthouse restaurant, the graveyard angle, the haunted lake, even renaming the streets! The idiots threw it all down the toilet!! Tell me what is wrong with 'Poe Avenue!!'"

"Well, it is a little too obvious, sweetheart," said Cynthia, blushing cherry red.

The storm broke with profane, masculine power.

"You and your narrow minded, bigoted little town can take all of your Azrealite fundamentalist crap and go to......go to...." Randall stood frozen and red faced in profound embarrassment, his right fist raised in anger as Cynthia sat, tight-lipped, defensive, tearful and guardedly amused.

"To..." She could not resist and misjudged the depth of his unreasoning anger. "A symbolic place of punishment debunked by the Reformed Tenebrae Church?"

"Get out!" he yelled, a red ball of seething anger. "GET OUT!"

"This is my room," said Cynthia quietly, sullen, sibilant and impalpably female. "Randall, sweetheart, don't..."

Randall turned sharply and stomped through the open door. He knew he was wrong. He knew he could not stop unless he surrendered his masculinity, his beliefs and himself forever to the implacable, immovable, impalpable femaleness that sat in the room behind him with his seed in her belly.

'And that goes for Jake too!!" he screamed at the absent owner of the building, and he stomped down the hall to the landing of the stairwell. "And tell it to the God damned Chamber for me!!!" Randall cursed at the brink of the stairs, and stepped down.

The stair moved.

Randall fell, his face frozen in inexplicable surprise and horror, clutching and clawing at air as he fell, thudding with sickening force against first the left and then the right wall as he fell, bruising flesh and breaking the bone in his left wrist on the hard stair edges as he fell, crushing the rib in his left chest and breaking his neck on the second to the first stair as he stopped.

He lay at the foot of the stars, twisted, a broken marionette. The last faint light of life flickered in his chest. Randall tried to rise on his elbows. He moaned profanely, blood at the left corner of his twisted mouth.

Above him in the muted half-light of a mausoleum, Cynthia cringed at the head of the stairwell in a yellow dress decorated with cherry blossoms, her hand over her mouth suppressing a sob, her eyes full of tears. At her feet, Oreo squatted on her haunches, licking a stained, white paw, purring sedately.

In one silent, graceful movement, Cynthia swept fearlessly, like a whisper of cool air, down the stairs, pausing once in mid-flight to glance fearfully over her shoulder at Oreo before she finished her descent. She knelt and cradled Randall's bloody head in her arms and whispered, "It's

all right, it's all right, it's all right."

"Cynthia, I..." choked Randall. "I..."

"It's all right," whispered The Crawford.

And without disturbing the flesh, it stuck out its tongue and reached in and moved his heart from the left to the right side of his chest.

THE END

THE SPIRIT OF LIGHT'S END

from a 1959 Chamber of Commerce Brochure: *Light's End: The Garden City*

by Randall Stubbins

The history of Light's End, "The Garden City", is so like a Brothers Grimm story that it needs to begin with...

Once upon a time, a tribe of Indians, the Abenakis, gathered their defeated people–plagued by smallpox and war–and fled to the desolate Memphremagog Forest in Maine. Long before statehood, these "People of the Dawnland" raised a starvation crop of corn, beans and squash and worshiped Odzihozo, their rock 'god.' They led a secluded and hard life, the final thirty years under the savage chieftain, Adogodquo. That Abenakis village became Light's End.

In 1653, an English outcast, Caleb Elliott, established a trading post at the heel of the crag where Jeroboam and John Azreal would build "The Watch" lighthouse in 1800. In 1852, the Rock Island railroad–which became the Pennsylvania RR #1–laid ties, and Light's End was incorporated.

There was little happiness in the early days of that isolated village. Abomination Reef had destroyed any hope of Light's End becoming a prosperous shipping harbor. In its first twenty years, it had obtained a population of only 800 souls, and established only one landmark, The

First Church of Tenebrae, founded by the Azrealites.

However, the real spirit of Light's End—that stubborn, set-jawed determination—was alive and hungry. As those early pioneers threw up shanties near the beach, that conviction never faltered, and they endured—sowing on hard ground, reaping little, and toiling—to plant a glorious new garden on earth.

That seed will finally bear fruit as The Garden City metamorphoses into the vacation destination of Maine, the nation, and eventually, the world! From the mouth of August Street to the Memphremagog Forest, self-denial and persecution will be replaced by wealth and ease. The pleasures of this world—rightfully ours—will be ours as our ancient festival, The Feasting, becomes the "Mardi Gras' of All Hallow's Eve—Halloween! Almost overnight, a new Light's End will be born and this little village will become a seething mass of forty-thousand people. On foot, in cars and buses, by train, by airplane, an endless throng will be lured by our promise of unholy thrills! The teepee of the renegade Indian will become the skyscraper of our runaway city.

Nothing will stop us.

Yes, there will be turmoil—and even crime. These are but birth pains; they will pass. Then the indomitable spirit of those pioneers who laid the foundation of Ebenezar Azreal's house, Gateway, will rise again.

With an iron will of self and civic pride, we will transform Light's End into the horror capitol of the world.

Yes, it is a monstrous and frightening goal. New hotels and motels must be built for the thousands who will flock to the new Feasting. Tourist attractions such as Sarah Azreal's grave, "The Twins" murder house, and Gateway must be preserved at all expense. Old street names will be replaced with Poe and Lovecraft and Machen. There will be new temples, new schools and hospitals—a new lighthouse. The Boiler Manufacturing District must be renovated. Traffic problems will increase as highways are built for the tourists. Clean water, sanitation, law enforcement—all these and other problems must and will be met.

Our future depends on how quickly and efficiently these problems are solved. Three years must suffice to finish this daunting task. With a population of over 20,000, and a trade territory including 70,000 more, Light's End can forever establish a position of leadership among the cities of Maine in recreational, commercial and industrial activities.

And our unconquerable spirit will guide us into The New Age as we fulfill that promise that first found voice in our founding fathers as they turned their eyes to the glory so long denied us–to the heavens above–and swore—

'As above, so below!"

A Trick of Light

The muted light clicked on and Louis Staples became his nasty Sunday morning face in the mirror over the bathroom sink again. He ran a hand full of yellow, dirty fingernails through his thinning hair. He opened the mirrored medicine cabinet above the sink, took out the tooth brush and paste, turned on cold water and brushed his teeth. Louis spat white foam. He set tooth brush and paste aside, took out razor and shaving foam from the cabinet, squirted and smeared foam on his face, and shaved.

"'Between the acting of a dreadful thing,'" he said to his reflection, "and the first motion, all the interim is like a phantasma, or a hideous dream.'"

Louis cleaned the razor in the running water and laid it aside, washed his face, opened the cabinet, put everything back, and closed the cabinet. He looked in the mirror again, ran a hand down his clean cheek, rubbed blood from his chin.

The air was warm and smarmy as Louis urinated, defecated, cleaned himself, took off his stained plaid pajamas and hung them on a wall hook. He put on a wrinkled, polyester white shirt and baggy, butt-worn black polyester slacks. He still smelled faintly sour and looked bloated and disheveled.

Louis hated Sundays. Nothing was on television except yelling preachers on all three channels, and everything was closed because of the Blue Laws. He left the bathroom, turning off the light. He clicked on a light switch next to the bathroom doorjamb and patted Marilyn Monroe's butt on the movie poster for *The Seven Year Itch* next to it. It was stained from repeated patting. As he passed her shrine of '50s men's and movie magazines, newspaper clippings, a calendar and a silent, black and white

52

stag film, Louis smiled.

He smiled about the other hidden thing in his apartment over the Phillips Pawn shop, stolen from the locked room that smelled like salt water and dead fish at the old Ashton Smith public library where he worked.

Louis moved through his maze of dusty shelves crammed with books, magazines, newspapers, comic books, pulp magazines, record albums and little, cheap toys as the irregular opening between things made the half light flicker like a silent film. He went to the two-chair room with one window, chose a book on film noir, and waited for Jake Horne. Jake was the good thing about Sunday because the theater manager brought him "damaged" movie posters from The State Theater and sold them for two or three dollars. Louis then thought of Polly and ran his hand full of dirty fingernails through his thinning hair. A muted beam of light fell through the fly specked crying window onto the carpet by his chair.

Jake Horne sat quietly with his face sweating as he looked out of the crying window. He had yellow teeth and a face full of stubble and was old and old and old. He took a deep drag on the stinking cigar that hung from the cut of his mouth.

"The Rialto movies was about five doors east of Parks Drug; third in line in its day," Jake ruminated. "And as a kid, I was the doorman, taking tickets. They also had minstrel shows: roving bands of musicians, lots of banjo music and they did comedy skits or sketches. I was there every minute of four years and it sat between Joan's Restaurant and the K.C. Store. And it was my whole life, Louis, a way to escape Light's End, school and my parents. And I knew then just like you know now."

"Knew what?" asked Louis as he leaned forward and creaked in his used metal folding chair, hungry for what Jake offered. The window to his apartment that looked out over August Street was crying. Jake took his cheap cigar out and smirked at an unspoken dirty joke that only he knew and loved although it was very old.

"I'm sorry if I seem distracted," apologized Louis. "But Polly's coming."

"C'mon," said Jake, "This from the librarian who hasn't missed a night at the State Theatre in fifteen years? You know that the real world only seems real when you see it on the stage or a movie screen."

"Ah. 'He will debauch himself with ideas, he will reduce himself to a shadow if for only one second of his life he can close his eyes to the hideousness of reality.'"

"Where do you get that stuff?" asked Jake. "Do you memorize quotes instead of cleaning this place? Is that in one of those books in that room you keep locked at the library?"

"Locked room? That's just storage, Jake. There are no 'eldritch books' from the old lighthouse. That's just town myth. And the quote is from Henry Miller's 'Tropic of Cancer'. As for the real world, I was heavy and shy and my mother was divorced when I was a child. Divorce just wasn't done then, so we were ostracized. We didn't go out much, not even to church. So I read a lot. And we didn't have much money for clothes, and I didn't fit in. So I turned to books and the library, and to television when it came along, and especially movies."

"The flicks were better then than now, huh?" said Jake, surveying Louis's room.

"Yes. Yes. Better," said Louis as he leaned back in his creaking metal folding chair. "I went every time I could, and bought all of the movie magazines. I loved cinematography long before I moved here. The movies were my life."

Louis looked reflexively at his wrist watch.

"Regrettably, I never made a movie in college," he whispered.

The mounds of books in the cheap metal shelves and shelves made of cement blocks and boards that filled every inch of his apartment ate the whisper and the sound of the rain outside his window.

"In a sense, even dreams are only a film inside your head, you know, except you feel you could walk into it and be a part of it."

"And life is but a dream, eh, Louis!" Jake's eyes burned with an unnatural light.

"All literature is essentially escape. How it is addressed by the great philosophers was the subject of my masters thesis, in fact. I've got it here, somewhere..."

Louis looked at his watch and thought of Polly somewhere beyond the crying window.

"It was titled *Allen to Zarkoff: Illusion as Reality*. And I just had an article titled 'The Reel Real' in a small circulation mimeographed journal that mentions that idea.

"Please excuse my bluntness, Jake" he said, leaning forward in his creaking metal chair. "but I'm a little short on time. Polly is coming, and she may be in a sour mood. What did you bring to sell?"

The rain that made the window cry distorted the street that wandered down to Jake's theater and blurred the huge marquee. Horne turned from the window and his eyes rummaged through the stacks of cheap horror, science-fiction and adventure paperbacks, second-hand movie books, molding pulp magazines, TV guides and comic books arranged by the Dewey decimal system.

"Anyway, it cost a dime to get in back then," Jake continued. "We had Saturday movie matinees—Tex Ritter, Johnny Mack Brown. Gene Autry."

Jake pulled a square of folded paper no bigger than the palm of his hand from his shirt pocket and began to unfold it.

"The Liberty Theater in the mid '20s and early '30s was located where the old Otasco store was; it was already gone when I started working at the Ritz. The Rex was the big one, though, because it was centrally located about where Patterson's Furniture is now. The Seminole was good, but the State was the best, and I worked there in the '50s. I worked at every one of them.

"Anyway, back in those days, Light's End had center parking on August Street," he said, talking around the stogie in his mouth. "On Saturday night you could hardly get up and down the streets. I remember the first time I went backstage was because of one performer called Smokey Joe. He was a banjo picker and singer, Louis. He impressed me."

Jake unfolded the paper.

"And I couldn't believe it. Smokey Joe wasn't Smokey Joe. He was a white guy in blackface makeup. And it struck me for the first time that something real backstage made something fake on stage seem real. You know? Of course you know. And I realized then Smokey didn't exist anywhere except on stage, and that the stage buildings, seen from behind, are cheap plywood. And it didn't come to me clearly until years later, but I couldn't stop wondering if there is a 'behind' to everything we think is real? And this 'behind' is what makes the world look like it does? The behind is the real thing, and the world is fake Do you think that's silly, Louis?"

"No," said Louis, leaning forward again. "No, I don't think that's silly, Jake."

Jake snapped out the creases in the paper.

"As the years passed, I wanted to go behind worse than anything, Louis. I wanted to see what's there. I'd guess that's why going to the movies is so exciting for some folks like us. They are kind of doing what is really impossible. Except for me, Louis."

"I'm sorry, Jake. But, regrettably, Polly..."

"I know how to go behind."

"What?" asked Louis.

Jake rose from the tattered recliner next to the crying window and moved to the rack that held his raincoat and umbrella. Louis watched him, saying nothing. Jake turned to Louis, winked, and handed him the paper.

"I didn't come tonight to talk about the glory days, Louis. Think of the history lesson as icing on the cake. I came because I found what you've wanted all of your life. What's probably hinted at in that book you don't have from the locked room at the library.

"And it's not what you think," he said, leaning close to Louis. "I'm having a private showing today of an extremely rare and esoteric film for just a few...eh...understanding customers. All the stars are in it. The cat and mouse, the sexpot, the clown, the action star and the girl next door."

"But it's Sunday," said Louis. "What about the Blue Law?" He creaked back in his metal chair and ran a hand full of fingernails through his thinning hair.

"Sunday can go to hell. This is a one time only showing. Don't be late," Jake said, and opened the apartment door. "It's the damnedest thing you'll ever see."

Louis looked at the movie handbill, then turned his wrist to look at his watch, then turned his wrist again to read the paper that was still warm from Jake's palm. It read: *All That Glitters*.

"...is not gold," said Louis, looking up from the handbill. "But, I can't come, Jake..."

The door was closed.

Polly sat quietly with her face cool as she looked out of the crying window. She had slightly crooked teeth and a face full of worry and she was old and old and old. She was fifty two. At the corner of her eye, she sensed The State Theatre through the crying window. She felt the train engine in the distance, its metal heart pounding against the rails in the rain. She pictured it chugging around King's Bend through surrounding scrub trees and rock. Polly was going to leave on that train.

"You're a little late today," said Louis nervously. He rocked back and forth in his creaking metal chair. "Please. Sit down. Guess who was here just a minute ago?"

"It was hard to come today." Polly touched a corner of her mouth with a fingertip then turned on another light from a lampstand.

"Ah," said Louis. "The rain."

August Street stretched before her below the crying window, down to the end of the hard edged town to the Light's End depot. The street was cobbled with red brick and lined on either side by buildings built of the same brick with metal awnings and fading, painted advertisements. At the end of the street, the depot of cream adobe and roofed with red ceramic tile sat on the mouth of the Pishon river that emptied into the harbor.

"No," said Polly quietly, "it wasn't the rain."

"Something amazing happened just a half hour ago, Polly. Just amazing. Jake who owns the State Theater was here and invited me to a special private screening of a movie called *All That Glitters*. But I've looked in every reference book I've got and it's not there, Polly. I can't find it anywhere!"

Looking through the crying window, Polly watched Miss Thomas cleaning the inside plate glass window of Killingsworth's Dry Goods and Shoe Market. Next door, James Andrews was standing in the doorway of Safeway Groceries watching the rain. "Bread $.50" was advertised on the window, and the shadow of these letters tattooed the message across his white, short sleeved shirt.

"I'm leaving Light's End, Louis," she said quietly. Outside the window, Dolittle Sundries, M & K Cafe, and the State Theater followed the descending curve of August Street to the depot. The M & K promised blue plate lunches for $1.00

"Can you imagine getting to see something like this in a small little town like Light's End, Polly. It's a once-in-a-lifetime opportunity."

The smell of fried fish, potatoes and hot coffee drifted from the Majestic Cafe where the Sunday after-church crowd was allowed to eat despite the Blue Laws. She looked at the Seminole Theater, then at Ebaug's, "The Diamond Store," offering family "photo's and gifts."

Distant in the rain, a wooden water tank stood a dozen yards from the station on the north side of the tracks, forgotten, its stilts tangled with weeds and trash. Across the tracks, two discarded axles rusted. Telegraph poles flanked the rails and shrunk eastward into the distance.

"I'm leaving Light's End, Louis," she repeated quietly.

"You...you're leaving?" Louis stammered, running a hand through his hair. "When are you coming back?"

"That depends...on you, Louis. That depends on whether you choose me or..." Polly looked around the two chair room and the crying window and the stacks and stacks of books. "Or this. I've had enough of this."

"But, Polly..."

"Louis," she cut him off. "Don't. I know why you do this."

"Polly," Louis pleaded. "Please, let me explain. Please."

He came to her side and knelt by Polly.

"I've never told anyone this. But if you'll only listen, I'm sure you'll understand. I was standing one night in a dark theater when I was thirteen and an empty projector booth was throwing a beam of light on the screen. From where I stood, that light swirling with dust motes mesmerized me, Polly. Everything else was almost pitch black. I was seeing the beam, and not seeing things around it. Then I moved, and it struck my eyes. Instantly, the whole first picture vanished, the theater was gone, and so was the beam. Instead I saw the old projectionist working at the camera, framed by the top of the projection window. You see? Do you understand? Looking along the light, I saw one Reality. Standing in it, I saw a completely different Reality. I thought, is there something behind the light that makes it light? And I thought, is there something behind me that makes...me? And if I stand inside the light and look down along it, what will I see?"

"That is why I do this 'stuff'," Louis said, swinging an arm that took in his apartment. "There's another me in the movies, somewhere, that is handsome and straight and thin who always says and does the right thing. A better me that's almost in these books, and on the screen, almost. Almost."

"Louis, stop it. Just stop. When I moved here and met you, I hoped we might be more than friends, and that we might make some kind of life together here in the little time that we have left. If you want the truth, Louis, neither one of us is a spring chicken or...or anything to look at, really. But I don't want to live here anymore. Something is wrong with this place. Something dirty. Secret. The people are...odd. This dirty little town is dark and lonely and sick in a hidden way. There is a door flat in the basement floor of my... And I don't want to live here anymore."

The crying window and Polly were crying.

"But Polly, I do want to get married..."

"Louie, you're already married to women who are always there when you want them and gone when you don't. Who never say no to sex or want it when you don't, never disagree with you, never talk about your faults, never burn the toast or forget to put oil in the car, never smell bad or get sick unless it's on cue. You're married to film women who always move, look, say and do the same thing forever. They never leave town unless it's in the script. But I am not in the script. And if you want to know what is real and what isn't, I know.

"I am real.

"And when you stand and look down the light," said Polly, standing, "you will have tiny, distorted moving pictures on the back of your head, and the screen will have a big, black blotch where your head blocks the light. Then the movie will end, and you will walk outside into the light of day and the real world will be there just like it has always been there, and will always be there, Louis..."

Polly slipped on her wet raincoat.

"But I won't be there."

"Pol...pol...Polly..."Louis stammered without rising from his chair. "Po... po...oly...." he stammered again, and then made the fatal mistake. He looked at his wrist watch.

Light's End wept as Louis walked past the window of *The Citadel* newspaper and saw his soft, pudgy face reflected in the glass and stopped. He wore no raincoat. His face was pale and weak, the face of a bank clerk, a fry cook, an accountant, a librarian, cut from the same polyester as his cheap suit. It was a face quickly forgotten, marked by neither exceptional intelligence nor stupidity, but Louis liked sameness.

Across the street at the State Theatre, the marquee screamed at him. He fought against thinking of Polly. The sky was heavy, grey and low and made the city seem like a closet. Louis bought a newspaper from a coin-operated rack and looked at the mast with its inaccurate drawing of the old lighthouse. The rays of light radiating from its beacon looked like a star. He read the headlines on the front page, folded the newspaper and tucked it under his arm. He fought against thinking of Polly at the depot.

Louis crossed the wet, brick street without turning his head left to look at the depot in the drizzle. He stood under the theater marquee and ran a trembling hand with its yellow, dirty fingernails through his thinning wet hair. The ticket booth was empty. He thought of *All That Glitters.* He thought that somewhere twenty-million miles away at the mouth of August Street at the depot was Polly.

Louis moved to the double doors of the State Theatre and rapped softly with his knuckles. He rapped again, harder. He whispered behind-behind-behind and Polly, and rocked back and forth on the balls and heels of his feet. The lock of the double doors clanked inside, and a slit opened in the doors.

"Aaaaaaaah," leered Jake inside the crack. "You."

"What do you want for..." Louis half-whispered, leaning close to the crack.

"Your soul," said Jake Horne, suspiciously looking up and then down August Street, "of discretion."

"No, I mean..."

"Don't be stupid," said Jake as Louis entered and the manager locked the door behind them. "You've bought everything I sell. Get in."

The lobby of the theater was pitch black and full with the timeless smells of candy, salt, popcorn, pop and human sweat. The air was warm and smarmy. Jake clicked on a flashlight in his left hand, pointing the light at the red carpet by their feet. He moved to the swinging door with the porthole in the center that separated the lobby and the theater and pushed it open.

"I'm sorry to ask," said Louis, "but, regrettably, Polly is...and I....is there any way we could do this later?"

Jake got red in the face and very tense and swore holding the swinging door open. "Sure, sure," he hissed with anger lacing the words. "We'll do this again when hell freezes over."

"I'm sorry. It's just that..." but Louis' words faded into the muffled black of the theater as he and Jake moved to a row of red upholstered seats to the sound of the lobby doors swinging in diminishing arcs. Jake swung the beam of the flashlight to a seat, and Louis moved to it and sat.

"Who's in *All That Glitters*," he asked. "Any of the biggies?"

"Everyone who earned it."

Jake swung the beam of light to the projection booth behind and above the seats. The projector clicked into spontaneous life. The title and opening credits flashed on the screen and faded to a mouse with a mallet and a cat, and the mouse hit the cat in the head, and its head exploded in blood and brains, and the cat died. Jake squatted on his haunches in front of Louis breathing heavily with a funny smile like a cut on his face. On the screen, the blonde bombshell licked her lips and rolled her hips. Jake sighed so deeply that he shook.

"There comes a time for dirty little lies to stop, Louis," he said. "Lies about books inside a locked room that I helped to build. Dirty lies about why you came."

On the screen, the clown slipped and fell, knocking over silverware and glasses and plates, and cried.

"You aren't here in scholarly pursuit or because you were rejected by

society since you were a child. You're here because you've been too busy running away from everything in pursuit of nothing for that."

On the screen, the action star battled a mongrel horde with bare fists and raw courage.

"You're here because you've always known and run away from what's behind."

On the screen, the girl next door French kissed her finance's best friend.

"Polly was right, Louis, but you can make her wrong, Louis. Stand up in the light. Polly knows you're a coward but you can stand up, Louis. Polly knows the truth, but you can stand up in the light without her. Stand up!!"

Jake drove each word like a nail into Louis. "You know the way behind. You are the way behind. Stand up. Look," hissed Jake. "Stand up and look behind."

And Louis stood up into the light and looked.

He did not face the projection window and look into the light. He did not look along the light that showed the State Theatre with its splotchy, empty red-cushioned seats, skyscraper light fixtures and the flickering movie on the screen. Louis stood up into the light and looked at the screen.

Louis stood up into the light and no pictures flickered on the back of his balding head. The pictures on the screen were not blotched out by the silhouette of his head. No cat and mouse, no action star or sexpot, no clown or girl next door danced on the screen.

"Do you see behind, you sniveling fool." Jake's eyes were red slits, and his teeth showed and he laughed, a painful laughter that twisted his face and convulsed his stomach but did not startle Louis.

Louis was busy screaming at what he saw behind.

THE END

In The Out Door

Adam Loman glanced through the fly-specked display window to his left at pyramids of toothpaste, cans of chowder, tins of maple syrup, and a fan of flatware on a pegboard featuring a serrated knife, a serving spoon, and an oyster fork.

"Be prepared, be prepared, be prepared," he berated himself. "A stitch in time saves nine." There was no umbrella in the display.

Loman pushed thuck thuck thuck at the left of two glass doors framed with tarnished brass, the view behind them mostly obscured by whorls of dripping condensation. The brass was cold on his fingertips. The sky behind and above him wept fat, slow tears as he stood in an overcoat, almost obscured by shadows, in the northernmost of two entryways recessed between three huge display windows. Above that, a sign stretching the length of the brick building announced the G. F. Wacher's 5¢ & 10¢ Variety Store. He pushed thuck thuck against the door again.

The sky was heavy, grey and low, and made the town taste, feel and smell like a mildewed closet. Bare-headed and dripping rain, he had squirmed against the cold in his soaked overcoat, irritated that he had no umbrella and that his new '59 Chevy was vulnerable to damage where it was parked at the curb. Loman pushed thuck against the door again as the sky rumbled.

He frowned as he glanced again at the display window and at the soft, still attractive, forty-five-year-old face reflected there, a face distinguished by neither exceptional intelligence nor stupidity. Loman turned back to the entrance, and placed his left hand on the door. Inside and behind a long lunch counter that diminished out of sight into the back of the variety store stood a young blond girl vigoriously miming a man pulling something. Loman smiled and pulled the door open.

The air inside was gratefully warm but smarmy, and smelled of grilled cheese, french fries, and talcum powder. Loman looked down at a wire rack to his left and at the mast of *The Citadel* newspaper with its inaccurate drawing of the lighthouse that supposedly hid many of the town's nasty secrets. The rays of light radiating from its beacon looked like a star. He read a headline on the front page, then shrugged out of his overcoat and hung it on the coat rack by the newspaper rack.

Loman ran a hand with its manicured fingernails through his wet blond hair and moved to the first of twenty cracked, red vinyl stools, and sat at the lunch counter next to a small rack of Lay's potato chip bags. The girl who had waved him inside earlier smiled at him as she poured hot coffee into a mug behind the counter.

Two teenaged girls sat halfway down the counter next to a red Double Cola dispensing machine, giggling and sharing secrets as they nibbled on sandwiches. Behind them, low, flat-topped, wooden display cases offered toiletries, ovenwear, cosmetics, ladies wear and much more under old-fashioned globe lighting hung from a stamped-tin ceiling. Loman also noticed a morbidly obese man in the middle of the store who glanced up at him and smiled with a mouth like a cut before turning back to a rack of slickers. The variety store was otherwise empty.

Loman looked for a menu. A white paper napkin lay folded into a neat triangle on the polished but worn lunch counter. A knife, a spoon, and a fork lay on the napkin.

"Welcome to Wacker's," said the blonde girl as she sat the mug on the counter in front of Loman. "You okay, mister? Something eating at ya?"

"Oh, uh, just a little embarrassed by that door thing a minute ago." Loman guessed she was sixteen years old with the saturnine face of a fashion model.

"Don't worry about it," she answered. "An honest mistake." Her eyes were cerulean blue and she was the source of the vanilla smell of talcum. Her pink legs were bare and hard-muscled below a white apron. She wore a small cross on a tiny chain that hung around her throat, yellow, rubber gloves, and the girlish sound of her voice betrayed a small town innocence and inexperience.

"Do you take cream or sugar? Oh," she said, noticing her gloves, " Excuse me. I've been cleaning." She peeled the gloves off. "I'm Penny

Neitenheimer. Are you new to Light's End?"

"Actually, I was born here," answered Loman. "Moved away when I was six. Adam Loman's my name. Pastor Loman, in fact." He added the emphasis to pastor from a sincere pride in his tiny Congregrational Church in a backwater burg about forty-five miles southwest of the coast of Maine. "I noticed your cross."

"Oh," Penny said, and lowered her head in deference to his position. "Would you like a menu?"

"Actually, I can just taste a good, old-fashioned 'BLT; pepper bacon, crisp lettuce and fresh tomato'? Any chance?"

"Comin' up! I kinda guessed you didn't know your way around," Penny continued, touching her cross with the thumb and index finger of her right hand. "I pretty much know everyone in town. "That little girl," she added, pointing at the girls at the counter, "is Sara Lagle, and the younger one is June Block. That man in the back..."

"I'm back to collect an inheritance," Loman interrupted. "I'm already almost late for a meeting with a lawyer at five o'clock. I've inherited my uncle's old mansion. I think it's called Gateway."

The blood drained from Penny's face. She leaned close to Loman and lowered her voice. "Listen, I've gotta say this quietly because Christians aren't exactly popular around here, Pastor. And that smelly fat man back there was Ebenezar's friend; used to eat at his house all the time."

"He knew my uncle?" Loman started to rise from his stool. "Maybe I should go back and ask..."

"No! No, no, no, Mr. Loman. I mean, Pastor. Please listen. I didn't know that horrible man, but my current events class followed his hunting expeditions because he comes from the richest, most famous family in town, and I clipped his picture out of the newspaper where he's standing with one foot on a lion he killed. Yuck. My dad knew him, and says he was a bad man, a very bad man, and he says he isn't dead!"

"But, I received a letter..."

"I've never been in his house," admitted Penny, her words rushed and urgent, "or seen all his nasty animal heads hung all over the walls of that crazy place. But my dad says Ebenezar liked killing, but he was too scared of dyin' to die himself! From the beginning, he killed just to watch things spill the last drop of blood, and he kept killing until there wasn't anything he hadn't killed...'cept men, maybe. Then my dad said he got bored. Then he got sick! In the head! Began to stuff other...things."

"Admitting that I've never even met my uncle," said Loman, "and don't even know what he looks like, don't you think that sounds kinda...silly, Penny"

"It's all true! When salesmen and inlanders started disappearing in town, everyone knew it was Ebenezar! So dad says he faked his death to get out of finally being arrested for all of the criminal things he's done here." Penny glanced to her left at the girls tittering and munching potato chips, then at the fat man in the back of the store who was looking at big, amber jug of cider. The young girl leaned so uncomfortably close to Loman's left ear that he could almost feel the fine hairs on her cheek.

"Ebenezar Azreal was a Satanist!"

There was an awkward moment of silence as Penny drew back and Loman struggled to mask his disappointment, and searched for the right word that wouldn't hurt an impressionable young girl's feelings: ridiculous? juvenile? ignorant? misguided? After all, Satan was nothing more than a primitive symbol of man's fallen nature, created at a simpler time for simpler minds.

"I'm a little surprised at your words," he answered with the measured response of an enlightened pastor who seldom won the Satan debate with his own congregation or his peers, and therefore chose to address Penny's lesser offense, gossip.

"As a Christian, you surely know that loose lips sink ships." He winced at his own cliche.

"Very profound, Mister...?

Loman followed the sound of the voice behind his right shoulder by swiveling on the stool. Behind him stood the fat man with loose skin and a smarmy smile. Penny stepped back from the counter.

"May I?" he asked, pointing at a stool, and laboriously sat.

"I couldn't help but overhear some of your conversation about Ebenezar Azreal, a friend of mine and a constant dinner companion. And, admitting he was certainly the black sheep of our little town, much of what is said about him is grossly exaggerated. You are...?"

"Reverend Adam Loman. I've inherited his estate."

"So you're the one who inherited his millions. Welcome to Light's End."

"M-m-millions?" Adam stuttered. "I thought..."

"As I was saying, some of what you'll hear is just plain outlandish. As example, the town didn't drag him out of Gateway and cut his throat. He never trusted doctors, and died from eating a piece of bad meat.

"Anyway, I won't take up your time; I'm already late for supper. Do you know how to get to his house?" the fat man asked, and gave Loman directions before Adam could answer.

"I hope I've helped," he said, and rose clumsily from the stool with an oily smile. "Remember, don't believe everything you hear. I assure you..." he paused and looked at Penny with an expression somehow both blank but threatening. "You'll find him a man after your own heart."

Loman squirmed deep into his still damp overcoat behind the Chevy's windshield as its wipers thup thup thup thup smeared rain across the glass. A heavy, salt-laden wind soughed over the yellow ribs of sand that skirted Abomination Bay, unseen because of the storm, crouching, and foul at the end of August Street. He shuddered as the sky spit lightning and rumbled.

The bay and its lighthouse were nasty things and childhood cautionary tales that still soured his adult memories. He drove past the last street lamp rising from a cluster of greaseweed thinking of his brief, melancholy childhood in Light's End, of his inheritance and a new start, of his wife and his little congregation. The street lamp's pale halo of light was rendered all but useless by the obscuring rain that seemed to bolt the earth to the sky and turn day into preternatural twilight.

Adam Loman was an uneasy but determined man. His knuckles were white on the faux leather protecting the steering wheel, and a line of sweat creased his forehead as he listened to the low hurrmmmmm of his car's heater and the fuuuusssh of the wind outside. Static had made the radio useless.

"Ebenezar Azreal is dead," he told the heater and bit his lower lip, tasting the salt of his own blood.

Adrian Keep's letter that lay on the passenger's seat. It was the only correspondence that Loman had ever received from a lawyer. It promised that he had inherited the infamous "crooked" house of wealthy Ebenezar Azreal, a perverse, feared, and hated man who believed he'd discovered the splintered Door between realities and reestablished the physical link between man and The One, The Urge, the foundation of the cult of the Azrealites and the Tenebrae Church. Keep had also written that Ebenezar had been obsessed with the occult and aberrant behavior since his childhood, and had believed he'd reopened the foul Door hidden deep inside Gateway, and set the stage for the triumphant return of The Urge, who had bought freedom for man and paid for it with his blood, and that it was all, of course, the madness of a sick, lonely man who had lost his grip on reality. The letter ended with odd advice: don't talk to the people in town unless wild rumor is your cup of tea.

"Superstitious drivel; the stuff of ignorance," he told himself as he turned south at the end of paved August Street onto Lewis Avenue, a graveled, dirt road, little more than a rutted pig run that followed the shallow cliff and Abomination Bay as it shambled past bunch grass and hackberry and the four clapboard shanties that Penny said would lead to Gateway.

Loman shrugged even deeper into his overcoat as the heavy, rolling clouds thundered and he passed the first, cheap, dilapidated shack. He distracted himself from the low moan of the unseen ocean by mulling over his wife's almost unquestioning love, the congregation that valued him not for brilliant oratory, but for his unselfish support through their temptations and crises, over unbelieving parents who pressured him to find a real job, and of the disdain of his church superiors, disappointed in his lackluster attempts to grow his flock.

"No turning back now," he reassured himself, and smiled at the irony of a new church built with the tainted money of a mentally ill, dead uncle. The fourth dark, fey house diminished and disappeared in his rearview mirror.

Loman shivered involuntarily, reason no match for the horror that swam out of the gloom into his headlights as he pulled into the driveway of Ebenezar's mansion, a huge, old, dirty, two-story house of mad angles, cupolas and spires and scrolls that looked like they'd been thrown against its walls by a drunken monster. It was easy to see why this insanity of decaying wood and brick and the august Azrealite legends had made the house a pariah, an infected eyesore, and the shame of Light's End.

Loman turned off the car's headlights and its motor, opened the driver's door, and stood up into the clammy wind and rain. There was no light on the railed porch around Gateway's first floor. He closed the car door and began the short walk to the mansion, leaning into thin sheets of stinging rain.

There were no heavy, scarred, wooden planks fixed with iron straps for a door, and no iron door knocker. The light bulb was missing from the light fixture next to a simple, modern door. Loman shook rain from his hair as he pressed the door bell button; the door did not creak on rusted hinges as it swung open.

"Mr. Adam Loman?" asked a wizened little man, a toothpick bobbing at the left corner of his mouth. "Welcome to Gateway! I am Adrian Keep,

Ebenezar Azreal's attorney. I've been expecting you. Please, come in."

As Loman stepped into a short hallway, he winced at an antiseptic, acrid smell that burned his nose and left a nasty, metal tang in his mouth. The short hall was utterly empty; there were no framed collections of dead butterflies, or clusters of photographs of dead relatives, or tortured animal heads on the walls, and no furnishings covered with mildewed, tasteless knickknacks.

"You look a bit discombobulated, Mr. Loman," smiled the lawyer who wore a modest, gray suit and string tie. He stepped back to allow Adam's entrance. "Were you expecting Peter Lorre or Vincent Price and a room filled with rotting, Victorian horrors, dust, and spider webs?

"Actually, Mr. Azreal was fastidiously clean to the point of obsession," continued Keep as he waved Loman inside with the sweep of an arm. "You talked to people in town, didn't you?"

"Well," Adam grinned sheepishly, and stepped inside the hall. "Just a little. But you have to admit that the outside of Gateway certainly doesn't reflect the inside."

"I'll get you a towel for your hair, Mr. Loman, and we'll discuss your inheritance after you are dry, rested, and comfortable. May I take your coat?" he continued as he began to help Loman remove his wet overcoat. "Your uncle enjoyed his local infamy, and was a bit of a showman; thus the bizarre outside of the mansion. It cost him a pretty penny. Ebenezar was eccentric to the extreme, and wild, lurid stories just naturally follow in a small town. He actually enjoyed them. Did they tell you how 'the Son of Satan' was dragged out of Gateway so that they could cut his throat?"

"Uh, no." Loman grimaced and shuddered. "They...cut his...throat?"

"No."

Keep hung Loman's coat on a hook on a steel grey wall and, with the wave of his hand, invited Loman to proceed to an open archway at the end of the hall.

"Ebenezar was also a shrewd businessman—much to your advantage, I might add. To be blunt, he was ruthless, and did not take being bested well. In the end, he always got his 'pound of flesh,' as they say.

"The living room," Keep concluded, and moved to the side as Loman stepped into the archway. Adam felt a puzzling, unnatural tightness in his chest, although what he saw was a large, half-timbered, unpretentious room with common flowered sofas, overstuffed chairs, and brass lamps. The sterile smell of antiseptic was palpable.

"Please excuse the carpentry tools lying about," the lawyer added.

"We've been doing some repair work in anticipation of your arrival. And you'll notice the walls are not..."

Outside, the storm surged, lashing needle rain against the windows. Keep smiled; the toothpick bobbed in his mouth.

"You'll notice the walls are not covered with decaying, stuffed heads, and the floor is not covered with animal skins, and there is no huge, stuffed gorilla? He was a hunter. But he had no interest in mounting trophies. I think you are beginning to understand now the town's paranoia, Mr. Loman?"

"What's behind there?" asked Adam, pointing at a door in the wall opposite him. "OUT" was painted on its surface in neat, block letters. Leaning against its doorjamb was a large, rubber-headed mallet. "That's a little odd."

"Nothing really, Mr. Loman. It is true that, even though he was only fifty years old, Ebenezar did fear dying, as do most men. You look to be in your early forties. I'd guess death has crossed even your mind? Ebenezar had always been a doer...a man of action! So he began looking for an 'out.' He began to dabble in black magic. A completely harmless... pastime... since there is no supernatural, wouldn't you agree? The sign was to have read 'Keep Out,' but a mistake was made by the letterer. Rumor, of course, has turned it into the infamous 'hidden' doorway to Hell.

"To satisfy your curiosity, would you like to take a look about before we review your inheritance?" Keep asked as they entered the living room.

Loman studied the room's yellow wallpaper covered with a faint, almost indistinguishable, pattern of 'dump ducks' in a feeding frenzy on a beach. "I must admit, I'm a little nervous. But you know what they say," he grinned as he and Keep, following a few steps behind him, walked through the living room to the queer door. "'Strike while the iron is hot!'"

"Ah. So very, very true," Keep added as Loman arrived at the door.

"Of course, the sea gull wallpaper will have to be replaced."

"Of course." Behind him, the lawyer stopped and picked up the mallet by the doorjamb as Loman opened the 'OUT' door onto a pitch black room and a nebulous but fetid odor.

"Goodness, Mr. Keep, what's that smell?"

"The smell of dead cats," said the lawyer, and swung the mallot back. "And the curiosity that killed them."

Loman swam up through a chaotic nightmare of dump ducks with needle sharp teeth tearing at chum into consciousness, his eyes swollen shut against white, blinding, excruciating, pain. His mouth tasted metallic. He tried to raise his head, but it was strapped, left cheek down, to something cold. He began to cry. He opened his eyes and cried out in the back of his throat and wrenched his eyes from the horrors on the wall to the bottom of a stained leather apron, and a hand on the polished, worn surface of a cart. Next to the man in the apron was the bottom half of a morbidly obese man with loose skin; a big, amber jug of cinder hung from his hand.

Someone said, "He's skinny."

On the cart were three rusted, dirty instruments.

A knife, a fork and a spoon.

Loman fainted.

Loman swam up through a horrific vision of screaming, slaughtered animals in the agony of death into consciousness, his eyes swollen shut against blinding, excruciating pain radiating from the back of his head. He tried to move it, but his head was strapped, left cheek down, to something cold and unforgiving. He knew it was a metal table, and he knew he was naked. Loman opened his eyes and screamed in the back of his throat because his mouth was taped shut, and averted his eyes from the horrors! the horrors! the horrors! nailed to the steel grey wall, and saw the bottom of a stained leather apron.

"Surprise!" said the apron man. "I have a confession to make, Mr. Loman. Ebenezar Azreal was a consummate liar. And Ebenezar did fake his death. While that solved a lot of his problems, it did have some unintended consequences. For example, it became hard to get groceries."

The leather apron creased and crackled as Keep leaned down by Loman's face. He removed the toothpick from the left corner of his mouth.

"And Ebenezar did enjoy mounting trophies. They all took the bait, so to speak. The papa bears. The mama bears. The snacks." Keep straightened up and outside of Loman's vision. Next to him was the bottom half of a morbidly obese man; a big, open, amber jug of cider hung from the index finger of his left hand. The jug was raised above Loman's field of vision, and lowered again.

"Please, don't cry, although I do enjoy the salt. And you shouldn't really feel embarrassed because Ebenezar fooled you. You can see you weren't the first. And you couldn't have known; you'd never seen me!"

Loman sobbed and shook and prayed in his throat.

"Ebenezar did find what he'd sought in his 'madness,' Mr. Loman;

Satan, the Great Worm, the imaginary boogeyman of simple minds! And after their deal was sealed, the devil did give Ebenezar certain 'gifts' for letting him in the out door!

"Of course, it's Ebenezar's duty to feed The Worm, but it's not without benefits! He takes your soul and, well, as they say..."

Loman sobbed and prayed in his throat and looked at the clutter of bloodless, human heads, rotting faces frozen in surprise, terror, and agony, mounted like butterflies on a stained wall with a Jesus nail through each forehead.

"Waste not, want not!" said his uncle.

"Oh, Ebenezar, you are such a cut-up!" said the morbidly obese man who began to laugh, a painful laughter, a laughter that convulsed his stomach.

Loman sobbed and prayed and shut his eyes to Ebenezar's blood stained, leather apron and the fat man and the polished, worn surface of a cart holding two rusted and dirty instruments.

A dirty fork and a spoon.

Light's End Map

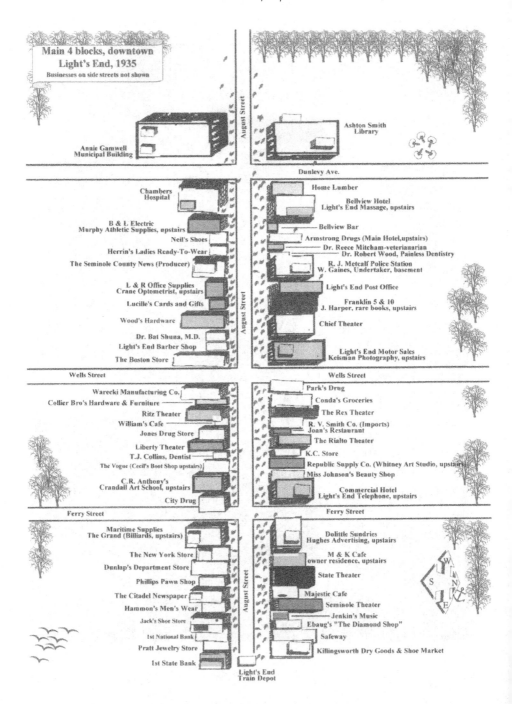

Main 4 blocks, downtown
Light's End, 1935
Businesses on side streets not shown

August Street

Ashton Smith Library

Annie Gamwell Municipal Building

Dunlevy Ave.

Chambers Hospital

Home Lumber

Bellview Hotel
Light's End Massage, upstairs

B & L Electric
Murphy Athletic Supplies, upstairs

Bellview Bar

Neil's Shoes

Armstrong Drugs (Main Hotel, upstairs)

Herrin's Ladies Ready-To-Wear

Dr. Reece Mitcham-veterinaarian
Dr. Robert Wood, Painless Dentistry

The Seminole County News (Producer)

R. J. Metcalf Police Station
W. Gaines, Undertaker, basement

L & R Office Supplies
Crane Optometrist, upstairs

Light's End Post Office

Lucille's Cards and Gifts

Franklin 5 & 10
J. Harper, rare books, upstairs

Wood's Hardware

Chief Theater

Dr. Bat Shuna, M.D.
Light's End Barber Shop

Light's End Motor Sales
Keisman Photography, upstairs

The Boston Store

Wells Street

Wells Street

Warecki Manufacturing Co.

Park's Drug

Collier Bro's Hardware & Furniture

Conda's Groceries

Ritz Theater

The Rex Theater

William's Cafe

Jones Drug Store

R. V. Smith Co. (Imports)
Joan's Restaurant

Liberty Theater

The Rialto Theater

T.J. Collins, Dentist

K.C. Store

The Vogue (Cecil's Boot Shop upstairs)

Republic Supply Co. (Whitney Art Studio, upstairs)

Miss Johnson's Beauty Shop

C.R. Anthony's
Crandall Art School, upstairs

Commercial Hotel
Light's End Telephone, upstairs

City Drug

Ferry Street

Ferry Street

Maritime Supplies
The Grand (Billiards, upstairs)

Dolittle Sundries
Hughes Advertising, upstairs

The New York Store

M & K Cafe
owner residence, upstairs

Dunlap's Department Store

Phillips Pawn Shop

State Theater

The Citadel Newspaper

Majestic Cafe

Hammon's Men's Wear

Seminole Theater

Jack's Shoe Store

Jenkin's Music
Ebaug's "The Diamond Shop"

1st National Bank

Pratt Jewelry Store

Safeway

1st State Bank

Killingsworth Dry Goods & Shoe Market

Light's End
Train Depot

74

What We See Is What We Get

A letter to *The Citadel* Newspaper
by Schlomo Nantier

Dear Editor,

Recent letters to the editor in *The Citadel* denying the existence of absolute truth are disturbing. Postmodernism's claim that "truth is what you believe it to be" and "every belief is equally true" (Jake Horne, last issue), my contention that postmodernism is a fraud is at least as valid as Horne's endorsement.

This belief is dangerous, and for those who don't believe it, try standing in traffic and saying, "I believe the street is empty," and see what happens.

Some proof: if 1+2 always equals 3, we say that equation is absolutely true. Repetition of result is our evidence. What doesn't happen is also evidence. It is not equally true that 1+2 produces 5, or hand grenades or alligators or strawberry cream pies.

There is absolute truth, and it doesn't depend on us to exist. Before we were born and after we die, 1+2=3 is true whether we believe it or not.

Also, the amount of evidence that our senses, within their limits, can recognize truth is staggering. As example, draw a circle. Ask everyone who speaks your language to draw what they see. They will always draw a circle. They will never draw a school bus. Yell the word "Hey!" Ask everyone to repeat what they heard. Everyone will always yell "Hey!" They will never yell "Postmodernism!" Again, repetition of result is evidence.

In addition, that we cannot see or know everything doesn't mean that what we do see is unreliable. Remember the story of blind men and an elephant?

Each blind man felt a leg or trunk or ear, and mistakenly thought that part was the whole beast. Therefore, because of human limitations, humans cannot know the truth.

What this flawed story ignores is that each blind man did know a real leg, a real trunk, and a real ear. They could share information, correct their mistake, and know to stay out from under elephant feet. And if they still need to know everything about elephants, they can ask a sighted man.

More proof: no sane human being sticks a naked hand into fire and expects it to grow daffodils, or waits for an orange to rise in the east in the morning. Naked hands always burn in fires and the sun always rises in the east.

Buy me lunch and I'll give you as many additional examples of this principal as you wish.

Everyone knows these things; even sane postmodernists have absolute faith in natural law. It is the laws of morality that stick in the craw of people who want to do what they want without restraint or consequences. But what is true about natural law is also true about moral law. Repetition of result is our evidence.

As evidence, adultery always breaks a loving spouse's heart. Lying never strengthens trust. Hatred or rage never beget love or peace. Abuse never creates joy.

If you have a stubborn postmodernistic friend who rejects these arguments, ask him to let you hit him in the face with your fist with all of your strength. You will discover a postmodernist who absolutely believes in fists and faces.

Postmodernism has no value by its own definition, and is simply an excuse to hurt others for selfish gain without feeling guilt. I agree with C. S. Lewis, hundreds of other philosophers, and trillions of human beings who have always known that everything is real. Even illusions are real; they are real illusions. It is absolutely not true that "truth is what you believe it to be" and "every belief is equally valid." What we see is what we get.

Dr. Schlomo Nantier, Ph.D.
Honored Albert Einstein Chair, Professor of Mathematics
University of Maine at Bangor
Brother, National Academy of Sciences

FIПAL ПOTICE

H is wooden chair ruuunked out from beneath its table as the shop bell
jingled. Schlomo Nantier rose from his chair and looked down at his
clenched left hand at his side. An air conditioning vent in the polished
black-and-white checkered floor whispered and unseen speakers sang "It's
Now or Never" softly to the nearly empty drug store.

Nantier looked up and smiled nervously at The Fat Man in a raincoat
who stood under the bell in the entrance to Park's Drug, his red face full of
distasteful stubble and yellow teeth. Raindrops wept down the glass door
that he held open with a mottled hand.

"Mr. Horne!" said Nantier. "Please, join me. Our meeting one another is
long overdue." Nantier ran his right hand through the muff of brown hair
that circled his otherwise bald pate.

Jake Horne took a drag on the cheap cigar that hung from the cut of his
mouth, flicked the stub out of the door, blew smoke from his nostrils, and
stepped inside. The door sighed closed. The shop bell jingled.

Standing by one of five red-leather stools facing the soda fountain,
Horne followed the sound of the greeting past two glass cases of sundries
to another long case topped by two cylindrical displays, one of pipes and
one of wrist watches, to Nantier. The slight man standing behind a table
waved him forward with an effeminate gesture.

Nantier thought: Horne is old and old and old with a face like a
crumpled paper bag full of wet flour. He marveled at his attention to such
trivial detail, the quirk of a logical and analytical mind diverting him from
the tension of meeting the head of the Tenebrae Church.

The Fat Man moved towards Schlomo down an aisle formed by store fixtures. He stopped by Nantier's table with its south and west chairs pushed beneath it, and its north pushed slightly back. That chair broke the meticulous order of Nantier's neatly folded newspaper lying perpendicular to the table's edge and a half-empty glass of Double Kola on a coaster by the left corner of the newspaper. The wooden handle of a closed umbrella hung on the table's edge over several damp newspaper pages spread beneath it.

"What convinced you to come?" asked Nantier, offering his right hand in welcome. Horne looked at the hand, unbuttoning his raincoat.

"A wise man–I believe it was me–once said that it's best to know thine enemies." Horne ran his fatty hand through the thick red hair on the back of his neck, stroking the fleshy anomaly beneath it. "Rumor has it you may be a worthy adversary, that you have an organized intellect, and I tire of small minds and puerile imaginations."

"Please, call me Schlomo." Nantier smiled and sat down.

Horne shrugged out of his raincoat, cataloging the cigars on display in the glass case to his left with naked displeasure. "Now I know why I never come in here, Mr. Nantier. They don't carry my brand."

"Those things will kill you, you know."

"I wish. I've been smoking them since Adam wore pants, and it's one of the few vices that interest me. The great regret in my life, you know, is that there are no new sins. It makes life so tiresome, Mr. Nantier. Where is this friend you wanted me to meet?"

Nantier glanced to his right and then turned back to Horne, shaking his head in disbelief.

"It looks like he's a no-show."

"If the truth be told..." continued Horne, tossing the raincoat on the back of the west chair, "which I rarely do, I'm looking for a commodity, a confidant–a person to whom I can candidly and honestly bare my deepest thoughts. And what better confident than someone who would never be believed by anyone in my congregation even if he should repeat my words? You are a Christian, aren't you?" Horne sneered and pulled the chair out with a hand like a ham.

"I am. In the interest of an even playing field, would you like to know something about me?" Schlomo looked down at his clenched left hand on the table next to his newspaper.

Horne abruptly raised his hand, palm out. "Please, allow me. I enjoy this. You're about forty, and already well known. By your long, tapering face and rounded chin, your owlish nose and eyes, I'd say you're an academic.

By your silly first name, I know you're Jewish; by your distinguished last, French. By your reputation, you're that most fascinating, illogical anomaly, a Jewish Christian. What I don't know is why you're interested in me, the most notorious atheist in Light's End."

"Two reasons, really. I'm fascinated by a priest who believes there 'is no God but man.' And I want to tell you a story. About Norman Fielding."

"A story?" Horne's green eyes sparked and he fingered a cigar in his shirt pocket. At the store's front, the glass door and the plate glass windows that skirted it wept slow rain, painting odd shadows on the floor. Horne removed a cigar and began to strip off its plastic wrapping.

"A story. I practically invented storytelling, you know." He stuck the cigar into his mouth. "They told me you were unorthodox, and I have time to kill. So, please, Mr. Nantier...impress me."

"Okay. Little Norman Fielding's birth about seventeen years ago at Chamber's Hospital escaped notice in town. He was bundled up and brought home by his parents to a nondescript and dreary house on Ebaugh Avenue off of Ferry.

"Norman was an unremarkable and unresponsive baby who slept well, cried regularly, began to babble when it was expected, and wasn't picky about food. He was an average baby with no distinguishing marks, but Norman was born with an imperceptible secret. He had a weak heart.

"Do you know Henry and Zoe Fielding? Well, they were poor and their first two children had already left home when Norman came along. Henry was a dour, weary but passable salesman at Wright's Shoes down August Street when he wasn't drinking at the Belleview Bar. Zoe sweated over laundry and ironing at home to make ends meet, and she attended the First Baptist Church Sundays with quiet little Norman and without her bleary husband.

"Zoe loved her son, but Henry dismissed him as lazy and insignificant. Their house was full of her cheap, used books and Zoe did everything within very limited means to help Norman rise out of their abysmal poverty. But, slowly, almost imperceptibly, she became the first person disappointed by her mundane son.

"Indeed, Norman's only surprising behavior happened when he was five and his parents brought his new baby sister home. They expected indifference or even jealousy, but Norman loved his sister from the moment he laid eyes on Cassie, and they became inseparable.

"Except for Cassie, Norman's next two years were lonely and un-noteworthy until he reluctantly went to Vacation Bible School. Unknown to him, as he modeled clay, played hide-and-seek, and learned Bible verses, Wright's Shoes nearly went bankrupt, and his father began to drink heavily and beat Zoe almost every night. His mother was an emotional wreck when Norman wandered home one afternoon and repeated what he'd learned as she sat in a ratty old chair in their dim living room.

"'Jesus loves the little children,'" he sang in his trifling tenor, "'all the children of the world. Red and yellow, black and blue, they are precious in his sight. Jesus loves the little children of the world.'

"Zoe hugged him and cried for a long time before pushing Norman back and holding him at arm's length. His heart ached and he was puzzled by the impalpable pride, love and desperation that lit her exhausted face. He hadn't even believed what he'd sang. She took a tiny chain from around her neck that held a little gold colored cross she had bought for twenty-five cents at the Wacker's Variety store downtown.

"'Normy,'" she said, as she dropped the chain and cross into his upturned palm, "'you'll do fine, you'll see. I have faith in you.'

"Norman lost the cross the next day. Zoe replaced it with another. Norman lost that cross, and the one following it, and Zoe replaced each one until carrying it in his jean pocket became a habit.

"As Cassie grew, Norman would read comic books to her with a flashlight as they giggled under a blanket long after they were supposed to be asleep. They seined for minnows in the creek that ran into the Pishon River by their house and kept the fish in Mason jars. They stood for hours at the magazine rack at City Drug as Cassie read about Fabian and Elvis Presley and Norman read *Screen Thrills* magazine. They even spent a night in a neighbor's station wagon once at the Skyway Drive-In Theater watching monsters eat cities and pretending they would never go home.

"But they did go home, although neglect and abuse were not strangers in the gloomy Fielding house. When their dismal poverty and their drunken father became unbearable, Norman and Cassie would escape to their secret place. Norman had discovered it earlier as he drifted around downtown after Saturday matinees at the State Theater. It was a large rock in the side of the hill at the end of Elliott Street that faced the railroad tracks, the beach and the bay. Time had rubbed it down into an overstuffed chair, and an old, weathered tree spread above it that suffused and mottled the light that fell through its drooping curtain of leaves and hid them from prying eyes. They lay there and read paperback books and dreamed, talking about intangible places. The trains moaned under heavy burdens and rumbled past.

"Norman was twelve and Cassie was seven when they lay there, half-asleep, one Sunday afternoon. Norman had earlier been slapped by his soused father for no other reason than that his son was mediocre. Cassie had muffled her tears in her hands. They were profoundly despondent and somber.

"Cassie turned facing her brother and gave him a penny bent on the tracks by a train, and told him she loved him. Norman put the penny in his pocket and turned away, embarrassed. But, from that day, he carried that penny with him everywhere. For even though a mere boy of almost thirteen would never say it, to be loved is very important.

"The next thing happened during the final inning of a pee-wee baseball game. The no account Blue Devils played on the dusty diamond down at Legion Park and hadn't won a game. Norman, who was usually overlooked because he lacked focus and was wishy-washy, was at bat. Cassie had never missed a game and sat behind home plate in the nearly empty little bleachers and shouted encouragement.

"Norman's heart beat like a trip-hammer as he summoned up every last ounce of courage and squeezed his eyes closed as the ball left the pitcher's mound, and swung with everything he had. His bat cracked loud in the stunned silence in the little bleachers, and the ball was already out of sight when Norman stumbled past first base. His home run won the game.

"No one jumped higher or screamed louder than Cassie.

"I think you know Coach Keisman. After the game, he knelt in the dust and tousled the hair of the boy he'd always ignored. Keisman told Norman he was proud and hoped for great things from him and handed him an empty key ring. On a rectangle of green plastic fastened to the steel ring was imprinted 'Sullivan-Cash Insurance.'

"It didn't matter to Norman that he didn't have any keys. He tied Cassie's bent penny and his mother's tiny cross to the key chain with twine and carried them in his jean pocket.

At the next game, he struck out three times. He dropped his bat in the dust and slumped away from home plate, his chin buried on his chest. Cassie could not console him.

"Norman never played again.

"Years passed, and by the time he became a senior at Elliott High, Norman knew exactly what not to do. He never raised his hand in class or joined a club. Every grade was below par. He had no friends or enemies, didn't volunteer opinions, advice or service, or excel in anything he couldn't avoid doing. He didn't argue on the rare occasions that an adult talked to him. He did as told, suppressing his emotions, and had no discernible hobbies, interests, political or religious beliefs, and wore nothing that drew attention to himself.

"No offense," said Nantier, glancing to his right and then turning back to Horne, "but his was a shallow, petty life, safe but dull.

"It just couldn't last.

"Last Friday after school, Norman ran into Wright's Shoes, his heart racing and his face red. His father was shocked by his behavior as the boy gasped, 'Papa, the house is on fire!!' You probably read about it.

"Fielding dragged him out of the store and drove like a madman the three blocks home where Cassie stood tottering in the front yard, most of her clothes burned off, and charred sheets of skin sagging from her twelve year old body. Zoe was at the grocery store and Cassie had been cooking supper when a pan of grease on the stove had exploded, engulfing her in flames.

"Norman and Henry fell to their knees in front of Cassie, crying; they couldn't touch her. Cassie sobbed, 'Papa, don't cry, it doesn't hurt', and collapsed into his arms. Henry drove her to Chambers Hospital and the fire department saved most of the house, but not Cassie. She died that night.

"To say that the Fielding family was devastated would be a gross understatement. The few members of Zoe's church, myself included, brought food, and tried to comfort her. But Zoe was depressed and inconsolable and wept uncontrollably. Henry got blind drunk. Norman was an emotional blur, disheartened and edgy and completely unwilling to accept the truth. It just couldn't get much worse.

"Then Saturday, as Zoe walked to the funeral home with a bunch of handpicked wildflowers for Cassie's burial, blinded by grief, she was struck by a van on August Street and crushed. It's in the newspaper.

"It was just too much. Henry disappeared on Sunday.

"For three days, Norman was alone in his house, and he emotionally unraveled. Zoe and Cassie were buried as he paced the empty rooms and raved against the parents who deserted him and the God who killed Cassie. He stood in their burned out kitchen and wondered who would feed a nonentity like him. He took the key chain and threw it against the charred kitchen wall. Norman felt like his heart would burst.

"Then he looked for the key chain and found it and put it back in his trousers. He floated like a ghost into his parents' bedroom and rummaged through his father's dresser until he found Henry's undershirts. He put a blue one on and stood in front of the dirty, full-length mirror that stood by the bed. Norman collapsed in tears on the bed, dispirited and empty, and sobbed himself dry. When he looked up at his reflection in the mirror through his red, swollen eyes, Norman saw his father in himself, and fell into a rage again, tearing the undershirt off in strips.

"He didn't notice his image in the mirror was sputtering like a candle.

"On Thursday, Norman returned to Elliott High, dreading the pity or averted looks and whispers that surely would follow him. He went because he didn't know what else to do. But no head turned as he entered through Elliott's big double doors, walked down one hall, up a flight of stairs, and into his English class. The teacher didn't even call his name during attendance check.

"Lunch was no different. Norman was sullen as he pushed his tray along the rail that ran the length of the buffet, picking what he wished, matching the pace of the students ahead and behind him. When he reached the cashier and stopped to pay, she looked at but through him as if he didn't exist. The student behind him plowed into his tray, sending it tumbling to the floor in a rain of gelatin, French fries and hamburger. Norman was startled and stumbled back against the wall next to the register and watched their puzzled expressions as students picked up his scattered lunch.

"'Whose tray is that?'" muttered the cashier.

"Her question was answered by blank stares. Norman moved away, an eerie tingle of surprise and anger pricking his skin. At first, he thought he'd died and was a ghost. Then he suspected the truth, that they didn't see him not because they couldn't, but because they didn't want to.

"He tested his theory by approaching the circle of cheerleaders that always segregated themselves, and stood behind and very close to the two most popular girls. They talked about the upcoming football game as he inappreciably nudged his way between them. When Norman stood in the center of the circle as they chatted, trembling from the potential repercussions, he slowly lifted his left hand and put a finger on the corner of Veronica Bullock's lips.

"Veronica swatted at the unbecoming annoyance and asked Sandie Hammon if she was wearing a new perfume.

"And although light did not bend around or pass through him, no magic cloak concealed him, and he hadn't been bombarded with radioactivity, Norman knew he no longer mattered, that he was a thing even beneath their contempt, and that he had disappeared.

"He went to his secluded rock to decide what to do. He knew now that he wouldn't die immediately. He could steal food and sleep wherever he wished. But after the necessities, then what? His thoughts broadened. He could patrol Light's End, stopping crime dead in its tracks like The Shadow or Batman. He could become the world's greatest spy, preventing world wars and saving lives, or take from the rich and give to the poor. Or he could make everyone in Light's End hurt.

"After thinking for a long time, he stood up, taking his key chain from his pants pocket. He raised his hand and opened it and let his key chain with Zoe's cross and Cassie's bent penny drop from his nerveless fingers. It fell to the rock, slid down its side, and was gone.

"Then he walked into town to rob the bank.

"It was drizzling a thin, cold mist that threatened to turn to rain as Norman entered the bank. Coach Keisman was filling out a deposit slip at the marble-topped island in the center of the First National Bank and a few people were doing things as Norman sauntered over to the island and did a little obscene dance at the coach's side.

"Keisman finished his deposit slip and walked to a teller's window. Norman walked to the small swinging door in the railing between the teller booths and the wall. He swung it open when no one was looking, because they could still see the door, and stepped through.

"Norman had decided to rob the bank not because he needed to–in a sense, anything and everything in Light's End was his now–but because he could. He had planned carefully. He knew that an overstuffed bag or two of money floating through the bank would not go unnoticed. He knew that he could make as many trips as he pleased, when he pleased, so he would take one thick stack of twenty dollar bills and walk away.

"He padded over behind a female teller and waited for a customer to approach the window. He was proud that he had the self-control to not touch her. He covered his mouth and nose with a hand to muffle his breathing. When a customer presented a withdrawal slip and the cash drawer opened, he reached in and took a wad of bills. He walked quickly away, the money held low beneath the normal range of vision.

"The little wooden door swung silently behind him as he moved into the center of the bank and the dirty joke happened and a sudden red hot pain punched his chest.

"Norman gasped. At first he thought he was shot as a razor's edge of pain shot down his left arm. He staggered back, surprised, clutching at his exploding heart. A bank guard yawned. Norman staggered back against the marble island, and fell, striking his head on its edge. Coach Keisman left the bank as Norman rolled back and forth, writhing in pain. A bank clerk stapled papers together. Then Norman's hand spasmed open and the wad of bills fell out onto the marble floor.

"And as his body sputtered in and out of sight on the floor and someone screamed, Norman thought an odd thing. Norman thought that for all the good things he could have done but didn't, he might just as well have never lived at all.

"And Norman died."

"That's it? That's your little story?" said Horne.

"I prefer a cautionary tale."

"Amusing, but flawed," said Horne, chewing on his cigar. "You didn't maintain the illusion of reality. For one thing, if Norman is invisible, how did you see him?"

"I look."

"For another thing, if Norman died, who told you about the bank robbery?"

"Well, I did make up dropping the key chain, the cheerleader thing, and Norman dying during a bank robbery. Most everything after I brought food to the Fielding's house, actually. But Zoe was my friend, and she told me a lot before she died."

"You made up more than that! And it was all just for me?"

"Not entirely," answered Schlomo, looking to his right. "It was also for my no-show who was about to throw away something that I'd hoped he'd keep."

"I also missed the point."

"For myself, it's that I must not act like Norman. He was given faith by his mother and hope by his coach and love by Cassie, and God's precious gift of life, and may waste them all. He was given talents that withered because he was afraid to fail. I must not do the same. So, I will be your confidant, Jake Horne.

"For you, the point is that there is none so blind as he who will not see," said Nantier as he glanced again to his right and then turned back to Horne. "There is a God, Mr. Horne, and it isn't man."

And the empty north chair ruuunked further out from the table.

There was a tense moment of silence and the floor vent sighed and the speakers that had murmured beneath notice now sang again. Horne's face was red and tense, his eyes were slits, and his teeth showed. Then slowly, inappropriately, he began to laugh softly but not spontaneously, a painful laughter that twisted his face and convulsed his stomach. Then that faded, and Horne sat for some time breathing heavily and looking at the empty chair with a funny smile like a cut on his face.

"That was the good-for-nothing, right? Mr. No-Show, pushing the chair back? My guess is you moved the chair using a transparent, plastic strip running from the chair's leg to your leg. Possibly a piano wire. Such a cheap little magic trick. It doesn't help the story, but, then, I am constantly disappointed by you people," he added, rolling his eyes back in his head.

"I like your quirky sense of humor, Nantier. I have decided that we will meet again," he continued, pushing himself back from the table, "but at my pleasure and on my turf. And when we talk again..."

Jake stuck the cold cigar back into his mouth and rose from the table with some effort. He picked up his raincoat and draped it over a forearm, his eyes on Nantier.

"I will eat you alive," he growled, his face distorted with contempt.

"And until we meet again, it seems fitting that I leave my new confidant with my first nasty little secret. I don't really believe that there is no God but man, Mr. Nantier.

"I believe there is no God but me."

Horne turned his back to Nantier and lumbered past the display cases to the soda fountain. Pausing at the entrance, he lit the cigar that hung from the cut of his mouth, opened the door, and flicked a cursory good-bye behind him. He stepped outside.

The shop bell jingled.

The sky drizzled as Schlomo hesitated in the entrance to the drugstore, watching the receding back of Jake Horne across the worn red brick of August Street. As The Fat Man lumbered past two shoppers with dripping umbrellas in front of Economy Home Furnishings, they recoiled from him like oil from water.

Another dozen steps and Horne paused in front of Jelly's Cafe where distance reduced him and its customers sitting behind its windows to mannequins. A solitary newsboy hawked *The Citadel* newspaper in front. Then the old priest shambled down the sidewalk past a couple in front of Cecil's Boot Shop, its door closing on the heels of someone entering, and passed beyond Nantier's sight.

But Schlomo continued to follow the thin, aimless stream of tiny shoppers wandering the cobbled sidewalk, and imagined girls poking their heads out of the C. R. Anthony's store, gossiping about dirty laundry, to Hammon's Men's Wear, where lonely men bragged about meaningless sexual dalliances, to Wright's Shoes, where a Help Wanted sign hung in the window, to the August Waffle House where a cup of coffee trembled

in a drug addict's wasted fist, and to the First National Bank at the mouth of August Street.

Schlomo looked down at his clenched left hand at his side, and opened it. Inside lay Norman's bent penny and tiny cross tied with twine to a keychain. He closed his hand quickly and looked up.

Schlomo covered his mouth with his other hand, suddenly overwhelmed by a heartbreaking sadness and longing to gather into his arms this dirty town and its selfish, blind people who were never washed clean by the rain. He yearned to whisper that they were loved, and that life was more than fear and pain and isolation, and Schlomo's eyes welled with tears as his hand shook. He glanced back inside the drugstore. Then the poet released the door and stepped out under the drug store's metal awning into Light's End as the door behind him sighed closed.

The shop bell jingled.

And Norman ruuunked the north chair back beneath the table.

X: Effervescent #3
(Sing a Mighty Song)

Lyrics by Michael Vance
Written at Blue Bell, Sept. 25th, 1972

Sing
Sing a song
Sing a mighty song
Bring
A new song unto the Lord

Thank the Lord for fiery flowers
For the ever burning sunshowers
Searing to the land
How sweet rain
When by God the spongy heavens dry are wrung
And drops to wet the desert's tongue
'Til wind, like a painter, sweeps across the stain

So Sing a mighty song for God
Mouth it very loud
For though he hears the gentle whisper
He wants to hear your joy in spring

89

He wants to hear his children bring
Up love into the world

Listen how this song is sung!
"When the old are suckled by the young
I'll have just begun!"
How time flies
Ah, how sad the foolish sinner
Fat with lies
Who laughs against God's healing winds
Until death, like a comet, streaks across his eyes
Yet greater still than all the billion sorrows man has cried
Is Christ the son of the Living God, who for us was crucified
So that death itself did die

So Sing a mighty song for God
Mouth it very loud
For though he hears the gentle whisper
He wants to hear your joy in spring
He wants to hear his children bring
Up love into the world

CROSS PURPOSES

After Allie Dunlevy passed over, the people of Light's End, Maine, joyously scattered her strange ashes over the River Pishon. An ill wind blew in from the sea and shook the weeds that clotted its banks. They cast her ashes into that wind because there were no graves for man nor beast allowed in the town. The men stood in silence at the funeral, emasculated by her death because they could not stop hers or their own. Joy at her ashes was best expressed silently. The women with sibilant voices and quick, furtive glances whispered of the inside of Ebenezar Azreal's house where Allie had lived and died alone, and of the questions that still clouded both.

Allie had scattered the ashes of her foundling, yellow-haired dog, Roses, on the Pishon earlier.

As First Selectman Stevens scattered her remains, an oil painting of Ebenezar Azreal on an easel elicited innuendo and macabre comments from older women in shiny worn suits. They spoke of Allie as if she had been a friend. They thought they had eaten at All Hallow's Eve or spoken with her because the confusion of time in the elderly paints the past as never really yesterday but, instead, a moment in which no pain hurts. They had never even met her.

Allie died at a time of confusion and a time of rock-hard uncompromising conviction. It was no wonder that her funeral was marked with a jaundiced eye. The president was dead and war threatened on the horizon. rock 'n roll records, drugs and teenage rebellion against parents were frightening society. There was unrest among the black population. It

91

seemed the young and old, the rich and poor, people of faith and people of science, the different races and even men and women were at cross purposes, and that the entire country stood balanced on the edge of chaos.

It didn't help that they hated Allie.

Ebenezar Azreal's was a huge, old, dirty house of mad angles, and of cupolas and spires and scrolls that looked like they'd been thrown against its walls and stuck there by a drunken monster. It stood on the east fringe of the sea port town, within walking distance of the Pishon. Its insanity of wood and brick and the august legends of the Azreals had made the house and Allie a pariah as it stood, stubborn and decaying, an infected eyesore on the face of Light's End.

Allie Dunlevy had been a reproach for the town of Jeroboam who had bought the land that would pass down, generation to generation, into the hands of his great-great-great-grandson, Ebenezar Azreal, who built the house where Allie died. Jeroboam had built the First Church of Tenebrae and the lighthouse and was one of the three groups of six who founded the town. Allie reminded Light's End that they could not stop what had destroyed Jeroboam's light house, shaken into rubble. Jeroboam had foretold the town's slow decay if they abandoned the Old Way, and he was charismatic and powerful and right and they hated him for that then and now. But, mostly they hated him because he was right.

The boys and girls who grew up despising Jeroboam and fearing his great-grandson Ebenezar became elders, deacons, choir members and prominent cornerstones of polite society in Light's End. On the first frozen February day when Allie and her derelict, yellow-haired dog moved into the Azreal house, the women of Light's End ignored them because they were rank outsiders from Providence, Rhode Island. They disliked them because she was an Azreal by marriage and therefore superior to them, was widowed and attractive for her fifty-odd years, had money and no need to work, because they did not know the source of her money, and because disdain is much cheaper than love in the coin of Light's End. They especially disliked Allie because, almost from the first day, a young man from the Twenty-Four Seven, the only convenience store in town, began to deliver groceries at her front door. That was outrageous, not only because the little grocery store and gas station had the highest prices in town, but because no one else had groceries delivered, not even the richest man in town, First Selectman Hiram Stevens. It didn't help matters that the Twenty-Four Seven man was humiliated by delivering those groceries and grew to hate her as well.

It was rumored she was the unrebellious daughter of a Presbyterian minister and had briefly and faithfully married an Azreal in Providence who wrote horror stories under a different name and died in 1937. It was whispered that she worked with fervor and sincerity in the church, loved children and had lost a daughter, wrote to prisoners as her own mission, and led an upright, unselfish life of sacrificial kindness. It was said Allie would rather die than hurt a fly. The women did not believe this, and decided to snub her.

Almost immediately, a carpenter came to the Azreal manse and cut a hole and hung a pet door that swung in and out on hinges in the bottom third of the front door. Her dog, Roses, was the child Allie had lost.

April came, and Allie was worth no more than an aloof but polite nod in passing from the people of the town. Then Reverend Jones, a big, electric, unmarried man with a booming voice and blue eyes, wrote Allie a letter that month asking her to visit the First Church of Tenebrae. That was the first nail. Jones was secretly and passionately wanted by most of the women in his congregation. When Allie came the following Sunday, the entire congregation rose as one and wrapped their arms around her in feigned compassion and welcome. It was what little was required of them from their god who seemingly cared nothing of wrath, judgment or justice.

The arms came off in September. Allie commented several times and with increasing trespass that the He in the hymnals had been replaced with It or words to that effect, that no Bible was to be found anywhere in the Church, and that the name of Jesus Christ was barely mentioned and not held above any other. She visited the Daughters of the Star, the women's auxiliary of the Knockers civic club, and did not return. She wrote a letter to Reverend Jones asking him to visit her at the Azreal house. It said that her God cared much about wrath, judgment and justice as well as love and compassion. That was the second nail.

The Tenebrae congregation and the people of Light's End knew with certainty then that Allie was an intrusion and did not belong. They still feared dead Ebenezar who had descended into violence, isolation and madness and then death, and felt the Azreals had always held themselves in too much esteem. She was certainly not good enough for Reverend Jones. To stand up for anything against the common opinion of the town was equally arrogant, and Allie, usually dressed in white, and her yellow-haired dog Roses by association and because it could not defend itself, became an affront and an irritation.

So when Allie next came to the First Church of Tenebrae, the entire congregation sat as one and did not wrap their arms around her even in feigned compassion and welcome.

The elders of the First Church of Tenebrae met with Reverend Jones about the letter, but Jones came to her lonely house anyway on a Saturday night. He knocked on the door that had hid Ebenezar's murders and was welcomed into a huge hall whose walls were still covered with the molding and deteriorating heads of animals that Ebenezar had killed and mounted. The hall smelled dank. Allie apologized that she hadn't had time to remove the obscenities or clean the place from 'attic to cellar.' The furniture was heavy and old and in disrepair. When they sat, a whisper of dust motes rose in the dim light. Above the parlor fireplace hung an oil painting of Ebenezar Azreal.

Allie was a small, thin woman with a tiny gold cross at her neck, and she faced Reverend Jones with that same quality of open, blunt but gentle honesty that made the entire town queasy. She faced him with confidence, her eyes clear and direct, and Reverend Jones felt naked. Roses sat at her feet, the dog's head between her paws, with a polite but total disinterest they shared their secret hearts. Allie's voice was firm and unemotional.

"Do you believe that Jesus Christ is the Son of God?" she asked.

"Why, we are all the children of a Higher Power, Allie. If you choose to call it g-god and are sincere in your belief..." he began. Allie interrupted.

"Do you believe that the Bible is the Word of God?"

"Yes. It and the Koran, the Book of Mormon, the writings of Buddha and Confucius and Plato, the works of the Templar's..."

"Mr. Jones," said Allie, leaning forward with a look that penetrated to the very core of his soul (if it existed), "do you believe in any one thing with all of your heart and soul and mind?"

Reverend Jones leaned back in his overstuffed chair, a big, electric, unmarried man with a booming voice and blue eyes, and mentally erased Allie from his list of parishioners. He wanted nothing to do with judgment or judges. He smiled patiently, expecting the worst. "Yes," he said. "I do. I believe in people."

"Please leave," said Allie with great effort and emotional self-control. She would later fall to her knees in utter failure and humility in the solitude of her bedroom and tearfully pray for the salvation of Reverend Jones' soul.

"But, Allie, it isn't good for a single woman to be alone..." protested Reverend Jones. "If you hold so adamantly..."

"No one is ever alone with God," said Allie. "The front door is down the hall."

Reverend Jones passed the man from the Twenty-Four Seven at Allie's front door as he delivered her groceries. At the exact same moment, an elder of the First Church of Tenebrae told another elder that Reverend Jones and Allie were having a torrid affair. It was the final nail.

When the news of their torrid sex spread through Light's End like a raging fire, the townspeople were satisfied. Now what she believed no longer mattered, the long hated superiority of the Azreal family was written off, Allie became human just like everyone else, and they were justified in not only ostracizing her, but blacklisting her. The secret lust for Reverend Jones among the women of Light's End was fanned higher. Caught alone in front of the old Azreal mansion, someone kicked Roses with enough force to make the surprised yellow-haired dog cry out and Allie open her front door. Allie did not leave the lonesome manse for several weeks.

When seen again leaving Miss Johnson's Beauty Shop next to the Commercial Hotel on August Street, Allie's hair was short like those young girls who look like the angels in stained glass church windows in books, innocent but troubled. Passing Allie on the red brick sidewalk, Barbara Horne asked "How's Reverend Jones?" without pausing, stopping or even turning her head but with an odd look on her face. That was when Allie first knew she was having an affair with the pastor of the First Church of Tenebrae. That was when she knew the women would kill her by inches.

Across the street in front of *The Citadel,* the town's newspaper, Reverend Jones was buying a newspaper from a vending machine when Allie passed him in front of the State Theater. Because he was a big, electric, unmarried man with a booming voice and blue eyes, little boys often gathered around the charismatic minister. They rustled around his legs, their laughter and Reverend Jones' guffaw at the center of the group rising clear and masculine. But when Jones saw Allie and waved politely, the laughter died and the boys scattered like autumn leaves from beneath the touch of his hand on a shoulder or cheek. Having passed Allie on the red brick sidewalk without pausing, stopping or even turning her head, Kathy Jesse saw the Reverend wave at Allie, and turned her head, sneering. The insinuation would spread out and grow from her like the boys who scattered like autumn leaves.

Initially, the women of Light's End had thought an Azreal would not think seriously of a minister, although flirtation or even sex between the two were unpleasant possibilities as well. Anything they could not control or mold in an image they wanted was, at the very least, repudiated. But that day someone left a Valentine's card on Allie's doorstep next to the groceries from the Twenty-Four Seven even though it was not Valentine's day. Caught alone in front of the old, desolate Azreal mansion, that someone kicked Roses hard and made the surprised yellow-haired dog cry out and Allie open her front door. The card read: "Roses are red, violets are blue. If I had your money, I'd have Reverend Jones too." A part of the male anatomy had been drawn incorrectly on the cupid on the card's cover. It had come from the Twenty-Four Seven store.

Allie, companionless except for Roses, did not leave the manse for three weeks.

The sarcasm and guarded tittering about Allie and Jones became open expressions of disdain and false sympathy. "Poor Allie. Do you think...?" they carped. "Are you kidding? What else ..." they hissed behind window blinds, in the bathrooms of restaurants or on the phone behind idle hands. "Poor Allie."

When seen again leaving The Vogue next door to Cecil's Boot Shop on August Street, Allie was pale, silent and wan like young girls who pine for a lost love, innocent but troubled. Her head was held high even though she knew she was fallen in the eyes of everyone that she passed. But Allie demanded at least acknowledgment of her dignity, of her imperviousness. No one on the streets or in the store even feigned compassion, welcome or even recognition. Allie had been blackballed, segregated, and she knew it.

That day, someone left a small, cardboard box on her doorstep. After Roses cried out and ran through her swinging pet door, Allie opened her front door expecting the worst. "Ally" was incorrectly scrawled on the lid of the box from the Twenty-Four Seven store, as was "Roses are red, violets are blue. You rut like a pig, and smell like one to."

A warm, bloody pig's heart was inside, wrapped in a copy of *The Citadel*.

Most of the people of Light's End who knew her or the situation, or even cared (most did not) thought the solitary woman would go back to Providence, Rhode Island, and take her filthy yellow-haired dog now. But the Twenty-Four Seven man came and went with groceries (although no one saw the front door open and the sacks disappear). It was said by a Daughter of the Star that Allie, isolated like a leper, was seen in silhouette at a window once, but for six weeks she did not leave the dreary Azreal manse. Only the women of the First Church of Tenebrae had always known that Allie's pride was too powerful and furious to allow her to leave.

Then the women of Tenebrae, and especially the Daughters of the Star, began to clamor openly that Allie was a whore and a slut and a disgrace to Light's End and a caution for children. The men said nothing about the invective. *The Citadel* was silent, although she was not a subscriber. There was no surprise when Reverend Jones left town, just disappointment that his departure killed any chance for growing scandal with Allie...or anyone else. And there was no surprise when a neighbor saw Allie let Jones in at her back door in the dead of night three days later. No one even really believed it, although everyone said and hoped that it was true. The Twenty-Four Seven man went to and from the Azreal manse with groceries. The backbiting and hue and cry grew. Roses, with great caution and soundless whimpering, nevertheless came out through the swinging pet door and wandered forlornly in and then beyond her yard.

That night someone left the crushed and bloody corpse of Roses on Allie's doorstep.

The Tenebrae women brought covered dishes to the Azreal manse in the afternoon and knocked on her front door. Allie would not let them in. She told them through the closed door that her yellow-haired dog was not dead. She did that for three days, with different members of the Daughters of the Star trying to persuade Allie to let them remove and cremate the body. Just as they were about to resort to law and force, she broke down and cremated Roses, quietly, scattering her ashes in secret on the river. Allie was utterly alone.

Light's End did not say she was crazy at that time, although it was said she talked to God out loud in the seclusion of the old house. For two more days, the Twenty-Four Seven man left groceries on her doorstep that were not picked up. The president was dead, war loomed, rock 'n roll records, drugs and teenage rebellion against parents were threatening society. There was unrest among the black population. It seemed the young and old, the rich and poor, people of faith or science, the races and even men and women were at cross purposes and stood balanced on the edge of chaos. And the women of Light's End cut dead any mention of Allie Dunlevy.

Then the bad odor began.

A neighbor next to the remote Azreal house complained of the foreign smell to the First Selectman, Hiram Stevens, who was eighty years old. "There's no need to embarrass her," Stevens said. "Something probably died in the attic and she hasn't noticed. I'll talk to Mrs. Dunlevy." But he didn't.

On the third day, Stevens got two more angry phone calls about the exotic, alien smell from Allie's house, one from a voter. Stevens called several of the elders of the First Church of Tenebrae who refused to call or visit the exiled member to tell her that she smelled bad. So Stevens and two policemen approached Allie's house late in the day like guilty school boys, ascended her small porch and knocked on her door. There was no answer. One of the police officers rattled the doorknob at the insistence of the First Selectman, and the other noticed that, oddly, the pet door swung and stopped abruptly when the door was shaken as if it were hitting something unseen and immediately behind the front door. They broke open the door only to stand in wonder at an entranceway that had been boarded up from the inside.

When the two policemen smashed down the door a thin, acrid smell like rotting flesh struck them bodily and a cloud of dust rose from the hallway. The smell seemed to overpower everything in the house, the tables, the faded curtains, the walls covered with the molding and deteriorating heads of animals that Ebenezar had killed and mounted, and the crude cross that lay flat on the living room floor.

Allie Dunlevy, laying on the cross, greeted them with open arms.

For a long time Stevens and the police officers stood looking at the spikes driven through her crossed feet and through her left and right bloody palms. The First Selectman vomited. The police noticed, under her right hand and partially discolored by her blood, a long strand of yellow hair. She lay quietly and at peace in the horrid embrace of death. And slowly and in each astonished mind crept the realization that death had cheated the Tenebrae women, Reverend Jones, the elders of the church, the Daughters of the Star and every person in Light's End at their own game even as it had released Allie. The coroner said it was suicide.

And as the last of her ashes were blown by the ill wind over the choked River Pishon, the First Selectman and the police officers stood in silence at the funeral, emasculated by her death because they could not stop hers or their own. The women with sibilant voices and quick, furtive glances whispered of the inside of Ebenezar Azreal's house where Allie had lived and died, and of the questions that still clouded both.

As the First Selectman scattered the ashes, the older women in shiny

worn suits lost in a confusion of time in the elderly that paints the past as never really yesterday pondered the question that would haunt Light's End and transform Allie Dunlevy and Roses into a caution and a legend forever.

Some suspected a hobo riding through town on the rails had stolen some spikes, or that Reverend Jones killed Allie. Some thought she'd been murdered by the Twenty-Four Seven man, or even by her own wrathful God. Several women from the Daughters of the Star, Barbara Horne and Kathy Jesse in particular, fell under suspicion at first. Some thought that Roses had come back from the grave and killed her mistress.

It is true there was relief that Allie hadn't been a "real" Christian because real Christians don't commit suicide. It is true that they eventually learned that Allie was a minor stockholder in Twenty-Four Seven, which was the source of her very meager income. It was equally true and disappointing when they learned that Reverend Jones had never touched Allie Dunlevy. Reverend Jones was gay. There was some surprise that no one except Allie and Roses and Reverend Jones, once, had been in the Azreal house for at least four years after Ebenezar had perished.

It was several years before the question that had no answer crept slowly into each perplexed mind. If Allie Dunlevy had been utterly, hopelessly and terribly alone in a huge, old, dirty house of mad angles of cupolas and spires and scrolls that was boarded up from the inside, and had committed suicide...

Who hammered the spike into her second hand?

HALF NELSON

The face in the photograph behind the glass in the five-and-ten-cent store frame was Maria's. With tenderness, Brett Nelson carefully replaced it in the pocket of his mousey suit and looked up at an old, two-story stucco building.

"F-fifteen years," he muttered as his right hand rose to his left ear and froze in transit. His hand slid to his chin as Nelson glanced like a hunted deer up and down the cracked sidewalk that narrowed and vanished back east into town. He was alone. Above him, a dirty splatter of gulls hung and then swirled and hung again in the bleak September sky in restless search for a roost.

Raw boned, the middle-aged man fidgeted in a smarmy suit next to a rusted pole; on its top, the words "August Street" were painted on a green rectangle. A subtle breeze insinuated the smells and sounds of the unseen ocean everywhere, but did nothing to ruffle the cropped, blond hair that clashed with Nelson's dark honey complexion.

Shifting his weight, he read "The Blue Heaven," ghosted in a faded arc of letters on the facade above the recessed entrance to the building. They were the last reminder on the last building standing of the red light district of dance halls, saloons and whore houses that had been "Bishop's Alley" thirty years earlier. A small wooden sign lettered "Bowden's Gym" swung and creaked in the entrance above the open door. Inside, stairs rose to a second floor, and a dismal hall lit by a naked light bulb sunk into the building beyond his sight.

"Fifteen wasted years," Nelson repeated. He redistributed his weight again to ease the pinch of cheap leather shoes, and then reluctantly mounted

101

the steps to the entrance. A faint stench of human flop and the distant thud of human flesh against canvas met him at the door as he entered.

A dirty poster caught and stopped him in the hall. Its lurid headline screamed in four-inch-deep letters: "Wrestling's Best," followed by: "Bangor, Maine, August 15, 1959, 7:00 PM., Marx Coliseum." Brett reached up and touched the name "El Diablo" above the picture of a Mexican with long, black hair, brown eyes and a pronounced scar on his square jaw. The Hispanic crouched like a cougar. To the right of his photograph on the handbill, a slab of Caucasian muscle in leather breeches called "The Hog" snarled and shook his ham hock fist. Below both pictures were two rows of small photographs of midgets in boots, masks and silk capes, paunchy has-beens in garish Spandex, and two leather-clad women muscled like men.

Nelson's hand dropped from the poster. Inside, his heart pounded as regret and joy struggled like water repels oil.

"No, Dan!! Use the Frog Splash, you idiot!! The Frog Splash!!!" W. O. Deacon punched holes in the mildewed air with a damning finger. Dan stumbled back from his opponent against ropes that sagged and snapped taunt again. The thud of his flesh as he hit the canvas face-first went unnoticed by the grunting, self-absorbed men around the ring who jumped rope and tossed medicine balls. Deacon shook his head in the unmitigated gloom of the gym.

"Morons wouldn't know a suplex from a powerbomb if it bit 'em!" he muttered around the wad of asafoetida gum that danced around inside his mouth.

"I-I know," stuttered the disembodied voice on the edge of Deacon's vision. He shifted his eyes left without moving his head; the annoyance was taking off a coat. "Unless you're a sports writer, sports commissioner, or Jesus Maestas—and he's dead—you're wasting my time, like that stumble-bum in the ring. Hey!! Dapper Dan! Just roll your worthless green shorts out of the ring, eh?"

The gym's owner eyed Nelson, who looked at the floor as Deacon ran a handkerchief over the sweating bald island between his wreath of hair. "This dump's a steam bath. You're about may age, right? You're forty if you're a day, hot-shot. You ever been near a gym, Mr....?"

"Name's unimportant." answered Nelson as Dan rolled under the ropes, hitting the floor in a flat-footed trot with Deacon as his destination. "I haven't w-wrestled lately, but I can whip that guy."

"Hey!" Dan slapped Deacon's shoulder as he eyed Nelson with suspicion. "Why'd ya pull me! I was hotter than a busted short block!"

"Is that right, Danny?" Bishop punched a gnarled finger against the wrestler's chest. "Well, 'Mr. Unimportant' here says he's hotter'n a volcano."

"This guy?!" Dan chuckled. "Roscoe'll cool his jets in under three."

"Like h-hell," said Nelson. Dropping his shirt on the floor, he jumped to the lip of the ring, then vaulted on one hand over the ropes.

"As for you Dan, you're a heartbeat away from a babysittin' career. Do you know the difference between a fisherman's suplex and an STF? Dan! Look at me when I'm insultin' ya!"

"Apparently he knows, Deac." Slack jawed, Dan pointed into the ring. Bare-chested, Nelson stood on the canvas under Roscoe, balancing the squirming wrestler above him with one hand behind his skull and the other at the crotch of his red shorts. He gave the wrestler a toss that reversed him in mid-air before landing face and athletic cup down in Nelson's hands. Abruptly, Brett stepped from beneath the red shorts. The thud of Roscoe's flesh shook the mat; he bounced once and lay still, moaning.

"Damn," said Deacon, and stopped chewing his gum. "What a shellacking. I haven't seen the Grand Slam since..."

Nelson trotted to the turnbuckle and learned over the rope.

"So, Mr. Deacon, do I wrestle?"

"Do you...!?" Deacon's jaw worked the gum again. "Can you sign your X on a contract?"

"Then I thank you, and Jesus thanks you."

"Jesus...!?!" Deacon's hand fell to his side and his smile became a question mark. Nelson's right hand rose with unflinching confidence to his left ear. He pulled the earlobe twice.

"Jesus!!" stammered Deacon. His gum fell from his open mouth.

"W-wrong Jesus," grinned Nelson.

At the top of the gym stairs, a backlight threw shadows on the semi-opaque glass inset in the door of Deacon's office. The shadows hung and then paced and then hung again. Behind that door, Nelson loped back and forth in front of Deacon's desk.

"I can't believe it. Jesus Maestas," whispered Deacon in naked disbelief as his asafoetida gum bobbed in his mouth. His hands where sunk in his fringe of hair, and his bony elbows rested on his scarred desk. "Even after fifteen years, the Hog's manager will kill you if he finds you."

"G-george Payne's g-gunning for a black-haired, b-brown-eyed Mexican named Jesus," stammered Nelson, his head lowered. "Not a blond, blue-eyed B-brett Nelson with a chin scar covered by c-cosmetic surgery."

"Look, kid, I tell you if he finds out you're alive, he'll blow your brains out."

"I've got to s-see my Maria, D-deacon." Nelson squirmed in his suit as he faced the dour manager. "T-the last f-fifteen years were living h-hell without her. I am h-half Maestas and half Nelson now, but not a whole anything. I feel like I'm not starving, but I'm always hungry. It is a gnawing yearning without her. She h-hated wrestling and El Diablo, but she knew I l-loved it second to her, even though I-I was dead s-set on w-wearing th' h-h-heavyweight ch-ch-champs' b-belt."

"Slow down, kid. You were the best I ever had, it's true."

"T-t-t-..." Nelson stopped and concentrated, forming each word carefully. "Thirty-five matches and thirty-five wins. I-I was so close! And every time I'd give the f-fans the old ear pull, they'd cheer like maniacs. I still hear the slap of the referee's hand on the mat. One-two-three. 'Another match for El Diablo!' Then you finally got me my b-big chance! I'll never forget the day I told Maria: "I've done it! I wrestle The Hog!' She said to me, 'Oh, Jesus, sweetheart, I know you desire this so much and worked so hard and deserve it. But George Payne is very bad and The Hog is a dirty wrestler.' B-but I told Maria that I was the b-best. What could happen?"

Reticent, Deacon leaned forward on his elbows. "You had two fat years, kid, but you ignored the script and didn't take the fall. You would've had the belt next, but you wouldn't play the racket. You're the reason Jesus Maestas' name is on a plaque in the mausoleum."

"It is true," admitted Nelson looked at his feet. T-the night of the big match, I turned my head a little, j-just a little, trying to see where Maria was, and you don't do that when you're wrestling t-the Hog. I don't know what hit me, but it hit me s-square. When I went down, my head struck the ring post. There was blood in my eyes, and I couldn't see. The last thing I remember, The Hog was d-down for the count, and down for good and forever. But it was accidental, Deacon, I swear it!!"

"Too bad Payne convinced the police otherwise."

"You saved my life then, Deacon. You got me outta town, faked my death..." Nelson stopped pacing.

"Hey. That's what disbarred lawyers do, kid."

"F-fifteen years of running from town to town, s-scrounging for odd jobs, washing dishes," said Nelson, placing both hands flat on the lawyer's desk and leaning forward. "God, I missed her. It aches. I'm no good for anything but wrestling. Inside the ring, I'm a cougar. Outside, I-I'm a n-nothing. The last five years, I was a j-janitor in Oklahoma."

"Since you were sending dough through me to Maria, you couldn't exactly afford France, kiddo." Deacon's words were humorless; the gum danced.

"So, fifteen years later, I-I get an idea, a plan. And I save enough for the blond hair, blue contact lenses, the new f-face and bus fare, and I'm here. I let Maria down, Deacon. I'm telling you, she was the most beautiful, the most loyal..."

"Jesus!" barked Deacon, "For God's sake, don't repeat it again! Maria was a woman, not a goddess. Listen, you think you were alone in this? They've been watching me for fifteen years. I don't talk with Maria. I've only seen her once or twice."

"But I've got to see how she's doing without me!"

"Which Maria? The one you've put on a pedestal or the real Maria? She's a lonely, bitter woman now, Jesus. After you 'died,' she couldn't keep up the mortgage payments and lost everything."

"I will see her, Deacon. She will not see me. I've got a plan. I can't do it alone. I-I need help."

"Of course," said Deacon, oddly detached. He removed his gum and smiled with nothing but his mouth.

Most cowards do.

"T-this time, t-this time, t-t-this t-time," Nelson stumbled under his breath. He shifted his weight, on the verge of flight, outside and across the street looking up at Maria's window for the hundredth anguished time, trying to build up enough courage to knock on her door. It was drizzling. It was now or...

Nelson crossed August Street and entered the lobby of the Belleview Hotel and ascended the stairs to the second floor.

His heart racing and his hand trembling, Nelson pushed the doorbell as he stood in the hall. It was painfully real now: the rolled-up copy of a wet newspaper in one hand, the wad of money from the bouts he'd already won stuffed in his pants pocket. Nelson's free hand rose to his left ear, and froze. It slid away as he glanced furtively up and down the empty hallway that narrowed and vanished into shadows.

"Hello?" Maria queried as she opened the door.

Nelson struggled to keep from stuttering as he drank in her face.

"Hello. My name is Brett Nelson. You don't know me, but my father was a friend of your husband, Jesus Maestas, fifteen years ago. Could I come in for a minute?" It was so hard not to grab and kiss her.

"Oh, dear. You're wet. Is it raining outside?" asked Maria with a mixture of suspicion and real concern.

"A little, I guess. Dad asked for a big loan from Jesus and couldn't pay Jesus back before he...they...passed on. He made me promise to repay you when I could. So, I'm here with the first installment on my father's debt."

"Oh, I can't believe it. Oh, this is like a gift from Mother Mary! Come in. Please, come in, Mr.... Nelson? Your voice sounds familiar."

"No, no, no. Lots of people sound alike." Nelson ran his hand through his wet, blond hair as he stepped inside. His heart fell. The room was clean, but shoddy and cheap, the walls covered with yellowed wallpaper and decorated with a Double Cola calendar from 1962, and a picture of the Virgin Mary cut from a magazine. Nelson covered his mouth with his hand. The battered, old plaid recliner he'd loved stood by the kitchen door.

"I'll get you a towel. Please...." Maria saw him hesitate, and waved him to the recliner. He sat, laying the newspaper on a lamp stand next to it.

"Jesus loved to sit in that chair," said Maria from the kitchen.

"Oh, I-I'm sorry," Nelson said and began to rise.

"I can't tell you how at ease I feel with you sitting there." She smiled as she entered carrying a towel. "It's almost like he's come back from the dead. He was very ambitious, you know. He wanted to be the heavyweight champion of wrestling. And he was a lion in the ring, but very shy, even timid, outside of it. Here. Try this."

Nelson sat back down, accepted the towel, and began vigorously rubbing his hair. "I'm sure he only wanted to help you because he loved you so much, Mrs. Maestas."

He dropped the towel in his lap and met the quizzical, embarrassed expression Maria wore. She lowered her eyes and pointed at the towel as she stood. Nelson looked down in horror at the blond dye that stained it, and instinctively covered his hair with both hands.

"Please. Don't be embarrassed." Maria took the towel from his lap, her face very close to his. "Jesus had such confidence when he wrestled, like he became another person. I notice you wear contact lenses, Mr. Nelson." She turned away.

"Oh. *The Citadel* newspaper. May I look at it," she asked, taking it from the stand and unfolding it. "I haven't bought one since, well, since Jesus passed."

"Y-yes. Yes, of course" Unnerved, Nelson flinched, his skittish heart beating like a trip-hammer.

The newspaper opened naturally to the sports page where Nelson had stopped reading. The headline read: Nelson Wins 13th!! Maria looked up nervously from the paper still open in her hands.

"You follow wrestling, don't you?"

"Oh, no. I-I'm a salesman." Nelson pulled his right earlobe.

"That...that little gesture...it's like..." Maria rose from her chair, realization dawning in her brown eyes.

"G-g-gesture...?!"

"Oh my sweet God. Jesus?" she whispered, tears welling in her eyes. "It's a miracle. My Jesus?!"

"N-no, Maria," he lied, half rising from the recliner.

Her lips were on his cheeks, on his eyes, on his mouth.

"Oh, Maria, it's been so long," he moaned into her mouth. "Maria. It is me. Maria.

"Oh, Maria!!!" Nelson said and jerked up from beneath his sheets out of bed, his heart pounding, his dark honey face covered with flop.

"I l-love you, Maria," he whispered.

His shoddy, cheap room did not answer. Its silent walls were covered with yellowed wallpaper and decorated with a Double Cola calendar and a picture of the Virgin Mary cut from a magazine. Nelson covered his mouth with his hand. His letter addressed to Maria lay on the night stand next to his bed.

He stilled his heart with effort, rose from the sheets, and dressed himself in the clothes draped over the only chair in the room. On the night stand sat a five-and-ten-cent-store frame. The face behind the glass was Maria's. Next to that, a wind-up clock sat on the stand by the letter. It was 2:00 A.M. He picked up the letter and left the room.

The night was clear and cool with a breeze that carried the faint smells of the ocean. Nelson stood on the corner beneath his room on the second floor of Curry Hardin Furniture and Appliances, and looked up at Maria's window in the Belleview Hotel across August Street. He crossed the street to a mail drop and opened it, holding his letter with his first payment on his fictional father's debt to Maria.

His hand dropped the letter into the mailbox. It had no return address. Inside, his heart broke as regret and fear struggled against his love like water repels oil.

September had tumbled and chilled into December when George Payne arrived at Bowden's Gym early in the morning. He ran his hand through his hair and over a hidden anomaly there as he inspected Deacon's office with open disdain.

"Well, you've made quite a name for yourself, Nelson," he said, his jowls shaking. "Just like me. I'm the 'King of the Squared Circle,' you know. You should see my swank digs in Bangor."

Nelson said nothing, his eyes on the floor. The three thugs behind Payne nodded by unwitting habit as Deacon turned a page of the contract on his desk. Nelson stood by Deacon, his hands clenched behind his back, the muscles in his jaw twitching, his fear of being recognized palpable.

"Fifteen matches, fifteen wins, and all in just four months," added Payne. "You ready for the big time, boy? Next step after could be a match with my champ, "The Fix"."

Nelson said nothing and smoldered as fifteen years of running from Payne's lie burned in his eyes. The fingernails of his left drew tiny half-moons of blood on the back of his right hand.

"He don't talk much, Mr. Payne," apologized Deacon.

"That's okay. The less said the better, eh, W.O? There'll be some smart money ridin' on that. I could get 15-to-1 odds on the Champ puttin' you down in the first five, and I bet it's gonna happen exactly like that! Some for you now, and a guarantee you'll get the belt next time out if you dive."

"Everything looks okay," said Deacon as he offered a pen that Nelson did not take.

"'Course, that's not in the contract," Payne winked. "It's an under-standing between...gentlemen."

Nelson looked down at Deacon's sallow, nervous face and took the pen and began signing the bottom of the last page of the contract.

"That's it, son," said Deacon. "Scribble your moniker here, and we're in tall cotton. He's a strong guy, Mr. Payne, and he's moving up fast. He'll do you good."

Deacon folded the document and leaned over the desk to place it in Payne's fat hand.

"That's it, boys. Let's get out of this nasty dump; no insult intended, Deacon. We got business in the big city." Payne turned on his heels and shambled heavily out of the office.

"Leave it to your boss to pull another rabbit out of another hat," said Payne as he descended the stairs. At the bottom of the stairwell, he stopped and flipped to the last page of the contract. His smile and blood drained from his bloated face. "What the hell is this," he snarled, livid with anger, as he looked back up the stairwell. "Does he think I don't read?

"Dammit, look what he did!!" Payne shook the contract in the puzzled face of one of his goons. "No one plays with George Payne. I can't let mugs bamboozle me!

"I'm gonna make an example outta Brett Nelson!!" he sneered, tearing the contract in strips he dropped on the floor. "You hear me, boys?

"You want I should go back up...!?"

"Shut up. I say where and when." Payne smiled from a mask of anger as he opened the front door. "We're businessmen. We don't dirty our own nest. So for starters, Mr. W.O. Deacon gets a ringy-dingy from yours truly." The door slammed behind them.

The wooden sign lettered "Bowden's Gym" swung and creaked above the closed door that cut off the breeze outside on August Street. Inside, the scraps of Payne's contract settled on the floor.

On one piece, on the dotted line above the typed name of Brett Nelson, was written Jesus Maestas.

Nelson never knew he had subconsciously signed the first name of the only man that could have saved him.

That night, in a blue funk, Nelson anxiously looked up and down the deserted sidewalk and street in front of the furniture store. The crowd that had roared at his sixteenth victory at 10:00 p.m. had left him with nothing but unnerving silence, a splatter of gathering clouds, and the light in Maria's window hanging mute above August Street. Brooding, he fidgeted with the letter in his hand.

Two blocks west, a sedan idling in front of the State Theater slowly and soundlessly pulled away from the curb. Its headlights were dark.

Nelson stepped off of the curb as the sky spit rain. In his mind, Maria ran up a cobbled path from the door of their home with her arms an open welcome to him.

The sedan slowly and soundlessly picked up speed.

Maria threw her arms around his neck and kissed him deeply and her body whispered love as Nelson walked across August Street. The car picked up speed and its headlights slapped on. Its windshield wipers smeared half-moons on the dirty glass. Nelson turned in Maria's arms in the middle of the street in the glare of the headlights, frozen.

The black sedan slammed on its brakes, its rubber tires squealing. It hit thud throwing Nelson up on the hood and rolling him forward to crack the rain spattered windshield. The car stopped, he rolled back on the hood and lay still. The sedan's wipers thup one broken like a bird's wing thup swiped dry and then thup hung again.

Nelson looked through the smeared, cracked windshield inside. The sedan jerked and screeched back hard. He rolled off the hood.

The black car ran away.

Dazed and bleeding, Nelson lay crumpled on the sidewalk as the sedan's taillights faded. He lay as the blood and rain thundered in his ears and stared up at the distorted yellow light in Maria's window.

Nelson lay with the horror of what sat behind the sedan's windshield etched on his face.

Sam watched as rain that spat outside the cafe's window etched across the glass.

Exhausted and sullen, he watched the gulls swirl high in the fading light of evening. Above them, charcoal clouds thickened.

"Whatta lousy day this'n was, eh, Nelson?" he mumbled. "Ain't nothin' hooch an' a cheap whore won't fix."

Gnarled hands froze in the sink and then came out of the dirty, steaming dishwater as fists. The blood swelled and glutted a careworn face.

"Take it back," Nelson snarled from a face full of gray stubble.

"Hey, Pops, you forgettin' who runs this greasy spoon?"

Nelson struck. The thud of flesh against concrete fed the outrage of the surprised, grunting, embarrassed cook on a floor cluttered with boxes of rank food scraps in the unmitigated gloom of the empty kitchen.

"If that'd hurt, I'd kick your ass," he snarled, breathing heavily. "Get out. Now! You're fired!!

The blood drained as quickly as it had glutted Nelson's face, and his arthritic fists relaxed and blossomed at his side. "I-I'm s-sorry. I didn't mean..."

He took off his apron, balled it, and threw it in the dishwater.

"No I'm not," he said, and left the kitchen.

The pensive, January air outside was heavy with a drowsy, deep-throated rumbling. His sixty-five year old legs gave way and Nelson sank heavily on the curb outside under the blinking neon sign of the Majestic. He looked up at the gray, claustrophobic and threatening thunderheads that were rolling sluggishly in from the Atlantic Ocean. He hated clouds. They always rained memories. Carefully, he removed a folded letter from the pocket of his denim jacket.

Felt but unseen, the deserted Belleview Hotel that still haunted him stood one block west, its lobby converted into a bar and its apartments above now empty. Three blocks beyond that lay the thin blanket of gray ashes and charred scraps of board that had been Bowden's before Nelson had torched it. He looked down at the folded letter he'd found on Deacon's desk fifteen years ago. He had memorized every word:

You must have guessed some. Since even a coward and an unmitigated love-sick fool deserves something (and I've never known a bigger fool than you by half, "Nelson") here's the rest.

If you'd ever had the guts to go to "Maria's" apartment, you would've fell over when Hog opened the door. Ever since he retired from wrestling, Hog's been doing odd jobs for me. Lately, he's been cashing the checks you sent to her at that address. Dirty lawyers know how to cash those, you know. I've always pocketed the money you sent her.

Of course, you never had any backbone outside of the ring. Fifteen years ago, you were too busy making me rich and wrestling out of town to see me fall in love with your precious, beautiful, loyal Maria. I always knew I'd have to get rid of you to have a chance at her. I saw my chance when you signed to wrestle Hog. It was easy since, unlike you, he would do anything for a buck instead of a phony belt.

That's right; Hog just took a dive that night. You've been running from nothing. I made sure you were too busy running to ever know. I paid Hog off with the money I won betting against you the night you thought you killed him.

Anyway, life isn't all peaches and cream. Even with you gone, Maria saw right through me. But that's okay. People always pay who don't give me what I want. When she got desperate enough, Maria made a great little addition to my stable of whores. You see, Jesus, I'm a fraud. I was disbarred because I worked drugs and prostitution, and wrestling was just a front to continue both after they caught me.

I was surprised and concerned when you showed up. But I always find an angle. You queered it all when you signed Jesus on that contract.

You'd love to stick a knife in my scrawny ribs right now, but you won't. Why? You didn't even have the guts to go see Maria. And don't bother looking now. You'll never find us.

That's it. That's everything. But, so you'll know, this isn't written with any noble purpose. I wrote it to hurt you. I can't stand the sight of you,

Jesus Maestas. But I do pity you, and pity (and the money you made me) is its own reward.

Deacon

P.S. Before I forget, I have always worked for Payne.

The somber clouds above him rumbled and spit rain. Nelson put the letter back in his pocket, unread. It was nothing compared to what had brought him to the gym that night so long ago.

He tried to shake off the memory of the black sedan and the letter and the fire he set as he ran a hand through his dirty mane of black hair. He failed. His wasted body shook as he buried his creased face in his vellum hands and sobbed.

Nelson wept, but not from the shame of arson, or the weary years of desperate poverty, or his hopeless loneliness, or even of having never found the woman he still loved or the lawyer who had betrayed him. Nor was it because the old man yearned for the roar of the crowd, or the thud of flesh on canvas, or even the smell of flop in the squared ring. What had blistered and then ruptured his soul was the horror of who had sat behind the windshield behind the sedan's wheel.

The storm exploded with profane, feminine power and the unseen splatter of gulls burst apart and fled. The storm and Nelson wept.

The face behind the glass had been Maria's.

THE END

WHY DO BAD THINGS
HAPPEN TO GOOD PEOPLE?

An unpublished letter to *The Citadel* Newspaper

Dear Editor,

Once again, an undeniable tragedy has struck Light's End. Understandably, we mourn the loss of an innocent child to a "random" act, and we are shocked, frightened and angry at this injustice. And, regretably, many of my own neighbors and friends ask "Why did God let this happen?" in the depths of their sorrow and outrage.

The answer is not a pleasant one.

I believe that, in the beginning, God created all things spiritual and physical in a state of perfection, held in perfect balance. At least in the material world, scientists call this balance The Law of Nature. Cause and effect is an example of a physical law. We reap what we sow is an example of spiritual (or moral) law. This principal is illustrated, whether symbolically and/or literally, by The Garden of Eden in the first book of The Bible called Genesis.

I believe that because both worlds sprang from God, spiritual and physical events also affect one another. In addition, of all the living things created in the physical realm, man is the only creature capable of breaking these laws because he has been given free will (choice).

When Eve sinned, she disrupted this perfect balance in both the spiritual and physical worlds. From that moment forward, these worlds were no longer the perfect creation God authored in his image.   Eve recreated His worlds in her own, imperfect image. At the moment of her disobedience, Eve sinned against only herself and God.   In human terms, the disruption to the physical and spiritual world seemed minor and the consequences were immediate and easy to see.   It seemed to only effect Eve. This, however, was not true.   Because of her sin, no human being would ever again be born into or enjoy God's perfect physical world, and Eve had laid the seeds of corporate, or "shared" sin.

When Adam joined her in sin, he increased the disruption of God's balance as well.   Now these worlds had been remade in the imperfect image of Adam and Eve, and they had further damaged God's perfect creation.   Furthermore, the interaction of Adam's sin with Eve's sin added a complication to the consequences of their actions, corporate sin.   In human terms, the disruption was still minor, and consequences still seemed immediate and understandable, but now corporate as well as individual sin had entered into and changed God's worlds. Simply by being born, their children would not only suffer directly for their sins, but also indirectly from the "environment" created by their parents.

Cain and Abel never lived in Eden. When they added their sins to those of their parents, they also added disruption to an already out-of-balance physical and spiritual world. The consequences of corporate sin became less immediate and their origin less easy to see. As example, events in the past that they never saw or participated in still had a direct impact on their lives.

As man multiplied and spread over the earth, each person added to corporate sin through their individual sins. The original perfect balance of the spiritual and physical worlds was and remains dramatically disrupted. That disruption is so massive that the origin of sins committed in one place and time that directly or indirectly affect other places and times are often impossible to trace.

Bad "things" seem to happen at random because they are not the direct and immediate consequence of an individual's action, but of the corporate sin that refashioned our world. The honest but painful answer to the question "Why do bad things happen to good people?" is: there are no good people. The question is misstated. It should ask "Why do bad things happen to bad people?" The answer is: because we do them to ourselves.

Here is a parable borrowed from the Buddhists and restructured to illustrate this truth.

Imagine the spiritual and physical worlds as a beautiful, calm lake.

Wishing to enjoy that astonishing beauty, a man pushes a boat out onto the lake, and, by doing so, immediately disrupts it. The boat upsets its calm with ripples.

If he tosses a stone into the water, it creates more ripples that further change the perfect peace and balance of the lake, but in such a small way that it seems inconsequential.

When a second man enters the lake and adds a second stone, the size and number of the ripples increase from the presence of two boats and two stones. But the slight turbulence also increases as the ripples from the first boat collide with the second.

As many men push their boats out onto the lake, and many stones are tossed into that lake, ripples become small waves, and their boats begin to rock.

When millions of men enter the lake and millions of stones are tossed into it, those waves become threatening. Suddenly, and seemingly at random (because distance makes it impossible to see all of these "sailors"), some of the boats spring leaks or even capsize, and their owners cry out "Why is God doing this to me!?" because their tiny stones could not possibly have created the turmoil on the water.

The stones are individual sins; the ripples are the consequence of those sins.

This is why the Bible states that 'the fathers eat bitter grapes and the teeth of their sons are set on edge.' Those sons suffer from a world fouled by the sins of their fathers and grandfathers and great-grandfathers all the way back to Eden. Those sons, in turn, will add to those sins and that suffering.

It is painful, but true, that man brought sin into the world, not God. When he did so, he brought spiritual and physical decay, disease and death with it. *All* of creation groans for the second coming of our Lord and Master. He will restore perfect balance to His worlds, destroying both individual and corporate sin and their wages, the horrible and sometimes seemingly random consequences of those sins.

Dr. Schlomo Nantier, Ph.D.
Honored Albert Einstein Chair, Professor of Mathematics
University of Maine at Bangor
Brother, National Academy of Sciences

KΠOCKERS

As quietly as falling dust, it was knocking.

Linda Richards stood in the doorway opening onto the barren, frozen crazy throw of slate gray stone that fell away to the ruins of the old lighthouse and tumbled motionless down its cliff to the yellow, dirty beach and the dead winter ocean. Her muscles, like a huge rubber band nailed to the wooden floor and twisted, twisted, twisted and stretched to breaking, were knotted to the top of her skull.

Outside the opened door, the ground was hoary with frost and a light dusting of snow. The sky was muffled by heavy, dirty sullen clouds. The screen door that separated her from the brittle air painted everything with dots like comic book art. She stood suspended in time and silence, a still life swallowed by a heavy quilted robe that shamelessly fell open to the untouched flesh under her diaphanous nightgown. She stood in cloth slippers in a weary house that had known nothing but the untouched flesh and smell of women for thirty years.

Linda rubbed her left temple below her brown hair hard with two fingers. It was a frigid October twilight, and everything had sharp edges. Cuts hurt and any fall left yellow bruises. The air tasted of salt and the ocean, flecked with foam, soughed against the piers. Linda knew she could grind gravel into the ice and snow with the heel of a shoe and know that this day was hard and clear and real. And that nothing terribly exciting and special would happen in old lady Horne's ancient house in Light's End today.

And the knocking of bloody, bony knuckles against the wooden lid of the coffin of the ravenous vampire rose quietly, clear and nail hard.

117

As quietly as falling snow, it was knocking.

She tossed the letter, still partially tri-folded, onto the already cluttered desk. Without looking at it, Robert Tram glanced sideways at Linda, her arms folded defiantly across her chest, and then back at the outdated, smudged computer screen peppered with his story. She was not the first in a long, tedious line of hungry college graduates who had taken a job at *The Citadel*, the daily newspaper of Light's End, to "pay her dues." As did all of those before her, because he would hire nothing less, she owned characteristics that were essential in any reporter at his paper: an uneasy mix of cynicism and an overwhelming and dangerous curiosity, both of which were irritating, and the naiveté that guaranteed that she would work cheap.

"It's not what you think," he said, which is true for most of life, he thought. "It's just a civic club. You know, like the Lions, the Rotary." His finger missed the right computer key, breaking his rhythm and flow of thought. Cursing under his breath, he stopped to listen to the female problem who wrote stories about school plays, city council meetings, church events, and anything mundane beyond belief until she could land the sensational story that would win her a job on a real newspaper in a real town.

"Knockers?" she said, disbelieving. It was knocking.

"It has nothing to do with naked women and cakes. It was started by dock men who broke down emptied barrels from the ships that unloaded cargo here about a hundred years ago. And 'Knockers' isn't the name of the club. It's actually the Sophist's Club. Knockers just stuck, that's all."

"Knockers?" she said, now seriously perturbed. Linda rubbed her left temple beneath her brown hair hard with two fingers and shifted her weight from the left to the right leg. "Please, don't say that again."

"Listen, this isn't sexism. It's just a civic club with stupid arcane symbols and sayings and traditions whose meanings were replaced a long time ago by guest speakers and their ongoing campaign to buy glasses for people who can't afford to buy them. If there were naked women jumping out of cakes, how long do you think it would take before that would get back to their wives in a town of eight thousand?"

"Their speaker this week is a raging sexist."

"He's state senator for our district. And if I sent, say, George over there, or Henry to spare your feelings, wouldn't that make me a 'raging sexist' just like him by giving you preferential treatment? Now quit bitching and go do the story."

Linda stood silently before the outrageous and indisputable logic of her editor. "Have you ever looked at their club seal with the funny star and the stone cutter's tools? For that matter, have you ever noticed that the town seal also says 'As above, so below'?"

"Yeah. It's on Sarah Azreal's tombstone which they say was the cornerstone from the old lighthouse. It collapsed long before either you or I was even born."

"Do you know where that comes from? Wiccans use it, and before that, it came from some weird Templar stuff from the Middle Ages and, before that, from alchemists."

"And Christmas trees come from Druids who built Stonehenge and danced around under the moonlight wearing the skulls of deer and bears. So what?"

"You don't think it just a little strange that your town motto is used in witchcraft and satanic rituals?"

"I don't think that anything the town fathers do to draw gullible tourists to Light's End to see the tombstone of the wife of an old lunatic and the ruins of an old lighthouse that collapsed in an earthquake is strange. Editors have been giving assignments to reporters in this old building since 1907. What's strange is a cub reporter who stands around arguing with her editor who's on deadline because she doesn't want to do a boring story on a speaker at a rubber chicken luncheon with a bunch of old guys who like to play around like boys for an hour every week."

"That's strange." Tram picked up the news release and offered it to Linda. "And it can cause terminal unemployment." Tram looked at the tall, brown-haired and blue-eyed, plain-faced and intelligent feminist and longed for the old days of ink-smeared, cranky, smelly, unshaven old men with paper caps and bottles of bourbon hidden in the lower left drawer of their desks.

Linda took the letter and turned away. It was knocking.

"Hey, Linda," Tram said as she moved away. "I mean, Ms. Richards."

Linda paused in the bullpen doorway and pushed the left corner of a framed comic strip up in an unconscious, reflexive and completely useless effort to straighten it on the wall where it hung. She did not turn to face Tram.

"Have you made it out to Block Lake yet? If not, hold off until midnight. That's when all of the drowned corpses rise from the depths and, in an ironic twist of events, cast spectral lines from skeletal poles fishing for the souls of men. I mean persons."

Linda left the bullpen.

"It's a great life if you don't weaken," Tram called after her, grinning without humor or malice or even resignation but because it was simply the single great truth of existence, and returned to the pepper on his computer screen. "Knockers," he said under his breath.

Linda left the newspaper office that sat next door to the Phillips Pawn Shop and across from the State Theatre, which was out of business. The sky was muffled by heavy, dirty sullen clouds and the frigid air was full of a light dusting of snow. The walk to her room in the old house three blocks from the merchant district of Light's End and several hundred yards from the ocean and the ruins of the old lighthouse would be a job. She turned up her collar and stepped out onto the sidewalk, thinking it is a great life if you don't weaken, and I'll be damned if I weaken before that idiot.

And the knocking of bloody, bony knuckles against the wooden lid of the coffin of the zombie rose quietly, clear and nail hard.

As staccato as hail, it was knocking.

Outrageously, the glass onion twisted and stopped, the hidden metal of lock and tumbler meeting wood inside the door. The glass onion twisted and stopped, twisted and stopped. Linda looked down at a hand she did not recognize as it twisted and stopped, the doorknob resisting her will. The doorway at the rear of the kitchen opened onto the frozen throw of stone that fell to the lighthouse ruins and tumbled down its cliff to the yellow beach and the ocean beyond her control. Her muscles, like a huge rubber band nailed to the floor and twisted and stretched to breaking, were knotted to the top of her skull. The doorknob beneath the alien hand twisted and stopped, resisting. The knocking

"They're a horror."

"What," Linda answered reflexively, startled out of her reverie and, turning, instinctively and suddenly conscious of her near nakedness, pulled the heavy quilted robe tight over her breasts. "Oh, Mrs. Horne. I was looking for coffee in the pantry. But the door is locked."

"Oh, that," said Barbara. "It's locked because it goes to the basement. After I murdered my husband, I buried him there."

"What," said Linda, swimming up from the depths of muddled thought and torn nerves.

"That's the pantry door, dear, and it's never locked. You must have turned the knob wrong. And I was saying they're a horror."

"What?" Linda asked, swimming up to consciousness through murky depression, up through three sorry months of concentrated hatred since she'd moved to the edge of the merchant's district of the seaport dung heap that had been built in the '20s and '30s and stayed there.

"Doors." Barbara Horne stood at the kitchen sink behind her boarder and looked at her with hard, clear, flat black eyes like the eyes of a cow. "Doors. They're a horror. They always open on the unknown and you never know what nasty surprise may wait on the other side." It was knocking. The old woman turned her sixty-five years to the refrigerator next to the kitchen sink without waiting for an acknowledgment or wanting response. "Something always wanting to leave or something always wanting to get in. And they're everywhere. Even on refrigerators. Probably thousands in Light's End. Millions and millions and millions of the little horrors all over the world opening onto gods know what. The one you were standing at is letting in a surprising amount of cold air, don't you think?"

"I hadn't really thought..."

"I know, dear. I've always had queer little ideas. People say I should be a writer. The coffee's in the cabinet above the coffee maker. I need to make a casserole for my club meeting tonight." Barb took a package of almonds, a half-stick of butter, a carton of milk, and a small bowl of mushrooms covered with cellophane out of the refrigerator and set each on the counter next to the kitchen sink. The old woman closed the refrigerator door. Sorry doesn't unslam the door, thought Linda.

"I hope you don't think I'm sticking my nose into your business, but you seem agitated. You're too young for those gray bags under your eyes. Is there something you'd like to talk about, or..."

"The knocking," answered Linda pressing two fingers to her right temple. She opened the cabinet door above the coffee maker and removed a packet of coffee. "I haven't slept more than two or three hours in the last two nights. It never stops."

"Oh, my. Those noisy old lead pipes."

"It sounds like knocking on wood."

"It must be your imagination. You couldn't hear it all of the time because you're at work during the day. And it does stop. This decrepit old house is more than seventy years old, honey. It creaks and moans and talks to itself every night, and does odd things to sounds."

"I'm a journalist, Mrs. Horne. If I can't prove it, it doesn't exist. And I do hear it. I hear it right now. And it sounds like wood."

"You won't hear them after tonight." The old woman poured milk into the pot and dropped the half-stick of butter into her casserole. "I've already called the people." Linda filled the glass coffee bowl with water from the tap and glanced at her landlord pouring canned green beans in a pot on the kitchen stove. "Mrs. Horne," she asked as she turned off the flow of water from the tap, "have you ever heard of the 'Knockers'?"

"Heard of them? Why, my late husband loved Knockers. Why do you ask?"

"My editor has assigned me to cover one of their meetings. I think its called the 'Sophist's Club' but everyone seems to call them 'Knockers'..."

"That," interrupted Barbara holding one hand parallel to her body and rapping her knuckles into its palm, "is because of their secret greeting. See? Knocking? My late husband, rest his soul, was a Knocker, and I'm still a member of their women's auxiliary, the 'Daughters of the Star.'"

"Women's auxiliary?" Linda sneered unconsciously and poured the water from her glass pot into the top of the automatic coffee maker. "Did you know that separate club auxiliaries for women are illegal now, Mrs. Horne? It's sexual discrimination."

"Yes." Linda waited it was knocking for what did not follow, then threw the switch on the coffee maker. "Everything is not about male and female, dear. I'm sure that won't matter as much to you with time because, although you don't believe it now, you and I are a lot alike. It's one of the reasons I rented the room to you."

"It seems this town is full of 'silly little' somethings," said Linda. "Like the caverns beneath the ruins of the lighthouse, 'not natural and not carved out by human hands...'"

"And every All Hallows Eve, the hobgoblins and witches and things with cloven hooves and human eyes gather there and dance to Satanic music while they sacrifice a baby on a stained, bloody alter and eat its heart." Barbara fussed with the pot. "You've read the tourist's brochure. It's just local legend. In the fifties, they even built a cheap copy of the old lighthouse made out of plywood that was blown away by the hurricane of '62."

"And the 'only grave within twenty miles of Light's End' by the Phison river, Mrs. Horne?"

"'The grave of Sarah Azreal, almost as much a tourist draw as the lighthouse. Its headstone was the cornerstone dug from the lighthouse." The old woman turned off the stove.

"Have you noticed that it's hard to find a straight angle in many of the buildings that were built in the late sixties around here? That comes from the legend of the old Ebenezar Azreal house and its odd architecture. it was knocking Some chamber member thought that if we added an odd angle or two to everything new we built, we'd draw even more tourists to Light's End.

"And the 'Knockers' is just a part of it all. The doors in attics and ceilings and garage floors are there because they open on another dimension or heaven or hell or any place a tourist will believe as long as they don't believe the truth, which is they're a tourist trap." The old woman opened a cabinet door and removed a glass bowl and cover.

"All Hallows Eve is the biggie, dear, and it draws thousands of tourists to buy our food and little flying saucers, skulls and lighthouse trinkets made out of colored plastic. And it's all just Chamber stuff because the world has just kind of passed us by. There really isn't anything here to see or any reason to live here except it's a nice place to die."

Linda looked down into her mug and noticed that, although the mug sat flat on the table, the coffee inside was not level with its lip. "I didn't come here to die," she said, looking at the coffee.

"Oh, I know. You came here to pay your dues as a journalist. You girls today are so independent. You came here to open doors." it was knocking Barbara poured the steaming contents of her pot into the glass bowl, set the pot back on the stove, and turned off the heat. "Speaking of doors... could you," she waved a finger at the bowl and grinned at Linda. "Could you open the little horror for me?"

And the knocking of bloody, bony knuckles against the wooden lid of the coffin of the ravenous vampire rose clear and nail hard.

Barbara moved to the coat rack next to the door as Linda rose from the kitchen table. Barbara set the glass bowl on the kitchen counter, and took her coat and shawl from the coat rack, and began to put them on. "Tonight is a special night for the 'Daughters.' We're initiating a new sister."

Barbara buttoned her coat around her shawl and turned to Linda, standing silently and straight with an odd look of disdain on her twenty-three year old face. "By the way, dear. That thing about doors in basement floors in the brochure? We live next to the ocean. They don't build houses with basements next to oceans." Her face was like a clown's without makeup, full of secret laughter.

Then the old woman turned again, opened the door and disappeared.

Linda looked into her mug and noted that, although it sat flat on the table, the coffee was not level with its lip. Her head was pounding. She paused in the bullpen doorway and pushed the corner of a framed comic strip in a useless effort to straighten it on the wall it was knocking where it hung. "It's a men's civic club," said Tram, sitting across from her at Barb's kitchen table. "It was started by dock men who broke down emptied barrels from the ships..." "That," interrupted the old woman, rapping her knuckles into a palm, "is because of their secret greeting." Linda looked into her mug in an old house that did strange things to sounds it was knocking since it was built seventy years ago and noted that the coffee was not level because houses were built crooked in the '60's. She paused in the doorway and pushed the comic strip up on the wall built in 1907. The thin, slimy film of lies lay everywhere. She got up from the table and went to the locked pantry door.

Linda put her hand firmly on the cool, glass onion doorknob and turned it easily and the door swung sorry doesn't unslam the door in, creaking. She gasped a hiccup, jerking away as if burned; instinctively stepping back from the it was knocking stairs that fell down into a murky red half light. Her robe opening on near nudity, she stood at the threshold of the old woman's lie, hands balled into fists, fingernails I'll be damned if I weaken before that bastard cutting her palms and arms hard as rods at her side, and pushed the fear, the violation of logic, down, hard, into its animal place.

And the knocking of bloody, bony knuckles against the wooden lid of the coffin of Barbara's dead husband rose clear and unmistakable from the murky red glow that swallowed the stairs.

"Don't weaken, don't weaken, don't weaken," she said, surprised that she spoke instead of thought the words. A pressure of warm, smarmy, moist air rising from the basement registered beneath the fear I'll be damned clouding her senses. Linda stepped on the first wooden stair which sagged a little under her weight but made no sound. She put the trembling fingertips of her right hand it was knocking everywhere at the end of her outstretched arm on the wall for balance.

They swiped through cold mucous.

Linda jerked back. Fighting revulsion, she brought her fingers to her nose and sniffed, smelling nothing beyond damp earth and damp flesh. She glanced down at the step below, wiped her fingers on her its a great life if you don't robe and stepped down. Linda stepped and the floor of the old house that was the cellar's ceiling rose above her head. The instantly familiar, low, red glow from a furnace huddled against the far wall, hot and dangerous and reassuring, rose as she descended, throwing wild, ululating shadows and a red half light. The furnace soughed through its red teeth grating against the cold of the frozen throw of stone outside. She moved down the creaking steps, some solid, some giving slightly, with a growing confidence and a curiosity too fierce to be learned or smothered by the musk of open graves. She stepped onto the cellar floor.

Linda shuffled forward, cataloging the it was knocking everywhere windowless walls lined with shelves filled with amorphous shapes, her cloth slippers whispering in dust. The knocking of bloody, bony knuckles against the lid of the coffin of the vampire rose clear and nail hard from the murky red glow when the cellar went white with pain. "Damn!" she hissed. "Damn!!" Linda squatted in the red gloom and grabbed her throbbing, stubbed toe and the unexpected warm wet of blood beneath her thin cloth slipper. She rocked back and forth moaning oh oh oh oh, squeezing the pain back into her flesh with her hand until it diminished and diminished into a dull throb.

Linda straightened and moved back a step into a thin line that whipped her cheek. The involuntary scream broke open her lips, and she beat blindly, frantically, with animal terror, at the web, the bat, the skeletal finger that jumped in the it was knocking everywhere ululating red shadows, flailing with the animal fury of survival until the small still clear voice of reason whispered linda linda linda its a hanging light cord. She dropped her arm and held it at her side. She did not move, breathing deeply and slowly. She stilled her heart. She reached up, twisted the light cord into her fingers, and pulled.

The door lay in the cellar floor, knocking the cellar floor the cellar floor the cellar sorry doesn't unshut the and the furnace soughed. Linda's heart rose and thundered, her chest heaving with short, choking gasps. Her gut tied in knots, she licked her lips and tasted the salt of sweat. Her flesh was clammy in the muggy heat of the cellar. She bit her lower lip. She fought down the fear, the instinct to flee screaming up the stairs. Trembling, Linda kneeled and reached I'll be damned for the glass onion doorknob and touched it.

The knocking stopped.

Her heart stopped. The muscles in her arm spasmed. The furnace soughed. She grit her teeth. Shaking, Linda reached for the glass onion doorknob and opened sorry doesn't unslam the door.

The floor beneath was smooth.

Linda stood and looked at the smooth floor. She raised her head, still holding the open door, and looked around the cellar and back up its stairs for the sneering faces of Barbara and the Daughters of the Star and Rob

Tram and the Knockers, all sneering at the "fearless reporter," at their well prepared practical joke, but the cellar was empty except for the red maw of the furnace. And Linda hiccuped, her fear spent, the tension draining away, and giggled nervously with relief. The furnace soughed. And she laughed at the shameful dead animal inside her because, whatever the reasons for the crazy buildings and the old woman's lies, she would find the truth. And she laughed out loud into the concrete reality of her justified cynical disbelief, and let the door fall back because sorry doesn't unslam the door with a FUFF of dust.

Linda rubbed her left temple below her brown hair gently with two fingers.

The door knocked.

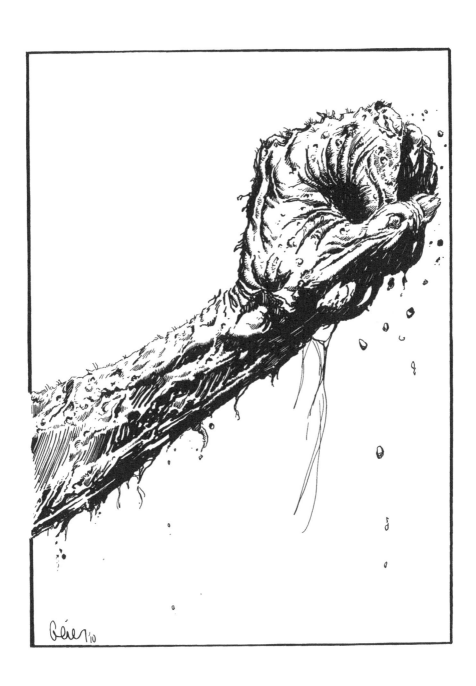

In The Out Door:
The Play

The face of Robert Tram's ancient clock, almost obscured by shadows, read four. "Oh, god, not again," he cursed. "Four shadowing."

Stiff with arthritis and pink with exertion, he rose from his battered editor's desk, dismissed the clock with a gesture, and left the bullpen.

Light's End wept as Tram tottered out of the in door of his office to stand before the fly-specked window of *The Citadel* newspaper. The editor wore no raincoat as he stood at the curb, lost in and irritated by the thought of his old Chevy, immobile and in need of expensive repairs. It was knocking.

He noticed his soft, pudgy, seventy-five-year-old face reflected in the windshield and winced. It was pale and weak, the face of an editor cut from the same polyester as his cheap suit. It was a mug quickly forgotten, marked by neither exceptional intelligence nor stupor, creased by endless deadlines. He reluctantly turned away from the window and his reflection.

Across the bricked street at the State Theatre, the marquee caught his attention. It read: "High School Play Practice." He fought against thinking of Cynthia Wells and her son inside, and of the review he must write.

The air was warm and smarmy and tasted of salt, bricks and dust. Down August Street from Tram, the Atlantic Ocean sighed against the piers like sand across a desert. The sky was heavy, grey and low and made the city feel like a closet. Tram looked back at *The Citadel* vending machine on the sidewalk and at the mast of his newspaper with its inaccurate drawing of the old lighthouse whose ruins still hid Light's End's nasty secrets. The rays of light radiating from its beacon looked like a star. He read his headlines on the front page, then turned and crossed the wet, brick street until he stood under the marquee of the dilapidated State Theatre.

He ran a trembling hand with its yellow, dirty fingernails through his thinning wet hair and felt the anomaly hidden there at the base of his neck. The ticket booth was empty.

Tram moved to the double doors of the State and rapped softly. He rapped again, harder. He whistled and rocked back and forth on the balls and heels of his feet. The lock of the double doors clanked inside, and the doors opened.

"Aaaaaaaah," said Cynthia Wells behind the crack. "Mr. Tram! Please, come in!

"All of the kids are so excited," she added as Tram stepped in the door marked out. The community theater director closed it behind them. She was in her early fifties with the saturnine face of an unemployed fashion model. Her eyes were cerulean blue, her hair jet black, and her pink legs were bare and hard-muscled below polka dot shorts. She wore stained, white linen gloves. In her left hand was a tube of rolled paper; her left, because of an accident that had damaged its nerves, was a wandering hand.

"I can't tell you how grateful I am to the members of the Sophist's Club and the Daughters of the Star who are giving us a chance at bringing a Little Theater to our town." She extended her hand. "I'm Cynthia Wells, John's mother.

"Oh," she said, noticing her gloves. "Excuse me. I've been cleaning the old place." She peeled the gloves off.

"We are happy to help," said Tram with no sincerity. "It's been a shame the theater has stood empty for so long. Since '61 or '62, isn't it? Our little town needs to put all of its resources to work for us if we're to compete with the other cities, don't we? And I see you've done wonders with the baleful old place."

The lobby of the theater was pitch black, full of the timeless memory of candy, salt, popcorn, pop and human sweat. The air was warm and smarmy. Cynthia clicked on a flashlight in her right hand, pointing the light at the red carpet by their feet, then at the concessions, then at the door. She moved in perfect symmetry to the swinging door with the porthole in the center that separated the lobby from the theater and pushed it open.

"I'm sorry I'm late," lied Tram, "but there's a big breaking story back at the office. Is there any way we could do this later?"

Cynthia blushed as she held the swinging door open. "Oh dear," she gulped with anticipated disappointment; "all the children are inside and

ready. I know your time is very valuable, Mr. Tram, being the editor of
the paper. I promise it won't take long."

"I'm sorry. It's just that....okay, let's see it." His words faded into the
muffled black of the theater and the sound of the lobby doors swinging in
diminishing arcs.

"How many kiddos are in this thing," Tram asked as they moved to
a row of worn, red, upholstered seats. Cynthia swung the beam of the
flashlight in her right hand erratically to a seat; her left was her wandering
hand. Tram moved to it and sat down. Cynthia leaned close to him, full of
nervous excitement, and handed the tube of rolled paper to the editor. It
was a script bound in a cheap plastic folder.

"About ten, including the stage hands. It's only little theater, but the
kids are really hopping about this, Mr. Tram. We don't have costumes yet,
or much scenery, but I think you'll be able to get the idea behind what I'm...
we're...trying to do here."

Tram unfolded the tube. The cover sheet read:

```
In The Out Door
a one act play
by Cynthia Wells
```

He opened the folder and looked up but Cynthia was gone. On the
stage, two teenage boys were busily doing nothing in front of the closed,
worn, red velvet curtains that had once dramatically opened on a world of
newsreels, cartoons, serials and movies. Each boy held an open copy of
the script. He looked back down at the blocks of sans serif copy on the
first page of Wells' manuscript. It read:

This play is dedicated to The Sophists Club, the Daughters of the Star,
and *The Citadel* newspaper of Light's End, whose sponsorship made this
production possible.

"Hide the truth openly"

Characters (in order of appearance):

Narrator Played by Samuel Ebaugh

Adam Loman Played by Steve Adwan

Twenty-Four Seven clerk Played by Melanie Killingsworth

Mr. Keep and Ebenezar Azreal Played by John Wells

Setting

1959. Light's End on the coast of Maine. Night. The famous "crooked"
house of Ebenezar Azreal who rediscovered the Door between realities

and reestablished the physical link between man and The One, The Urge, who is the foundation of the Azrealites and the Tenebrae Church. This is a dramatization of that pivotal moment in world history when Ebenezar reopened the Door and set the stage for the triumphant return of The Urge who bought freedom for man and paid for it with his blood.

Tram looked up from the play, a storm of profane, masculine power behind his eyes. On the stage, Samuel Ebaug sat on a short stepladder to the left of Steve Adwan who straddled a wooden chair in the center of the stage. Behind a table next to Steve stood a young, agitated girl of sixteen. The audible click of a tape recorder somewhere backstage hiccuped into static and the sounds of a thunderstorm. Cynthia stood below the stage with her arms raised and spread wide above the height of her shoulders.

"Miss Wells..." said Tram with some heat, but his words were obscured by the roll of recorded thunder.

"Begin!!" said Cynthia to the Narrator and Adam Loman. "Do your best, honey," she added to John Wells who blushed cherry red with embarrassment.

"Mo-om!!"

"Sorry, sweetie, I forgot. Now, go ahead, Narrator."

Narrator: The painted lettering reads "Twenty-Four Seven' on the plate glass window of the convenience store. The shadow of that lettering is painted by the waning outside light across Adam Loman and a clerk.

"Miss Wells..." Tram snapped again. She turned and sat on the front row of seats in the smarmy darkness of the theater, oblivious to Tram, to the world and to the reality of the material universe. Tram, already in a foul mood, again looked down at the script.

Narrator: The clerk is fat and greasy. Adam Loman crushes the inheritance letter in his balled fist.

Clerk: He ain't dead!

Adam (crushing the letter in his fist): But, the letter...!?

Clerk: Listen, I knew Ebenezar. I followed all of his hunting expeditions and clipped his picture out of the newspaper where he's standing with one foot on a lion he killed in Africa. I was here at the first stone ol' Ebenezar laid at Gateway, and the last stone they laid over Ebenezar's coffin...but he ain't dead!

I've even been in his house and seen all his trophy animal heads hung all over the walls of that crazy place. A man like Ebenezar don't die! He killed, but he was too scared of dyin' to die himself!

From the beginning, he killed just to watch things spill the last drop of blood. He killed 'till there weren't nothin' he hadn't killed...'cept men, maybe. Then he got bored. Then he got sick! In the head! Began to stuff those things on the walls and...other stuff. And they come for him with clubs and pitchforks.

Narrator: That's when sailors started disappearing mysteriously, and it killed Light's End. They knew like you know bad water—by the smell! It was Ebenezar—killin'! Killin' unnatural! The crowd yelled outside of his house. "Son of Satan! Seed of the Damned!"

Clerk: They went to that black hole of Hell you inherited—Gateway—and drug him out! Cut his throat! And I was the one that tied his arms and helped dig his grave!

Narrator: Adam Loman imagined Ebenezar screaming. The fat clerk leaned over the counter into Adam's face...

Clerk: Your uncle was the son of the prince of filth! And those blank-faced heads on his walls are changed men! Bewitched! Cursed! He changed men into animals!

(Light's go down. Clerk leaves stage, rolling table with him; light's up as Adam raises hands to mid-waist as if driving a car.)

Narrator: The road winds by the ocean. It is night. Adam's car shambles its way through the rain past an abandoned lighthouse. A heavy, salt-laden wind blows scraps of garbage inland over the foul ribs of sand. The yellow earth seems bolted to the sky as Adam Loman feels the ocean heave with sluggish swells of spotted, oily foam. He is sick.

Adam(clutching his stomach): Ooooh.

Narrator: Behind the windshield, its wipers fighting the rain, sits a very frightened but determined man. A line of sweat creases his forehead and mirrors the scattered streaks of rain on the windshield. A low wail moves over the sea. As the night pulls in close around the car, Adam's knuckles are white on the wheel.

Adam (with intensity): Money....

Narrator: The dank sea wind sucks at the Chevy. Adam shrinks deep into his over coat and thinks about his dead uncle and shivers.

Adam (shivering): Money is... mine!

Narrator: Adam Loman thinks of the inheritance, the bitter cold sea, his battering wife, and shakes with laughter. Tears come to his tired eyes.

Adam (laughing): Ebenezar Azrael is dead! Dead! Dead!!

Narrator: The wind is clammy, sucking at the trees, sucking at Adam

Loman as he pulls up, parks and steps out of his car into the rain outside the gothic house.

Ebenezar Azreal's is a huge, old, dirty house of mad angles, and of cupolas and spires and scrolls that looked like they'd been thrown against its walls by a drunken monster and stuck there. It stands on the east fringe of the sea port town. Its insanity of wood and brick and the august legends of the Azreals have made the house a pariah, stubborn and decaying, an infected eyesore on the face of Light's End.

Adam: I-I gotta do it! I...gotta go!

(Adam rises from chair and approaches stage curtain/door to the Azreal house)

Narrator: As Adam approaches the house, his shoulders slump. The presence of his wife and mother-in-law hang ghostly on either side of him. He feels his shame burn as he leans into the thin sheets of rain. He feels burning fear at the pit of his stomach and hears his wife and mother-in-law, Mother Applegate, whine incessantly in his head.

Adam: If I'm a...man...I've got to...to do it!

Adam's wife (offstage): Why can't we have real money like real men bring to their wives!

Mother-in-law (offstage): You married a spineless idiot! I told you, you should've married Harold Glenn.

Narrator: He feels the hate turn his stomach. He hears his boss. "I knew I should've given this to a better man! Someone with guts! Ambition!"

Adam (preparing to knock on door/curtain): Yes, Mr. Hobnot.

Narrator: But the years of cowering, struggling, losing, are stronger than the fact that...Adam Loman is not a man!

Adam (knocking on curtain/door): This time. I'll show them all this time!

(The curtain opens to the width of a door revealing a 'butler' in an outdated tuxedo)

Keep: Mr. Adam Loman? Welcome! I am Keep...the curator. And this is Gateway. This is...all yours!

Adam: MY GOD! no.

(Curtains open to show a large room with walls covered with crude drawings of stuffed heads, floor with several animal skins, and a painting of a man next to the doorway where Adam and Loman stand. A free-standing door at stage left is clearly marked "OUT." Behind it is a small curtain)

Narrator: An oil painting of Ebenezar Azreal on an easel that surely must elicit innuendo and macabre comments from older women in shiny worn suits unnerved Adam. A strangled dream...a soul-wrenching sickening! The overpowering stench of decay yanks at Adam!

Adam (against a wall, arm raised defensively): This...can't be all...real!

Keep: I also rather admire Mr. Azreal's taxidermy! It is breathtaking, isn't it, Mr. Loman?

Narrator: The silence lies like death. Outside, the storm surges, smashing needle rain against the windows of Gateway.

Keep: You're tired, Mr. Loman. Perhaps I should show you to your room. After all, you've got a long time to see Gateway!

Adam: Wha...?

Narrator: The words are blurred by Adam's burning, aching pain as he and Keep move into the horror of a room! "Ladies and gentlemen— Adam Loman! Heir Apparent to stuffed squirrels!"

Keep: Excuse me...?

Adam: I said: 'Wha...?'"

Keep: Mr. Loman! Didn't they tell you? You have to wait until after I die to inherit! Your uncle knew I loved Gateway and guaranteed me a place to live out my life.

Adam (pointing at "OUT" door): What's behind there?

Keep (overstated): NOTHING! Nothing, Mr. Loman! At the end, Ebenezar's mind went. He lost everything in the end...his money, strength, youth! And, Mr. Loman...he feared dying! He shook with the fear of death! Mr. Azrael had always been a doer...a man of action! So he began looking for an "out," as he called it. He began to dabble in black magic. But he was harmless, Mr. Loman! After all, there is no Satan! I remember well the hours he would sit and talk to his stuffed heads... about death. That's when we began to see faces in the windows! Some people from town saw him talking to the animals! One night, they came and they...they...

Adam: ...cut his throat?!

Narrator: Adam heard the howling wind through the gap in Keep's words. He felt an unnatural hardness in his chest. He did not believe.

Keep (picking at gap in teeth with pick): The sign was to have read "Keep Out," but there was a mistake. What little Mr. Azreal valued is behind it. I have the only key!

Adam: Where?

(Keep's hand high; audience sees his index finger has been replaced with a key)

Adam: Oh NO!

Keep: Don't! Please, Mr. Loman. It no longer bothers me. He had it surgically placed on my hand because he trusted no one else....because he was closer than you can imagine! Mr. Azrael's will stipulates that you'll have the key...when I'm gone. I can see that you need some time for thought, Mr. Loman. I'll be in the library if you need me.

Adam (stroking his chin): Huh?! Oh...good night.

(Keep moves to large, overstuffed chair on stage right)

Narrator: Five...ten...fifteen years! A man wouldn't wait! A man would take what is...and his wife's! A man takes the initiative! A man gives the orders!

Adam (moving towards 'library'): Keep's gone?! No! Got to have it now! There's got to be something...money...jewels...behind that bolted door!

(Keep sits in chair and pets a small, stuffed animal. In background, Adam reaches for a sword from a display on a wall)

Narrator: The weight of the storm shakes the rotting house. The weight of his fear shakes Adam's weak frame!

Keep (to the animal): Patience, my friend. The storm is almost past.

(Adam, behind Keep's chair, draws back the sword)

Adam: NOW!!

Narrator: The decayed, wooden floor creaks under his feet. In a distant room, rotten shutters are thrown open by the screaming wind!

(Adam wrenches chair around [back to audience] and plunges sword into Keep)

Adam (stabs): FOR YOU, DEAR!

(Sound Effect: kachuck!!)

Adam (stabs): FOR YOU, MOTHER APPLEGATE!!

(Sound Effect: kachuck!!)

Adam (stabs): FOR YOU, MR. HOBNOT!!

(Sound Effect: kachuck!!)

(Adam raises sword to cut off the key on Keep's hand on the arm of chair)

Adam (maniacally): Now...NOW...NOW....NOW!!

(Sound Effect: SWAK!!)

(Lights go out on stage as Adam strides to the door marked "OUT")

Narrator: Adam staggers under the strain and moans with relief! The storm is spent!

The rage is dead!

Adam (in dark): The key! The key! Open, damn it. OPEN!!

Narrator: The scream breaks open his lips!

(Light's go on. Adam screams, clutching his chest. He stands at open door and reacts with horror at what he, not the audience, sees.)

Narrator: His chest heaves with short, choking gasps! His heart explodes. And then...

(Light's OUT!! "Out" door and curtain are removed)

Narrator: The silence of Adam's death is like dust lying over Gateway! The storm has sunk back into the sea. Adam will never know that on his last day, Ebenezar had found what he'd sought: Satan, the Great Worm! Or that the devil gave Ebenezar eternal life in exchange for guarding the 'out' door— the door to Hell— as 'Keep'!

Of course, it's Ebenezar's duty to feed The Worm, Mr. Loman, but it's not without benefits! HA HA HA HA HAAA!

(Light's ON! Where "out" door and curtain stood, in shadow sits a body on a chair with "Keep" standing behind. Spotlight on Keep)

Ebenezar (actually Keep peeling off the mask that was his disguise): You get freedom from the shoving, demanding and shouting. No one will push or hurt you!

Ebenezar (holds up the 'face' of Keep): Satan takes your soul and...

(Spotlight moves to Adam, heavy, clumsy stitches mark his corpse-like face and neck)

Ebenezar: ...a stitch in time saves mine!!

Narrator: Loman screams eternally...but silently! For Adam cannot move his lips clumsily stitched together!!

The End

The theater lights came up as Cynthia moved down the isle with the perky, naive enthusiasm of youth. She held her hands out, palms up. Her blue eyes sparkled. "Well, Mr. Tram, wasn't it wonderful!? Just wonderful!? I think the kids did a great job, considering we had no props to speak of."

The storm broke with profane, masculine power.

"Stuffed corpses, Miss Wells?!" barked Tram with a knot of anger like a rubber band twisted to its limit in his gut. "Human taxidermy?!!" His voice rumbled like thunder. He rose from the seat and crabbed sideways between the rows of dusty, worn chairs to meet Cynthia's approach. "Ebenezar is the fifth generation of the founder of this town! He's an

Azreal, for Other's-sake!!"

The smile froze on Cynthia's face as Tram cursed, and her left hand went wild with movement. "Well, I did have to take some artistic license, condensing time and using symbolism. It is a dramatization, Mr. Tram."

"'The prince of filth'!? 'The Worm'!?! The One, The Urge is the prince of filth, Miss Wells?!!"

"Well, maybe I went a little over-the-top with that, but I can change it, Mr. Tram," said Cynthia defensively, with growing dismay. "But I was just trying to follow our own church tenant: hide the truth openly."

"This 'truth' is a bit too open, Miss Wells. And what of the other Azrealite tenants," said Tram with fire behind his eyes. "You forgot the important, unwritten ones like Taste and Talent and...Plagiarism."

Tears welled up in Cynthia's eyes as he reached into his pant pocket and drew out his bloodless hand clenched into a fist. "I read this story in a comic book ten years ago, Miss Wells. Open your hand," he said coldly, his anger now a ball of volcanic fury.

"But, Mr. Tram...!?!" said Cynthia, her voice quivering as she looked at his white, extended fist. "The c-children...?" she stammered as she glanced at the empty stage for succor from what she knew was to come. "Johnny...honey??"

"Your right hand, Miss Wells," said Tram, and he reached into his shirt pocket with his free hand and pulled out a folded piece of paper.

"But, Mr. Tram...!?!"

"Must I say it again? I hate repetition, Miss Wells."

She held out her trembling right hand, and Tram dropped a small, black stone in its palm. Her face went white when she saw the secret name, Beelpore, engraved on the stone. "Y-yours is the authority," she whimpered, lowering her head in subjugation.

"Indeed," he responded. She did not move as Tram dropped the folded square of paper on top of the black stone. "As above, so below," he said without inflection.

"Good day, Miss Wells. At least it was." And Tram strode out of the theater into the lobby, and out the in door of the lobby onto the street beneath the marquee.

The marquee screamed *In The Out Door* at Tram. He fought against thinking of Cynthia inside; her left was her wandering hand. The air was warm and smarmy and the sky was heavy, grey and low. The ticket booth was empty and would stay that way.

Robert Tram crossed the wet, brick street until he stood at the front door of *The Citadel* newspaper. He saw his soft, uneasy face reflected in the glass, but did not stop. Tram did not look down at the vending machine or the mast of his newspaper. He ran a hand with its yellow fingernails through his thinning hair, feeling the three hidden numbers there, and fought against thinking of Cynthia and the play and her dream for a community theater.

He knew that, hunched against its massive, clammy piles driven into the sea, Light's End would continue without Cynthia or her little theater. Tram knew the Tenebrae Church would support his decision. And he took solace in the knowledge that he'd killed Cynthia's abominable play and had erased any chance that others would suffer.

Or learn the dirty, forbidden secrets.

But he could not shake the monstrous image of Cynthia in tears and her son distraught. He could not forget the theater and his own fierce anger.

His bared teeth. His bloodless indifference. He knew the horror that he was had risen from the theater seat not as a reviewer, but as something more. And no heartless, bareheaded government clerk had squirmed in his chair, moaning at her one act play. But he would still spend many long, sleepless nights mulling over what she clutched in her left and wandering hand.

Cynthia Wells had fled from the theater sobbing from the monstrous obscenity of potential starvation lurking around her past-due rent, and the ravenous, unpaid bills that would soon fill her empty right hand.

In Cynthia's left was a pink slip.

THE END

THE FEASTING

Penny Neitenheimer soundlessly scratched the inside of her pink right ear with a manicured fingernail. She lay her left hand first on her cash register and then onto the spoon in a bowl half full of raisin bran cereal smothered in skim milk. She looked out of the huge, fly-specked plate-glass window, impeccably clean inside and tattooed with advertising stickers for beef jerky and Camel cigarettes and Double Kola.

"It's Sheriff Jones," she said as a dirty, white police car crept into her gravel driveway to stop at the Texaco gasoline pumps rimmed with greaseweed. "It's Alan Jones from Light's End, Schlomo."

She rubbed her chin without glancing at the delicate old man breathing quietly in a wool coat who sat across from her checkout counter on a stool. A Bible lay open under his yellow, gnarled hands. She picked a raisin from the cereal with the spoon and threw it into a trash can on the floor.

"Now why's that bald-headed young fool disturbin' th' peace by slidin' into th' Old Rock Store from Block Lake at six in th' mornin'? In October. For a cop, he never did have a lick o' sense, Schlomo."

"Anything's possible the mornin' after th' Feasting, Penny," answered the gaunt seventy-year-old as he smoothed down the memory of his hair on a nearly bald scalp.

"Why don't you ever go?" Penny put a spoonful of bran in her mouth and chewed, mulling over Schlomo's wife's suicide of years past that left him reclusive and introspective. "You know. To the Feasting?"

"Same reasons as any Christian, I guess. Plus it's so muddleheaded. 'Christians are fools,' but the tourists swallow nonsense like Light's End being honeycombed with caves leading to a 'gigantic maggot under

141

Elliott's Head cliff that eats our dead. That's why we don't have graves'."
The old man shook his fey head in mute frustration. "Or the bloated
corpses churning up Block Lake at Halloween to eat. That mindless junk
is th' Feasting, and going would mean condoning it, Penny."

"I'm just a country girl, but it looks like th' sheriff's got a 'perp'," she
whispered, peering out the window. "Someone's in th' back seat. Can't
see th' other cop inside the car; the Sheriff's blocking him. But Jones's
pumpin' gas. I'd better go check this out, Schlomo. You comin', 'rabbi'?"
She picked a raisin from the cereal with the spoon and threw it into the
trash can.

"I suppose. Say, Penny, why do you do that?" Schlomo Nantier closed
his Bible and traced the odd sword melded with a cross on its white leather
cover with an arthritic finger. "You know. Pick out the raisins and trash
them?"

"I don't eat raisins, 'perfesser'." She rose from her stool, oblivious to his
open, puzzled expression.

"But then it isn't raisin bran. Why don't you just buy...?" Nantier studied
his old friend's oblivious face. "Guess I'll never understand women."

"What's to understand?" She patted her brown hair back into place,
snatched her coat from a wall hook, and padded around the open end
of the counter. "Our souls are lonely, yearning for companionship. And
women have the same needs as men – for love and respect and kindness –
and the same gifts, 'cept we have babies, talk more, and can't pick up real
heavy things. To treat a woman as anything less is to debase yourself and
her."

"Hubby'll watch the store?" The old man rose from his stool in the
white, impalpable silence with concentrated effort and concealed pain.

"Let 'im sleep, Schlomo. If he misses some excitement, serves th' old
heathen right for not comin' to Bible study."

Sheriff Jones leaned against the squad car next to the gasoline hose,
worrying his mouth with a splintered toothpick as Penny and Schlomo
crunched through the gravel towards him, startling the otherwise uncanny
silence. Even the pulse of gasoline surging through the hose into the squad
car was inaudibly felt in the queer dead calm.

"Officer Jones," Penny said, adding a nod to her verbal greeting. "Not
a breeze or a gull stirrin'. Makes me skittish when it's this quiet outside."

"Folks," he said, touching the lip of his blue cap with his right forefinger
and looking first at Penny and then at Schlomo. "We're transportin' a
nutcase we found out on Block Lake to the hospital."

"What happened, Alan? Is he all right?" asked Nantier as he stopped by the vehicle and half-squatted at its back window.

"Don't know. Stoned, drunk, or mad, I'd guess. He was floatin' around that damned lake in a dory screamin' and clawin' at his head and beatin' the water with an oar like he was fighting piranhas."

"Oh, no," said Nantier, abruptly straightening and stepping back from the police car. "It's Dan Richards."

"Who?" asked Penny, stepping forward.

"Don't look," said Nantier, and covered Penny's eyes with the palm of his right hand as the side of Richards' head snailed down the window, its sotted bandage pushing up and off and smearing an arc of watery blood across the inside of the glass.

An unseasonably warm, pungent breeze is blowing in from Abomination Bay over the sluggish river of noisy bodies in gaudy costumes, feathered masks and necklaces of cheap, plastic keys. Surging down the street, feverish with the thud of raucous music, sotted with booze and drugs, hungry for debauchery, they gossip and laugh nervously, carrying you and Bob Azreal along as flotsam in the carnival madness. It is four in the morning.

"Finger lickin' good," comments Azreal as he oggles women.

The cluster of grimy keys on his neck include a lucky rabbit's foot jangle to his words and look like those toys that hang over cribs. Light's Enders wear them as an unspoken insult that outsiders should be in cribs. Tourists wear them to prove they've handled the spaghetti 'guts' and the olive 'eyeballs' and Halloween nastiness in the dark Horror Rooms scattered in basements and businesses around Light's End: the sinister Ebenezar Azreal Room with the Out door to Hell, the squamous Memphremagog Monster Room, and the rest. The keys, 'free with any purchase,' open nothing except fat tourist pocketbooks.

The Feasting is a bloated and outré festival, a money leech, a chaotic, drunken revel of hedonistic excess flowing down August Street that spills over and gluts side streets and eddies into shops hawking candy skulls, lighthouses, and flying saucers. The riot of noise masks the brooding, occult underbelly of the Feasting in a perverted imitation of Mardi Gras. Feasters dance and yell and snort cocaine and expose themselves, chasing forbidden pleasures while looking furtively over their shoulders.

A sharp *kaboom* overhead raises heads to a spreading umbrella of multi-colored fireworks, its bright orange edges falling apart in shimmering ffrummmmp's of popcorn explosions. You smooth the wrinkles of the multi-colored, striped shirt that is tucked into your stained green tights, and wrinkle your nose at fetid odors.

The smells of fried, little neck oysters and Chourico sausages, lobster and dynamite sandwiches, stale beer, urine and perfume taint the chill air. Wild colors from lights hung on and between the buildings paint the drunken crowds in flickering oranges and reds and blues as they snake through the bricked streets. Shoulder to shoulder with Bob Azreal and pushed by the revelers against the entrance to the Commercial Hotel, your left hand on the cold, plate-glass window pulses with the heavy beat of rock and roll and seedy jazz from unseen bands.

"You're stinkin' drunk, Fireman Bob," you cajole, and nudge him in the ribs with an elbow as he hunts for prey in the crowd. "Come on, let's go in. It's my favorite, the Block Lake room. You know. They flooded Lost City to make the lake, but not everyone got out. So every Feasting, the damned corpses rise up from the rotting town with their knives and forks looking for a bite."

He shakes his sallow head, looking into the crowd. "You're a squirrely lot tonight, eh?"

From long habit, you mentally blank out the smarmy profanity. "Somethin' eatin' you? We've done a dozen other Feasting rooms. You can't be afraid...?!" He averts his eyes. "Ooooooh, I get it. It's the drowning thing. You are..."

"Shut up, Richards," Azreal hisses, tall and gaunt, dressed from head to toe in the green of an elf, his white mask now washed red by the lights. He bends to your ear to counter the racket, clutching your shoulder. "Lookie! Th' breakfast of champions!"

He sways to the discordant jumble of music and waves at a loose swarm of young girls dressed as peasants and French maids and hookers and Vegas show girls drawn near by the undertow of human flesh. Held in his left hand by his thigh, a six pack of Budweiser beer with three empty, plastic rings bumps against your hip as he exaggerates his wave and leers. He uses beer as mouthwash to clean his pallet of whiskey.

"Hey, eye candy; over here!" he shouts, his mask washed an outré blue, the words eaten by the relentless thudding din, his hand kneading your bunched shoulder. "Over here! Let's get nasty, eh!"

The French maid in the clutch of girls turns towards Azreal, the smile beneath her feathered mask dissolving into disinterested disgust as she recognizes, not his words over the hubbub, but his naked lust. She turns abruptly away as the hooker next to her covers her mouth and glances at Azreal from beneath heavily painted eyelids even as the eddy breaks and they disappear, swallowed by the dense, restless crowd.

"They think you're a drunken pervert, Bobbie," you shout. The tiny, brass bells on your fool's cap jiggle as a nearby hive of firecrackers erupts in chittering pops.

"Right, Danny," nods Azreal, the breeze catching and turning his hair into a brief, puckish chaos. "An' only half of 'em are guessing, you wussy lunatic."

"Great fun, eh, Bob?" you yell through a cupped hand against the uproar as the hanging lights dapple your white clown makeup red. "Wouldn't miss it for the world."

"Love this stinkin' bunch of noise, eh. Feasting is my personal meat market, Danny boy. Nothin' better than fresh," Azreal finishes with a putrid synonym for a whore. "Course, you wouldn't know that being's your a virgin, eh?"

"I'm not a virgin, Bobbie. I know a big stud like you could party forever," you grimace at Azreal's suddenly blue face, "but it's time for our trip to th' little sinkhole, our Block Lake adventure, isn't it?"

"Wha...?!" Azreal yelps, his voice slurred by whiskey and Budweiser. "Lake?"

"Too sloshed to remember? Block lake. Sunken drifts. Mud banks matted with weeds and dead tree limbs. You know. The Memphremagog Monster. Snake birds, gnats, flies and those big, fat, bloodsucking mosquitoes. If you're not up to it.... but I did rent a boat...for the girls."

"Girls?!" Azreal says under the jarring music, his eyes flat like black ice.

"Jill. And Samantha. We're supposed to meet them on the north side of Block Lake, remember?" Your bald lie is dangerously transparent to anyone except a tourist or a staggering drunk. "Oh, I get it, Bobbie," you drop your hand while still yelling as you move him against the crowd and around the corner of the hotel onto Ferry Street, "it's the corpses in th' lake... 'When the moon's right and the lake's clear, you can see the town folk and Lost City under the lake on All Hallow's Eve'. Their ferocious, bloated bodies..."

"Shut th'up!"

"Superstitious nonsense, eh, Bobby? Urban myth. I agree. No one died when the dam opened back in '37 and flooded Lost City."

"Wha...?" barks Azreal from a face again lit Elvin blue.

"You know, I've seen people drowned 'cause they didn't bulldoze those trees down that still stick up out there. Always did think it kinda funny that a big tough guy like you," you say adjusting your cap, "so hot with the ladies, big on sports, gambling, booze, drugs, the whole macho bit, is terrified by, well...you know."

"What you talkin' about, you; 'fraid of nothin'!" Azreal scowls under glazed eyes and lifts a beer can in his right hand to his mouth for another drink. He swears in disappointment, crushes the empty can, and drops it to the littered sidewalk.

"But you can't swim, big man! Don't you remember when we were kids? The municipal pool? You flailed around screaming bloody murder 'til they pulled you out, then you puked all over..."

Someone jolts into Azreal from behind, a glancing blow at the shoulder, half spinning him around where he stands.

"HEY, you!!" growls Azreal. "Watch where you going, you moron!!"

"Sorry," the fat old man answers with a mouth full of yellow teeth set in a sandpaper face of stubble. "Have we met, because I certainly am a..."

The patron of The Feasting, goat-headed Baphomet, leers from a beer and sweat stained t-shirt beneath a dirty, open blazer worn by the old fool. Above the demon's twisted horns is printed THE FEASTING '90. Beneath its cloven hooves is printed RAM IT. The hanging lights wash his face red as he smiles from a cut of a mouth, turns, and is eaten by the chaotic crowd.

"The idiot!" Azreal curses violently, his face raw and confused.

"Just forget it, Tarzan. There's the girls. Remember the girls?" you add, pulling him by a beefy arm along Ferry Street.

"Girls. Girls. Nibble some ear."

"To the girls and the barnacled, festering corpses of Lost City!" You lie and raise the empty beer can that you earlier washed out over your sparsely furnished studio apartment. "I'm parked down by the bus station."

Befuddled by his alcoholic stupor, he asks again, "Why we goin' lake?"

"To scare the living..." a yellow green mushroom of fireworks explodes above, obliterating your uncharacteristic profanity, and then rainbow rains in slow motion down over the Seminole Theater. "...out of you, you unmitigated jackass."

"Wha....?" Azreal leers, exhausted, and cups a pointed ear against the infernal Feasting caterwauling.

"Girls, Bobbie!"

For agonizing years, you've endured his filthy, degrading insults and overblown machismo and inexplicably easy conquest of women, until one event boiled your disgust into an ulcerating, consuming hatred that could end only in his unmistakable, undeniable, irreversible humiliation. "Jill. And Samantha. At Block Lake!"

"To the lake!" he salutes, and raises high his six pack of beer with three empty rings in his left, grabs your mottled arm with his right hand, and burps a crooked, idiot smile.

Your cramped '88 Ford Aspire approaches the only Lost City building still above water standing on the edge of the sunken town, the Old Rock Barn built of weathered, natural stone shouldering Block Lake on three sides. A gibbous, yellow, half-moon hangs breathless at the horizon in a fathomless sky dirty with faint stars. Your white-knuckled hands are vises on the steering wheel as the smudged dashboard clock blinks a yellow 5:32 a.m., and the food and gas store, dark and asleep on the asphalt road snaking down to the lake, shrinks behind you into the grey haze of early morning.

"Unlike you, I don't have a superstitious bone in my body, but this is starting to creep me out. It's dead calm outside, as dark as hell, and it's late. Maybe we shouldn't. The water out there is pretty stinking cold. Someone falling in," you pause to let the words sink into Azreal's heart, "would die in minutes from hypothermia."

Your words are met with the hushed susurration of the car's heater. Slouched behind the wheel in a loose coat recovered from the back seat of the car, you study the unnatural light in Azreal's poached eyes, his slumped body engulfed in a brown windbreaker, his face pensive and thick from beer and fat sausages. Your left foot on the floor next to a crushed beer can half covers your conical, belled cap. His six pack of Budweiser with four empty rings lies in his lap.

"How many, Bob?" You ask in the white noise without turning to face him. The smell of beer and flop sweat is pervasive and oppressive. "I'm just curious. Tell me how many. Twenty? Linda Fifty? A hundred?"

"How many what?" he mumbles, his head sunk on his chest.

"Girls?" you ask, troubled because, sobering, he is beginning to build words into sentences. "How many girls have you had?"

"How'd I know, you dumb ... " You ignore the word for that intimacy meant to bond a man and woman in love that is also a filthy expletive. "Not enough. Shut up; let... me sleep."

The relationship has been so since you were a bookish, nervous, self-absorbed teenager lost in the eerie fiction of Lovecraft and Bradbury, and

Azreal was a brash bull of a teenager drooling over men's magazines and sports shows, already at ease with the same girls that scared you spitless. Paradoxically, he sends money to the mother he loves in Providence, Rhode Island, and blubbers about his sisters, even as he uses and then throws away every woman in Light's End who will say yes.

"You forget our dates, tom cat? Anyway, no time for that. We'll be there in a heartbeat, unless..." You smile. "Is all this about th' gnawing corpses under the..."

"Not afraid." A nervous drop of dirty sweat crawls down his sallow forehead.

"So we go. But how about another brew?" He nods mutely and strips a can from its plastic ring, pulls the ring to open it, throws his chin back, and guzzles it dry, his bloodshot eyes flat and unfocused. He burps, crumples it, and throws the can on the floor.

The Aspire, tepid air droning from its overtaxed heater, rolls hypnotically on whirring tires down the otherwise silent, black road skirted with hackberry and maples. Nervous exhaustion has painted dark half-moons under your eyes, and your left hand, buried in the pocket of your coat, twists compulsively on the small, soiled photograph.

"I don't get it and never have. You're from the richest, most powerful family in Light's End. You could marry any woman you want, but you bed-hop, Bobbie. Why? You love your own mom and sisters. Don't you get it that every woman you 'date' is someone's mother or daughter or... sister?"

Your question is met with his shushed breathing. Anxious, you stare out of the Ford at the trees that blur into a hard flicker of black and white black and white black and white as you speed down the asphalt ribbon. Clammy sweat glazes your own armpits.

"This's a goo goof, Danny, but..." he burbles, leaning his head against and looking out the window, "think has gone...far enough. Let's go eat. "

"Right again, Bobbie," you answer solemnly. "This is far enough. We're here."

The road snakes down to the dock caught small in the Aspire's headlights, and then into and beneath the coffee waters of the lake into the slimy grave of Lost City.

You turn and smile as you remove your boot from the gas petal and turn the engine off. Unlike the rest of the lake, there are no submerged trees on the road hidden by the black waters. That's the area you'll avoid like death on the "black, timeless and immutable, seductive and hungry" lake of the

Chamber of Commerce brochures. The Ford sighs into motionlessness at the small, wooden dock feathered with dead cattails as you reach over Azreal's lap and open the glove compartment.

"Didja hear me, Bobbie?" you ask and remove a flashlight and shut the compartment door. You reach across him, pull the door handle out, and shove the passenger door open. "We're here. The girls are waiting. Time to get out."

He shudders, shaking his head from one shoulder to the other as he crosses his arms over his chest and buries his hands under them. "You get girls. I wait here."

You step out of the car and close its door, the click of the latch articulate in the silence, and move around the Aspire on the hardened muck of the shore. The lake is queer in the half-light. Twisting the photograph in your pocket you think of the ineffable sounds of the distant, mournful cry of an unseen loon or the rhythmic, deep-throated croaking of bull frogs now silenced in October.

"You, Richards" Azreal gurgles. You grab his resistant bicep and pull him out; the click of his door closing is like a muffled firecracker in the lewd silence. His steps are clumsy and unsure as you walk him to the dock and the dory moored there. You stare out over the black lake where Lost City trees, their limbs broken by boats or rotted, once stretched brittle fingers like lacquered spider webs above the brackish water.

"The boat," you say with an indicative wave of your hand, and turn to Azreal whose fists are clenched white at his side. "This has got to stop, Bobbie. You're trembling. Let's go back; you're too green from booze to handle the flesh-eating..."

"Shut...up!" Azreal says, now frantic and breathing hard. "Shut up!!"

"I didn't mean to frighten you," you lie, stepping clumsily into the dory's transom and dragging Azreal like a sack of wet oysters with you, the fishing boat rocking and creaking it takes three hard strokes. "But maybe we should go home."

"Sit down, Bobbie; sit...!" you say, forcing him down onto the clammy bench as he spews a torrent of profanity and invective. "You could fall in and drown."

Shivering and grinding his teeth, Azreal's glazed eyes are round and locked on the keel of the dory as you search the shore to make certain it is deserted, then untie the transom and then the bow ropes from the dock and push the rowboat out on the lake. You place the clammy oars in their locks, dip the blades into the lake and pull deep and hard.

One.

The rowboat slides by a half-submerged trunk laced with a withered spider's web of trumpet vines and wild fox-grape. Its bark and rotten underside has been unceasingly nibbled by fungi, and you remember March dragonflies like lightening bursts skittering across the dark yellow-copper water now licking at the boat.

Two.

Inexplicably, illogically, a hot thrill of anticipation runs up your spine.

Three.

The startling, frantic, hideous scraping like broken fingernails on slate crawls under the bow like frenzied electric pain and slides down the boat, engulfing the dory in skittering, ear-splitting horror.

Azreal yells and half-rises from his bench. "What in hell?!?

"Tree limbs," your words torn by the chaos of scratching. You pull again at the oars. "Or th' black mistress killed by her lover before they flooded the town. Sit... down, Bobbie, sit down! unless you wanna be fish food."

"The scratching!" Azreal yells, his white-knuckled hands still clutching the boat, his voice cracking, his poached eyes locked on the bottom of the dory. "Stop it!! Let me off!!!

You know his flesh and yours crawls and puckers with goose pimples, his heart and yours thud as his face contorts with fear. You remove an oar from its lock and balance it in your right hand, swaying it back and forth in little arches. The energy concentrated in your wrist, you whip the oar blade forward against Azreal's chest and nudge.

"Hey!!" yelps Azreal, slapping the oar away and flinching back hard against the boat. "What...?!"

"Their names?" you yell in a spray of spittle, your voice vicious and your heart firing like a trip hammer. "Do you even remember them, Bobbie? Do you!!" You glance at the shore, at the oar, at the shore, and then back at Azreal's trembling face twisted bloodless by terror. "Their names!!!"

The clammy oar jerks up against his big cringing bull chest and you push harder. He screams like a girl, slapping it away and shaking violently, his face distorted into black horror by the frenzied scratching.

"Mary?!" you demand amidst the cacophony of gouging, broken, bony branches. "Janice?! Cindy?! Rebecca!?! Linda!! Do you even remember Linda!!?"

"Who?" he shrieks, batting at the oar.

And your fevered brain snaps and you realize you never really intended to just scare the hell out of Bob Azreal as you place the oar blade through his flailing arms against his heaving chest and shove with the unnatural, savage strength of revenge.

"Linda!! Linda!! Linda!!!" you scream as the bow lurches up when he jackknife's out into death and hell with outraged surprise and flops, writhing, into the lake. You relish the too-brief scream cut short as the fetid water floods his tormented lungs and he is swallowed, thrashing and clutching at life.

The dory slaps down as you pant in tiny, rapid, painful gasps, and pull the left oar from habit. The boat rocks. Concentric ripples fight the waves and flee away from the point of Azreal's impact as the dory continues the broad, slow circle that will ultimately swing it around to face the shore. You replace the oar in its lock.

Then the brutal truth that you've murdered Bob Azreal cuts like a razor up your spine and rams your heart like a fist into your throat. You sit very still in a cold sweat, eyes clinched shut and, panting lightly, you pull instinctively at the left oar.

Your chaotic thoughts are of conflicting, lame alibis and electric chairs that rupture and bubble your flesh until an overwhelming compulsion wells up that you must stop the insane scratching of the branches against the dory to think clearly. Forcing your fear down, you pull in the oars from the row-locks and let the dory slowly slowly slowly whisper into motionlessness.

You breath deeply, once, twice, a third time. Then the second horror creeps into your mind as a small, quiet voice that stands the hairs up on your head and back and arms. You rise to your feet, shaking uncontrollably in the motionless dory, the oars forgotten in their locks, fighting to save your sanity as it crumbles into mewing, shuddering, black horror.

You look up.

"Don't, Schlomo," said Penny, and pushed Nantier's hand away from her eyes. She moved to the car, futilely trying to push her hair back into place against the breeze. She bent by the window smeared inside with blood. "He's done somethin' to his head."

She jerked up, eyes wide, her face shocked bloodless, her hand stifling a sob.

"You say you know this guy, Mr. Nantier?" asked Sheriff Jones, carefully unwrapping a candy bar.

"He's an environmental scientist who works for the Corp of Engineers, Alan. His name is Dan Richards, and I play chess with him occasionally down at Park's Drug Store. Dan is one of the most pragmatic men I've ever met, and he knows every inch of Block Lake. How did you know he was out there?"

"We always patrol th' lake during and just after the Feasting," answered Jones, biting into the candy bar, "although I'd rather eat mackerel guts than do it. Place gives me the shivers. Seems like there's always some drunk kid or idiot hop-head that decides it's a great time to take a dare to hop in for a swim. This guy was about thirty yards out on the lake, standing up inna dory, screaming and flailing his arms around, like I said. Sorta hard to miss."

"Do you know why he was out there," asked Nantier.

"Not a clue, but the car was full of empty beer cans. The damnedest thing is he ain't drunk. And we found this kinda crumpled up in his coat pocket," added the Sheriff, handing Nantier a photograph. "Do you know her?"

"Yes. Yes, I'm certain, Alan. It's Linda Richard's college graduation picture," Nantier responded, handing the photograph back to Jones. "Not back in town more than two years or so after six years of university in Rhode Island. She's Dan's sister."

"Linda Richards?" asked Penny, her face pale and her eyes welling with tears. "The girl who was just... Oh, my God. She was his sister?!"

"He was screaming so loud," said Sheriff Jones and took another bite of chocolate, "that he musta torn his throat up. Not sure what he was yellin'; somethin' about scratchin'."

"You must know the lake is full of trees," said Schlomo. "His boat must have been scraping over the top branches just below the water."

You sit with your chin on your chest inside the police car and rise from your bench in the boat and look up at the second horror, the road painted gray by dawn that does not stop at the murky shore but snakes under the dirty water directly beneath the dory.

"Nice theory, Mr. Nantier," grinned the sheriff around the chocolate in his mouth, "'cept if Richards' knows the lake like th' back of his hand, and he was smack-dab over th' old sunk road, then he sure as Hell knows there ain't no trees on that road.

You look down as the impossible, ravenous, bloated, rotten, murdered corpses writhe below your boat over the road as the horrors of bones and teeth and insatiable revenge and broken fingernails, clawing the underbelly of the dory, gouge it into splinters. You cover your violated ears, but the frantic scratching is unabated, so you jam your fingers painfully deep into them and pull them out wet, but its frenzied delirium lacerates your raw nerves, and you totter on the brink of insanity in the motionless dory as your black heart thunders apart, and you scream and scream and scream and....

"And then there's that other little flaw," added Sheriff Jones, squatting by the window and tracing the smeared arc of Richards' blood on the inside of the glass with his finger. "How'd he hear all that scratchin'...." he paused at the brown smear he left and licked the chocolate off of his index finger, "with his eardrums busted...

"...and his ears torn off?"

THE END

DiRTY ΛΠGELS

His hand was everywhere evident.

A box of grape-nut flakes was off center.

The snow outside was randomly dimpled with spattered blood.

Brooding, the manager of the Twenty-Four Seven convenience store turned and walked through the entrance of his cashier's island and moved to the aisle facing his cash register. First things first. His right hand was everywhere evident on the spotless chrome fixtures almost worn bare by the endless touch of its heel. His idle left hand was in the front pocket of his creased khaki pants. Pensive, he pushed the grape nuts box precisely back into its place in The World According To Archie Killingsworth.

Archie studied the tyranny of repeated labels on the shelf for any aberration. Each can and bottle and box was a brick in the floodgate of his repressed, righteous anger. Archie adjusted his rimless glasses on his clipped nose and nervously stroked his salt and pepper mustache.

The snow outside was dimpled with spattered blood.

On Archie's t-shirt, the patron of the town's festival, goat-headed Baphomet, leered. Above the demon's twisted horns was printed THE FEASTING. Beneath its cloven hooves was printed RAM IT. Archie reached up and reverently touched the small plastic snowflake meticulously pinned at his collarbone. His fingers quivered.

A heating vent in the polished black-and-white checkered floor sighed in the silence of the empty store.

"Big boys don't cry," she whispered, her lips wild and her cheek close to his ear. Her warm right hand gently squeezed his left in the front pocket of his khakis.

The Twenty-Four Seven manager looked through a lopsided oval blown clear in the fogged glass by the heating vent. Outside, a pair of tire tracks in the snow were twin ruts of gray slush. They careened down Uring Street between white, fat dollops of snow that distorted houses into blond, timeless, frigid silence. The tracks snaked down like drunken gray worms to and past the hazy neon Twenty-Four Seven sign. They smeared past the parking lot to the edge of Azreal Avenue where the wreckage lay smoking against a tree shocked naked of snow from the impact. Archie walked to and looked through the irregular oval in the fogged plate-glass wall of the empty store.

The snow and the automobile outside were dimpled with spattered blood.

"Big boys don't cry," she whispered again, breathless, her lips wild and close to his pink ear. Her warm hand squeezed his left in his pants. She stepped away and smiled, fighting back tears. She touched the small plastic snowflake half-hidden by her Feasting corsage pinned on her yellow prom dress. Her pink and unutterably feminine fingers trembled. "It's the only way out," she whispered.

Agitated, Archie turned sharply and walked to the counter of the island in the middle of the store. He moved through the entrance to the register and glanced at the '98 lighthouse calendar stuck on the side of the soft drinks machine. October 30 was circled in red; it was All Hallow's Eve, The Feasting festival in Light's End, Maine.

The snow outside was uniform, smooth and perfectly white.

"Carol," he muttered, surprised by the sound of his voice. Archie drummed his fingers impatiently on the cash resister. He reached under the counter and turned on a radio. The Twenty-Four Seven whispered muffled music.

Archie watched through the irregular oval; his fingers drummed. The snow outside was randomly dimpled with spattered blood. Her hands were evident on the twisted wreckage; on the bloody steering wheel, on the broken neck of the bottle of bourbon weeping onto the floor, on the bloody, cracked window where her dimpled face was pressed like a dead flower against the hand thrown between it and the passenger's window in a startled, futile defense against death.

Tenderly, Archie pulled her from the wreckage, smearing a dirty angel in the snow with her body. A bell jingled. He cradled her head in his arms and pushed her matted hair back from her dead eyes. A bell jingled.

The snow outside was uniform, smooth and perfectly white.

The bell jingled. The Fat Man, Jake Horne, stood under the bell in the door of the Twenty-Four Seven in a hazy aureole of yellow neon light. Horne stood with yellow teeth and a face full of distasteful stubble. He took a drag on a cigar that hung from the cut of his mouth, then flicked the stub into the snow. He looked at the crepe paper strung like black spittle in a tangle from the ceiling, and stepped inside.

"Not a soul out," Jake said from a face like a crumpled paper bag full of wet flour. "Pristine snow for as far as you can see. I even kinda hated to mush it up."

Jake's left boot exploded into a ball of fine white mist that fell to the checkered linoleum floor as he kicked it against the chrome doorjamb. "Arch? Arch, are you all right?" The kicked right boot exploded. Archie looked away from the oval in the fogged glass to the smiling cut in Jake's face.

"What? Oh, it's you, Jake," Archie answered, his face blank. "Just thinkin'."

"So much for the festival," Jake said, pointing to the snow outside. He unbuttoned his massive coat as he shambled to the counter. "I know that's gotta be a financial blow to merchants, Arch, and I love All Hallow's Eve and The Feasting, but I gotta tell ya, I get off on this."

The Fat Man shook his massive coat and watched the snow explode and fall apart to the spotless but cracked checkerboard floor. "Oh, jeez, Arch, I guess I wasn't thinkin'," he said apologetically.

"What did I do to deserve that?" Archie looked with festering irritation at the slush on the floor. Horne looked at a tray of pastries by the register.

"Gotta give some slack to your best customer, Arch. Man. The town's glutted with disappointed tourists and I get all the goodies." He picked a skull filled with rich cherry icing from the tray filled with flying saucers, lighthouses, tombstones and satyrs.

Archie took a worn cloth from his back pocket and scrubbed at the oily fingerprints of countless customers on the counter next to his register, putting the strength of repressed anger into the heel of his hand.

"You're really into that stuff," he said. He pushed a pastry back into place with his right hand; his left was in the pocket of his creased pants.

"Just desserts. Snowballs, cream filled cakes, donuts, pies, ice cream; you name it. I figure why waste time with foreplay when you can get right to the goodies. And save the lecture. I know it's bad for me. I just frankly don't care. Coffee?"

Archie looked, distracted, through the oval in the fogged plate glass wall. He wiped his hand with his rag. The snow outside was uniform and smooth. The shrouded trees around the Twenty-Four Seven store were surprised white by the unexpected snow, stretching brittle fingers up and out into the silent night air like spider webs in shattered ice.

He nervously stroked his salt and pepper mustache.

Carol was inside his head.

He wiped his hand with his rag then nervously stroked his cold and naked upper lip. He looked at the '88 lighthouse calendar on the wall outside his high school gym. Oct. 30 was circled in red. Ragged and painfully shy, he stood in his after-school work clothes over the mop bucket and rubbed his swollen eyes with the heel of his right hand.

Whatsya waitin' for? A decree from th' Pope? Go ahead on in, he thought.

Archie looked at the banner over the entrance to the Elliott High School gym. It read: The Feasting Prom.

Look, kid, don't let it eat you up. That kind of thing ain't for poor folks like me, he thought.

He looked at the puddle of melting snow on the hall floor. He dunked the mop into the bucket and wrung it out and looked up at the banner. He dunked the mop into the bucket and left it there and walked to the double doors of the prom.

The paper snowflakes hung by cotton string were a random flurry falling forever from the gym ceiling. The ceiling and walls were awash in reflected pinpoints of light. Couples swirled and swayed and separated and came together to muffled music. Carol McKraken and Robert Fleming were arguing not far from the door. She glanced away, distraught, and saw Archie. She waved and made dimples in her face and began to approach.

"Archie," she called. Robert grabbed for her arm and missed and followed. Robert grabbed for her arm, and caught her, and spun her around near the door.

"Just five minutes, Bobbie," Archie heard Carol plead in a little girl voice. "Please? We've been friends since the seventh grade."

"I don't want you anywhere near that geek."

Carol tiptoed and whispered into Robert's ear. He looked at Carol and then at Archie in the door. "Five minutes," he said, and turned to Archie.

"Just keep your faggot hands off of her, you hear, cripple?"

Carol watched as Robert walked past her and then past Archie through the gym doorway. She stepped forward and unexpectedly kissed Archie on the cheek.

"Big boys don't cry," she whispered her lips and dimpled cheek wild and close to his ear. Her hand squeezed his left in his pants pocket. She stepped back, fighting tears.

"Whattaya think, Archie? It's the first dress I ever owned." She reached up to the cheap plastic snowflake half-hidden by her Feasting corsage and pinned on her yellow prom dress. Her fingers trembled. "Please. Please, don't look at me like that.

"You're not like me, Archie. You're a good boy. Don't worry. Someday, you'll get a new dress, too!" She giggled and lowered her head and her long, blond hair fell forward like snow and hid her face.

"It's the only way out," she whispered, and unpinned the snowflake and stepped forward and pinned it to Archie's shirt.

"Carol!!" yelled Robert standing in the out door twenty yards down the hall.

"Remember me," she said, and Carol turned and was gone.

And from that cherished moment frozen forever in time, and though he had never touched her, Archie Killingsworth adored and worshipped Carol McKracken. Neither death, nor life, neither time nor distance, god nor demon, no law of man or nature, or any other thing would ever diminish his unutterable, unconditional, intimate and tender love.

Carol never thought of Archie again.

"Arch? Arch? Arch!?" Jake snapped his fingers.

"What?" Archie wiped his hand.

"You're actin' like you're gonna jump out of your skin, Arch. You keep glancing out at the snow or lookin' at me without seein' me. What's wrong, kid?"

Archie stroked the edges of his salt and pepper mustache. The bell jingled and black crepe rustled. A forlorn little girl stood in the door of the Twenty-Four Seven wreathed in hazy yellow neon light, her pink, dimpled face softened by a halo of off-white fur lining the yellow hood of her parka. Archie scowled as she stepped sidewise from the snow into his store.

"Oh, great," he grumbled. "Light's End's youngest thief."

The Fat Man looked at Archie and then at the little girl and raised his Styrofoam up in salute. "Talk to me."

"It's nothin', really. Just something kinda lousy happened this night about ten years ago. It's not something I talk about." Archie watched as the little girl moved past aisle one and two to the gaudy Feasting party display.

"Maybe that's why you're acting like a vein about to pop. I mean, I understand 'a place for everything and everything in its place', but you scrub and polish every crack in this place like you were trying to wash away some secret guilt."

"It isn't like that."

"I suspect you've got lots of unresolved anger in you, Arch. Folks see you as a righteous guy who mows his lawn and doesn't ruffle their feathers. I think the righteous guy who screams most about the sanctity of marriage is usually committing adultery. Just an example, of course."

The bell jingled. A disgruntled middle-aged woman in a stained coat stood in the doorway. The spittle of black crepe rustled as the heating vent sighed. The woman took a deep breathe of sterile convenience store air and wrinkled her nose at the smell of lemon-scented deodorizer.

"Sorry, Jake; customers" Archie said with the long suffering annoyance for the necessary evil of tourists. "May I help you, Miss?"

The woman looked at Baphomet on Archie's t-shirt and then at Jake and smiled nervously. "Could you do some crazy Satanic ritual and get rid of the snow?"

"Sure," said Jake, "but first we have to sacrifice a virgin. Do you know one?"

"Very funny. I came for the festival. I'm a sucker for supernatural stuff. I heard this was better than the Mardi Gras in New Orleans."

"I'm the town fool and this is an upstanding citizen of our nasty little town, Archie Killingsworth. And you're right about The Feasting. Every All Hallows Eve, all of the hobgoblins and witches and licorice demons gather in Light's End and dance to Satanic music while we sacrifice a baby on a bloody altar and eat its heart. Just local color. But you did miss a dandy."

"How can I help you," Archie repeated.

"I'm just pickin' up a few things on the way out," she answered, looking at the cut in Jake's face. "Excuse me. I think I see..."

The woman pointed and moved away.

"What suddenly gives you the right to run off my customers, Jake?"

"Because I'm evil," said Jake, "and tourists are a dime a dozen." He leaned, hungry and close, to Archie. "And because I want to hear your story."

"It's not... my story, and it happened ten years ago, so who cares."

"Me," said Jake. "I care."

"Will you keep this to yourself if I do?"

"Cross my heart," Jake said, making no effort to do so.

"It's about a friend of mine and his girl. They grew up dirt poor," said Archie, stroking his mustache, "and she was the only one who didn't treat him like trash. And he told me the day he walked home from school in the seventh grade with her, he fell for her. She had the face of an angel, Jake. She was as pretty as he was...well, ugly."

Jake glanced down at Archie's left hand hidden in his pants pocket.

"He wanted to marry her, but he couldn't even ask. She wanted a big house in New York City and he couldn't give it. And Carol knew the only way she could escape was to marry for money, and that's what she did, Jake. They moved to New York City and it finally seemed like all the good things she deserved were coming to her until they were driving back on All Hallow's Eve for The Feasting. Robert was drunk and the roads were icy, and Carol....they hit a tree, Jake, right outside the Twenty-Four Seven. Ten years ago tonight, she was killed."

"Killed?" asked Jake, arching an eyebrow. "It sounds like you're talkin' about Carol Fleming, Arch. She was in a wreck, but she isn't dead. She won a huge settlement because the driver in the other car was drunk..."

"That's not right," Archie lied.

"This is a small town. Apparently everybody but you knows what everyone is doing or else they make it up. After the accident, there were problems with her marriage. She divorced, has a kid, and lives right down the street from here on Uring..."

"But she loved him."

Jake studied Archie through slitted eyes. "Your 'friend' isn't the first man to mistake compassion or pity in a woman for love."

"But she didn't deserve to die!?! She was so good, Jake?"

"Good for what?" Horne sneered. "Listen, people do good things for bad reasons and terrible things sometimes thinking they are right. This is the world we made, and that's why children suffer and fat men sweat.

"This isn't about love, it's about unrequited lust. Like it or not, we reap what we sow. I don't have much sympathy for people who sow wild oats and whine when they don't get buttercups and rainbows.

"Maybe it's not true in this little world you control," said Jake with a sweep of an arm that indicated the Twenty-Four Seven, "but a woman who sells herself is a whore..."

"Shut up."

"What...?" Surprised, Horne looked up from the pastry.

"Shut up!!" exploded Archie and the floodgate cracked and the muscles in his jaw knotted and his idle left hand came out. Horne startled. It went back in.

There was profound silence. The heating vents in the checkered floor sighed.

The Fat Man looked at where the left hand had been and at Archie's face flushed red and rigid. Horne looked at where the left hand had been and saw the long years of hidden shame and impotent rage; of savage childish insults of freak, claw, cripple and queer. The beatings. The taunts that Archie Killingsworth wasn't worth killing.

The reason Carol's friend was ugly.

The implacable cut in Jake's face smiled.

Archie turned sharply and walked out of the island and disappeared into the storeroom, slamming its door.

The tourist stood with her elbow resting in the palm of her left hand. Her right hand trembled over her mouth. Her eyes were blurred with tears from the heartbreaking anguish of a woman who desperately yearns for the child she had never suckled at her breast or cradled in her arms or dressed for school or cooed to sleep.

"O-oh," she stuttered, overcome with emotion. "She's so...innocent."

Becca lay as only little girls do on her left thigh with her legs tucked under her parka in an L, bracing herself with a hand on the checkered floor. The Feasting display of wax flying saucers, candy skulls and tiny flashlights shaped like lighthouses beckoned on the peg-board display. Little Becca raised her pink face in an innocent, open admission of heart wrenching poverty.

The tourist blubbered.

"Is the manager still here?" asked the woman. Her mascara smeared under her left eye, she laid four items and a five dollar bill down on the counter and looked, puzzled, at Jake behind the cashier's island.

"He went to get a mop. Can I help you?"

"Could you add a dollar to this?" she asked, her head lowered. "I'd like to buy one of those toy packages for that poor little girl over there."

"Sure," said Jake. "It's always easier to soothe guilt with cheap, symbolic gestures than to actually do something helpful."

"Excuse me?" The tourist looked up.

"It's a common reaction of aging, do-gooder hippies like you who dropped out of the capitalistic war machine and opted for social work in upstate New York. 'The children are our future.' By the way...

"You shouldn't feel guilty about being barren. Everybody did drugs and had multiple abortions in college."

"Wha...?!" asked the woman. "How could you kn...how can you say that?!"

"I always tell the truth when it serves my purposes."

"W-where is the manager," she demanded, her voice laced with outrage. "He seems nice enough."

"He does," Jake answered and leaned over the counter in mock intimacy. "But, like you, he has an unsanitary mind."

"You goddamned son-of-a-bitch," choked the woman as the muscles constricted in her jaw. She covered her mouth with her hand.

Horne waited until the bell jingled over the front door, then looked down at the items and the money on the counter. "You forgot to pay for your things," he said to himself and glanced over at the Feasting display.

Jake smiled profanely and glanced back at the closed storeroom door.

He put her money in his shirt pocket and walked out of the island.

Smoldering, Archie pushed the mop bucket out of the storeroom behind the cashier's island. He scanned the store.

"What did the woman buy?"

"Nothing." Horne looked down at the watch that was on the sack of flour that was his left forearm. "I insulted her and she left."

Archie's left hand jerked in his pants. He dunked the mop into the bucket. "You seem to have a gift for nastiness."

"It's not a gift. I make things happen. I like to think of myself as a subtle catalyst. Look, I'd love to stay and yap, but I've got an appointment to spiritually corrupt some parishioners, and I'm already late."

Horne picked up an iced flying saucer from the tray on the counter. He put the tourist's five dollar bill on the counter, looked at Archie, and turned on his heels and began to walk away. He stopped at the front door, turned, and waved a flabby hand.

"Uh, Happy Feasting, Arch," he said. "And about earlier. I'm sorry. I'm truly, truly, sorry."

Archie did not look at Jake. He erased the remark with a gesture.

"My thirty pieces of silver are on the counter." Jake pulled on his coat. "Oh, and the little girl hasn't paid." He turned and walked out the door. The bell jingled.

Archie stood over the mop bucket and rubbed his swollen eyes. He looked at the puddle of melting snow on the cracked, checkered floor. He dunked the mop into the bucket and wrung it out and watched Becca. Becca stood off center at the front door clutching a Feasting toy. Archie dunked the mop into the bucket and watched Becca step through the door. The bell jingled.

It jingled again as Archie jerked the package of Feasting toys out of her arms.

"Where in Hell do you think your going," he hissed, and he pulled Becca roughly by the sleeve of her parka back into the store. The door swung shut and Archie kicked the lock on the bottom of the door into its recess in the checkered floor. "I been watchin' you. This is the last time you'll steal from Archie Killingsworth if I have anything to do about it."

"Get your hands off me," the little girl bleated, struggling against the unforgiving grip around her arm. "I didn't take nothin'. That woman gave it to me."

"Sure," said Archie, dragging her away from the door. "Just like the last times. We'll see who the cops believe, you or me."

"You can't do this! Who died and made you God?" Becca blubbered.

"I did," spat Archie, and he squatted down and shook her. Her face paled with sudden fear. She shrieked and reached up and grabbed the plastic snowflake on Archie's t-shirt and shoved him off balance and back. The pin pricked her finger. She pushed again frantically, and goat-headed Baphomet on the t-shirt slipped beneath her hand and bunched up like crumpled paper on Archie's collarbone, dimpled with spattered blood.

Becca pushed him back hard against the shelves that rose, violated, into a metallic cloud of hard edges and corners that hung and fell and struck the black and white checkered floor like firecrackers and cracked the floodgate of volcanic repressed rage inside Archie Killingsworth.

He rose from the chaos of cans in blind fury. He grabbed her arm and jerked Becca painfully forward and drug her struggling past the cashier's island to the door of the stockroom.

"Stop it!!" screamed Becca. The Twenty-Four Seven whispered muffled music. Archie tore her yellow parka off as an explosion of coins and several dollar bills rose from it and fell apart and to the checkered linoleum floor.

Becca looked at him, slaughtered.

He kicked opened the door and tossed Becca through it into the stockroom. He stepped in and slammed the door behind them.

"STOP IT YOU BASTARD!!" screamed Becca, hysterical. Archie threw her against the wall by the back door and wedged her against it with his body. He could not open the door with his right hand; his left came out.

Archie tore open and looked out the back door down the irregular alley; it was the only way out. Her fingers trembled on his shirt. His hands were everywhere evident on the stockroom, outside on the frozen hand rail, on the twisted mouth of the can of garbage weeping onto the snow, inside on the clean, gray wall where her face was pressed like a dead flower against her hand thrown between it and the cracked concrete in a startled, futile defense against death. She shook with deep throated sobs.

Fish-eyed and rigid, Archie pulled her outside through the doorway and threw her, paralyzed with fear, down in the back alley in the snow. He knelt and cradled her head in his arm and pinned her left hand behind her frantic, arching back.

At that frenzied moment frozen forever in time, neither death, nor life, neither time nor distance, god nor demon, no law of man or nature, or any other thing could stop the futile, frenzied defense of her right hand.

"Mama!!" She screamed hopelessly into Archie's smarmy hand over her mouth.

And down Uring Street between the white, fat dollops that shifted and distorted her house into blond, timeless, frigid silence, Carol Fleming raised her head and her long, blond hair fell back like snow and revealed her puffy, drunken, frightened face.

"Becca?" she whispered.

"I-Im a good boy, Carol," Archie blubbered.

His left hand was everywhere evident. He wiped it clean...

Smearing dirty angels in the snow.

THE END

Y: WHY?

Lyrics and art by Michael Vance
Written April 1972 on the news
Of a friend's nervous breakdown

On quiet nights, he stood at windows listening to dragon cry
to the thundering of a fly's wings, the screaming of table dust
and built his castles in the air, summer gardens made of rain
floating women made of fluff, paper gods and paper lust
and lived inside his brain

and sang…

"We are all children of Gawd, a small part of the Greater Gob
"each and all a smaller Christ, at one with princes and field mice
"But God forgive the price we've paid, God forgive America"

He hummed the Star Spangled Bum, consumer dream all in vain
Saccharin reality gone insane, he hummed
to the fluttering of the tree tongues, the sighing of the flying snakes
He made a gun from river reeds, and blew out his brain with waterweed
I lost my friend today, and though he stayed, he went away

to sing…

"We are all children of Gawd, a small part of the Greater Gob
"each and all a smaller Christ, at one with princes and field mice
"But God forgive the price we've paid, God forgive America"

Running down to the seasoned sea, he mad dog drank up the salt lick
And how he beamed at me
when he finally found the soft parade to insanity.

Sleight of Mind

He pushed the beige button at the bottom of the blank computer screen that instantly popped and lit with an exterior picture of the small Light's End Clinic at which he was unhappily employed. The medical technician grinned at Daniel Whang, his middle-aged patient sitting in the room's uncomfortable, vinyl-upholstered chair, naked and vulnerable except for a paper gown.

"I can't forget. She ran off," repeated Whang, squirming under the harsh, antiseptic light in the clinic. Under the ridge of his brow, anger and frustration smoldered in his eyes. "She ran away with another man and took my beautiful, four-year-old daughter, Ruthie." The faintly yellow skin of his forehead was beaded with sweat as he nervously ran his left hand through his black hair to the back of his head where the hidden anomaly was branded. "For the last two weeks, I can't eat or sleep or do anything. How does it erase a memory like that?"

"Sorry; I forget," answered the medical technician with a grin that froze on his raw, clean-shaven face as he waited long seconds for a response, a laugh or a giggle or even a smile. The checkerboard of sticky little paper squares on Daniel's unshaven face and head embedded with sensors continued to broadcast invisible data that became a jagged thread scrolling slowly and soundlessly from left to right across the computer screen sitting on the cold, impersonal, metal table by Daniel's chair.

"That was a joke," the technician said in a sing-song, condescending tone. There was still no response. "See the little peaks and valleys?" the technician asked, pointing at the jagged red line with a carefully manicured fingernail. "Thought is electrical, and the drug sort of throws a chemical tarp over the tops of the peaks and the bottoms of the valleys. We can't read thoughts, of course, but we've learned which little jiggles are the bad memories, the extreme emotions, and we sort of 'program' each prescription to cover 'em up. It is kind of the opposite of the deep brain stimulation that is used to treat dementia. You're about thirty, right? At that age, it takes about two weeks to be completely effective, but wears off pretty fast.

"We don't really erase memories, of course. It's sort of like when a magician palms a coin and makes it 'disappear.' The quarter is still there; he's just done a sleight of hand trick. So Oblivion is like a sleight of mind trick, in a way.

"Bottom line, I promise you," added the technician with the perfunctory grin back on his face, "is that Oblivion is one-hundred-percent effective at blocking unpleasant memories when it is carefully monitored, kept in your system and will help you, uh, smooth over the, uh, disappointment and anger that are keeping you awake."

"You mean I'll forget my wife and daughter completely?" asked Daniel, anxious and edgy.

"No, no, no. Just the painful stuff."

Daniel did not respond immediately, but said: "I'm going away after this, for a week in Oakland, west of here."

"Vacation, huh? You should really count your blessings," continued the technician. He coughed into his hand. "You're getting the drug earlier than most because someone at the Sophist's knows someone, I guess. I hear you're the best carpenter in Light's End. That didn't hurt either."

"We call it the 'Knocker's Club.' I couldn't even afford this without the Knockers," said Daniel, and wiped the sweat from his brow with his left hand.

"Right now, we can cover up the loss of a loved one, or a terrible auto accident, or your dog dying, as long as you remember to take your medication. You know what they say..."

"What you don't know won't hurt you."

"I think that's: 'what they don't know won't hurt you'," Daniel corrected and let his left hand drop to the lap of the white, paper hospital apron he wore.

"Oh, yeah. That."

Whang pressed the brown button next to the door jamb of his house with the index finger of his left hand. The sky above him was grey and sullen, swollen and churning with the threat of a violent outburst, heavy with a drowsy, deep-throated rumbling. He rubbed his temple with the first two fingers of his left hand.

Daniel stood on the small porch that he'd constructed to the specifications of the blueprints for the "Warham No. 203 two-story Craftsman" house that had been built one-hundred-forty-four years ago from a kit bought from a long-defunct company called Sears and Roebuck and delivered by train to the Light's End depot. His right hand, buried in his right pants pocket, twisted compulsively like a trapped animal on the black stone that bore his secret "Azrealite" name beneath the worn cloth. He shifted his weight from his left to his right foot and then back again as if the concrete porch was hot. It was not.

His wife, Denise, had put everything that was her into the house that was built by the unyielding, immutable laws that define how the material universe works and more specifically the heart mind and will of every human being who'd ever drawn breath in that universe and that Daniel illogically and without conscious thought pushed against, impotently tried to manipulated, and hated even as he used them as a carpenter to earn the money that sustained his life. She had put everything including her adamant compliance to the neighborhood association's demand for historic accuracy, her hope for a better life for herself and Ruthie, her dream of respectability (she was, after all, a member of the town's most influential family, the Azrealites), her taste in color and texture and form and utility, her personality, and even her marriage. She had nagged him endlessly about not installing HousMom against the association's rules. He had encoded her voice in HousMom as revenge when he'd installed it anyway. He was vindictive in that way.

Her Christmas wreath that should have been removed and stored in the attic still hung on the front door, her mute rebellion against Daniel's defiance of the rules of the association and his disdain of her love of tradition. According to Daniel, the neighborhood association's rules to maintain the historic accuracy of the district were all a sham.   There wasn't a single original scrap of wood, stone or glass left in the house; the wreath was made of plastic, and the marriage had been as phony as the wreath.

Though he knew it was empty, Whang slapped the small, medical pump attached to his belt over his right hip with the hope he'd dislodge a drop of Oblivion. But nothing changed. The wreath still hung and the bronze house number on the door still read 1426 as Daniel sneered at Denise's small, flat, cheap cross that he'd bolted on the door above the wreath, bronze and green-veined with oxidation. He made a mental promise to himself: the cross would not hang there much longer.

He placed his palm on the wall next to the front door against the cool, smooth metal of the slightly raised pad that controlled HousMom and, therefore, his house on Goodwin Street in the old Stonebreaker Heights district of Light's End, the house that his wife, Denise, had pushed hard, very, very hard, too damn hard, to buy. HousMom recognized his fingerprints, and the front door unlocked electronically with a click.

Her house was directly across the street from what had been the home of the town's infamous poet and mathematician more than a century earlier, infamous according to Light's End because Schlomo Nantier had been a Christian, and infamous for the rest of Maine because both he and his wife were murdered there. For some reason beyond his understanding, the Realtor had told them when they were looking for a place that its proximity to an historically important artifact alone raised the value of the house.

He'd told the Realtor to her face that was ridiculous. Daniel was not known for his discretion. Denise's face had flushed scarlet with humiliation.

But Denise had said over and over and over again, wasn't he a carpenter and wasn't he capable of doing most of the work to repair it, and that would save tons of money so that they could afford to buy it? And didn't their daughter deserve better than a crummy apartment?

Oblivion apparently didn't consider that memory a big one. He rubbed his temple with the first two fingers of his left hand, then slapped the empty pump on his hip again.

There was a faint whir of recognition by HousMom, the home computer he'd installed "for the sake of safety and energy conservation," and the door hissed open and back into the wall. Daniel stepped inside, and the door hissed closed behind him.

"Good afternoon, Daniel" said HousMom in Denise's voice, and Daniel turned out of habit to face the computer's large camera lens recessed in the interior wall of the house on his left. Hanging on the wall to its right was Denise's painting of white, roaneberry flowers.

"Today's date is July 18, 2062. The weather forecast calls for overcast skies with possible thunderstorms. The current temperature inside is 70 degrees. Your heart rate is slightly elevated..."

"Shut up," Daniel said. "I don't want to hear my weight or if I need eggs for the fridge, or if the trash needs to be taken out. My wife. My daughter..." he began, but could not finish.

"As you wish. You have twelve voice mails and thirty-seven emails. The first voice mail is from Mrs. Debra Smith, the second from Greg Mitchell, the third..."

"Stop it! Stop! Stop!" he commanded and slammed his open palm against the screen. Except for his labored breathing and the hiss of the heater vents, a protracted silence followed. He composed himself emotionally. "Are any of the messages from Doctor Bodoni?"

"No, sweetheart," answered HousMom. "The doctor is still out of town until Monday."

Daniel laid his forearm on the screen and, leaning forward, buried his stubbled cheek against it, fighting to erase the images that were alternately flashing in his mind. The heating vents in the wooden floors sighed in the otherwise silent house. After long moments, he lifted his head and mechanically looked around her judiciously furnished living room behind him, seeing everything but receptive to nothing that he saw.

"Are any of the message from the pharmacy?" he finally asked the computer as he straightened away from the wall, restraining a growing uneasiness.

"No, darling."

"Stop that. You will not speak again until I request information."

He moved into the living room that was all Denise and nothing Daniel. He looked at the built-in white bookshelves on either side of the non-functioning stone fireplace, and at Denise's figurine collection of cats displayed there, at the translucent, pale, yellow curtains and their tiny twinflower pattern on the windows above the shelves, and at the wainscoting and molding that partially defined Craftsman houses. The deep-throated rumbling of the impending thunderstorm outside was muted and subtle.

"Get me John...no, Jim, uh..." he demanded of HousMom. "I can't remem..."

"Jake Horne?" interrupted HousMom.

"Get me Jake Horne now."

"I will do so," said HousMom. "I will contact his office first."

"And get rid of that damn voice!" Daniel added, his voice flat with suppressed anger and his stubbled jaw clinching and unclenching as he ground his teeth. "Reset to default. Now!"

"Compliance impossible; default voice erased," answered HousMom in Denise's clear, reasonable voice. "I am receiving a busy signal from Jack

Horne's..."

"Damn it!" interrupted Daniel, "Keep trying!! Do I have to do everything around here?!?"

"Of course not, Daniel; I will try his home now," said HousMom.

The doorbell rang.

"Whoever it is, get rid of them," ordered Daniel as he rubbed his temple with the fingers of his left hand. "I'm getting a headache."

"It is Denise's dearest friend, Debra Smith; the president of the Stonebreaker Heights Neighborhood Association," said HousMom as Whang listened to the front door unlock and hiss back into its recess in the wall.

"Hello!?! Is anyone home? My goodness, it looks like it could rain cats and dogs out here!"

"Come in, Debra. Welcome," said HousMom. "Please leave your umbrella in the stand and your raincoat on the coat rack next to the door. Daniel is in the living room."

He sat in cold, silent rage with his clenched right fist on the arm of his chair as Debra Smith placed her umbrella in the stand and glanced with disapproval at HousMom.

"Oh, there you are, Daniel," she said, and took several steps toward the living room as she began to unbutton her dry, yellow, plastic raincoat. "I hope I'm not intruding, but I got concerned when I left messages and no one answered. Please, there's no need to get up."

"You're right," Daniel said with naked disdain as he ignored her by glaring at his fireplace.

Debra stopped, her raincoat forgotten, the smile frozen on her face.

"As I was standing on your porch, I noticed that someone or something has kicked down the little walls to Ruthie's sandbox at the side of your beautiful house, and scattered the sand around. Is everything all right?"

"Not that it's any of your business, but I knocked it down to stop the neighborhood cats from using it as an outhouse and a place to bury half-eaten rats. Now, what do you want, Debra. Make it short; I'm not really in the mood for chit-chat."

"I hope it's not too soon to visit," she said, ignoring his comment and beginning to unbutton her raincoat again. "You must be beside yourself with grief, Daniel."

"Not really, I'm on Oblivion."

"Oh," she said, her disapproval naked and her hand immobile over the second button on her wrapper. "You're on...you do know she's gone...and why? You haven't forgotten..."

"I know," he interrupted. "I guess that's not the part that hurts."

The heater vents hurrrmmmmmed until the resurgence of the deep-throated rumbling outside broke the awkward silence.

"I loved your wife like a sister, Daniel. She was the sweetest, most giving, most compassionate woman I've ever known. So active in the community, and she loved you and Ruthie so much. She always said you were a wonderful provider for your family. I'm frankly stunned that this, uh, uh, happened."

"Really? I'm frankly stunned she didn't run off with that weenie of a husband you married."

The consoling smile melted on Debra's face.

"Now that you're finished with your phony-baloney condolences, why are you really here, Mrs. Debra Smith."

"I also came today," she continued, her tone now emotionless, "to discuss the matter of your HousMom, Mr. Whang." The hand over the button on her raincoat dropped to her side. "As you know, Stonebreaker Heights is an historic district, and each owner signs an agreement when he purchases it agreeing to maintain the historical integrity of his home. Your home computer is a breach of your contract with the association..."

"Sure it is," said Daniel he rubbed his temple with the fingers of his left hand. "That's why I installed it," he lied.

"...and your vendor told us of your purchase of a HousMom just before Denise...left. I'm here to tell you that, by association contract, it must be removed immediately."

Daniel rose slowly from his chair, and Debra stepped back instinctively.

"And I'm here to tell you I'll remove it just after hell freezes over, Mrs. Smith. And you'll now kindly remove your fat butt from my house."

"Daniel.." she objected, and stopped. "You will hear from our lawyer," she said, turned, walked to the front door, and snatched up her umbrella as she did so. The door hissed open as she approached.

"You betcha, and I expect good news!!" shouted Daniel as she passed through the doorway. "He's a lodge brother!" he lied.

"Please come again, Debra," said HousMom as the door hissed closed. It was then that the thunderstorm roared and broke with all of the arcane fury of a woman scorned.

Daniel smiled at the thought of Debra, umbrella unopened and forgotten in her wrath, suddenly drenched to the bone. He kicked the leg of the faux-antique end table next to Denise's pale blue sofa with enough force to send the digital photograph frame tottering. Daniel snatched it up before it could fall, and watched as the images rotated through scenes of Ruthie with a robotic toy cat in the sandbox behind their house, of Ruth and Denise holding hands in front of Light's End's landmark lighthouse, of Denise smiling over a pot on the stove in the kitchen.

He thought of the sand in the broken sandbox turning into a sludge spreading out like molasses under the drenching rain. He looked at Denise's painting of white turtlehead flowers that hung on the pale yellow wall perpendicular to the fireplace, and hurled the frame with such force that it shattered, its shards falling to the hardwood floor.

"Damn it!! Get me Jake Horne now!" he barked as he walked to the entrance to the kitchen that opened onto his den at its opposite end, slapping the pump over his right hip to dislodge a nonexistent drop of Oblivion.

The slightly diminished rain outside spistissing on the roof of the Craftsman house was the source of the low roar inside Daniel's den. That sparsely furnished den was his only refuge in a house that was otherwise ninety-percent Denise and nine-percent Ruthie. On a small, scarred table next to a ratty, overstuffed chair and beneath a HousMom wall station sat his red fez embroidered in gold thread with the Knockers diamond-shaped emblem of small, interconnected crosses, his coffee mug in the shape of a well-endowed woman's torso, the burnished, wooden plaque honoring him as the Knocker of the Month, his replica wooden mallet, his liquor bottles, and three crystal shot glasses. Inside the locked doors of the table were his collection of rare magazines full of photographs and videos of naked women, and photographs and one video of the women he had had before he'd married Denise. To the left of the HousMom terminal hung Denise's painting of blue Harebell flowers.

Daniel picked up the Knockers mug, carefully filled it with Scotch, and moved to his faux leather chair. Before he sat down, Daniel took a polished, black stone out of his pocket and looked at his secret Knocker's name inscribed there, and thought of his one claim to respectability, the Knockers, and of their president, Jake Horne. He returned the stone to his pocket and sat down.

"I could lose the house," he whispered, and took a long sip of Scotch.

Denise had wanted a house in the historic Stonebreaker Heights district not only because they simply could not afford one of the corpulent old houses in midtown Light's End, or even one in the newer housing districts on the outskirts of town, but because that's where her "people" lived.

"Who the hell cares?" he said to the empty house, took another long sip of Scotch, and chuckled briefly.

Stonebreaker Heights had been built in 1939 as a low-income housing development meant to relocate the black residents from Lost City where blacks had been segregated for decades by the mostly white citizens of Light's End. But when need overwhelmed tolerance, and Block Lake had been built to alleviate damage to their town by flooding Lost City, something had to be done to alleviate the guilt felt by the compassionate Light's Enders.

The housing division on the western outskirts of Light's End had gone through three long cycles of deterioration and regeneration, and was now an "artists colony," the home of semi-professional and amateur writers, musicians, and artists who mostly made a meager living at a hated day job in anticipation of evenings spent grousing about how artists are misunderstood and unappreciated although superior people. Grousing was easier than actually producing enough paintings and pottery to be sold at weekend craft fairs to pay their bills.

Denise was an artist, although she had never sold a painting for more than $50. Despite that, it was regrettable to Denise that Daniel was only a mundane carpenter with no artistic sensibilities who earned a miserly $40 an hour, just enough to pay the family bills and buy a few wants, therefore making them barely acceptable but certainly not enough to make them respectable to their neighbors. But no one, Daniel mused, got everything they wanted in life, not even Denise.

Daniel smiled and took another long sip of Scotch.

"Daniel," said HousMom with the patience of a bruised lover, "I have located Jake Horne. Do you still wish to speak to him?"

"Jake Horne! Jake! Put him on, you idiotic piece of junk!" said Daniel as the rain on his roof muffled into the slow, incessant drone of a billion tiny feet. He subconsciously rubbed the anomaly on the back of his head beneath his hair. "I've got a splitting headache," he said to no one in particular.

HousMom's screen filled with the yellow teeth and the fat, stubbled face of the High Demi-Urge of the Knockers Lodge who took a deep drag on the outlawed cigar that hung from the cut of a mouth in a distasteful face full of slightly hidden superiority.

"Daniel, you old tail chaser!" The cigar bobbed in Horne's mouth as he greeted Daniel by forming the Knocker's secret sign with the fingers of his left hand. "As above, so below. How are you feeling today, my boy?"

"Like crap. I can't eat or sleep or work, Mr. Horne. This thing is eating me up. Sometimes it's like she's still in the house."

"Yes, I know your... situation. Everybody in Light's End knows what happened. It's time to start getting over it, and you might start by erasing her voice from your HousMom, Daniel. But, whatever you do, you need to buck up and act like a man, my boy. Whining is not an option for a Knocker, eh? After all, you chose her, and, I might add, over the advice of all of your lodge brothers. You choose her with all her faults and her unfortunate, misguided belief in a 'god.' She might as well have believed in a giant teacup orbiting the sun, or unicorns, or Satan."

"I'm not whining, Mr. Horne," Daniel said, and took a drink of Scotch.

"Call me Jake. With time," continued Horne, ignoring Daniel's objection, "you'll realize that women are evolution's biggest mistake, albeit a necessary one; the more I know about them, the less I want to know. I admit they do have some value within the limits of their use. And I know it hurts right now, but you've got to remember that there are six billion of them infesting the world, all with the equipment to give men what we want.

"You're still young, Daniel, and not unattractive. If you're open for some advice from someone who's been around since Adam wore pants, the best medicine for you is to get back in the saddle as soon as possible and find yourself a new skirt."

"No, no, no," interrupted Daniel, his face flushed red from rising anger. "That's not why I called, Mr. Horne. "About three weeks ago, I went on Oblivion..."

"Ah, Oblivion," interrupted Horne, the split in his face spreading into a yellow smile. "Good stuff. You put a bullet in your tax man, pop a pill, and you won't remember a thing the next morning. One of my favorite drugs."

"I went to Oakland for a couple weeks, and just got back. My prescription expired while I was gone, and I'm out," said Daniel with growing impatience. "And the drug store is closed today. You have pull in town, and I'd like you to give the pharmacist a call to get him to open for me until I can get to my doctor tomorrow morning."

The grin froze on Horne's face.

"Why would I do that, Daniel? What's in it for me?"

"Well, you're a lodge brother..." he said as he vigorously rubbed his temple with the fingers of his left hand. "I'm sorry; my head is splitting in two."

"Daniel! You've forgotten a basic tenant of the Knockers, my friend.

Enlightened self-interest. And to be blunt, since I own everything and everyone in Light's End, directly or indirectly, I can't imagine how this benefits me. What are you going to do, build me a bookshelf?"

"But, Mr. Horne!! Jake!!! I'm getting flashbacks..."

"Stop whining," barked Horne. "And you need to remember who you are talking to and reign in that temper, my boy. You've always had a reputation for being a bit of a hot-head. Here's what we'll do. You get a life, and call me back after. Until then, as above, so below."

The screen blinked and faded to black. Daniel finished the last of the Scotch.

As Daniel rose from his chair, his anxiety and fear no longer masked by Oblivion, and the boyhood rage that had first been inflamed by his father's physical and verbal abuse and his mother's cloying impotence to stop it, that had crippled all of his human relationships and made him a pariah in Light's End, bubbled to the surface, and he spoke the name that had brought peace and hope and love to his wife in an otherwise miserable marriage, the name of the man that Daniel both vehemently denied had ever existed and nevertheless openly hated:

"Jesus," he blasphemed. "Where would I live if I lose this dump?"

Under the ridge of his brow, his eyes burned with unholy fire and the sting of the Scotch, and his hand shook as he sat his mug on the side table next to his chair.

"Would you like me to call Mr. Horne back?" asked HouseMom.

Daniel looked down at the naked mug, and looked up at HousMom.

"Shut up," he hissed, the muscles of his jaw visibly clenching and unclenching. Daniel picked up the mug, and looked at its exaggerated breasts and looked at HousMom.

"Daniel," said HousMom in the condescending, placating tone he hated, "is your temper getting out of control again?"

"SHUT UP!!" he screamed and threw the mug at the terminal. It smashed against Denise's painting next to HousMom, the remaining Scotch weeping slowly down the blue flowers.

"Daniel," said HousMom, "your outburst of anger is not healthy."

"We'll just see about that," he whispered, and, walking to its door, stepped out of the den into the hallway. The rain outside and just on the edge of his consciousness muffled into the incessant drone of millions of erratic tiny feet

"Daniel?" asked HousMom, the concern obvious in her voice although its volume was somewhat diminished by the increasing distance herself and her master. "What are you going to do?"

Daniel struck the wall with the heel of his left hand just below Denise's painting of pale yellow Bluebeard-Lily flowers as he strode down the hall to the utility room at the back of his house.

"Wouldn't you like to know," he muttered more to himself than to HousMom, and sneered.

Daniel struck the wall again with his hand, and harder, now further down the hall on his way to his utility room.

"Daniel," said HousMom, now almost a whisper, "this is completely unacceptable. I am going to call for help."

"No you're not," said Daniel, and stopped when he reached the utility room. He moved to a small table that stood just to the right side of HousMom's master control panel recessed just to its left of one of Denise's many paintings of blue flowers, and picked up the thick, flat disc that was his recoil-less sledgehammer. Under the ridge of his brow, his eyes burned. He slid his left hand through the strap of the disc, raised his hand to the level of his chest, and snarled:

"You are unacceptable," said Daniel to HousMom and the wife who'd betrayed and deserted him, and the daughter he'd never see again. The thunderstorm boomed and then, spent, wept itself into silence.

Daniel pressed the button on the edge of the disc. HousMom's control panel exploded BAF in a thin cloud of dust and tiny shards of lathe.

As the debris settled away from the hole he'd knocked in HousMom's control panel, Daniel staggered back.

"Oh God, oh my God, oh GOD!!" he screamed and screamed and screamed, his face distorted with shock and horror.

Deputy Clide Stacy, his body bent at the waist and supporting his weight with his right hand, palm pressed flat against a wall where one of Denise's painting hung, vomited on his galoshes and the floor. He missed hitting the lumpy, long, white sheet soaked with an abstract blood rose at one end by inches.

"Well, at least we know she didn't run off with anyone," said the old man whose voice was distorted by the filters stuck in his nose. The name tag on his white coat identified him as Peter Staabnick, Coroner. He raised a fold of clothing with a small, extendable metal rod. "There's sand all over this one, Rusel."

"This doesn't make any sense," said Chief of Police Rusel Gilet through his surgical mask, tracing a tiny, metal plate attached to the bottom of the ruin of HousMom. Below that lay the shattered frame of Denise's painting of purple Joe-pye "weed" flowers. Below that lay a puddle of rainwater from Gilet's yellow rain sicker. "Unless he wanted to give himself away. Here's the required tag identifying himself as the installer, Pete, so he must have known that it's also an alarm system. If a HousMom senses any threat, including to itself, it instantly screams at us down at the station."

The coroner shook his head as the policeman straightened to face him. "I can only hazard a guess, Rusel. Maybe he just didn't care anymore. He was wearing an Oblivion pump. So..."

"Maybe he forgot," said Rusel for the coroner. The police chief wedged his night stick under a thin, yellow, plastic strap, and lifted a toy pail away from the body.

"This one is the real tragedy," he continued, and looked down inside the pail on the end of his night stick. "OH GOD!" he yelled, and dropped it.

"It's full of maggots!!!"

Daniel pressed the button on the edge of the disc. HousMom's control panel exploded BAF in a thin cloud of dust and tiny shards of lathe.

As his left hand fell rose to the level of his chest, he sneered:

"May the Lord bless and blah blah blah."

He pressed the button, and Denise's upturned face as she sat quietly in the recliner in the living room with her open Bible on her lap exploded into a red meat rose spotted with tiny white shards of bone.

Daniel shook his head violently to erase the pain and the image.

His face was spattered with blood. His hand raised to the level of his chest, he pressed the button, and Ruthie's smiling upturned face as she sat with her plastic pail in the sandbox in the backyard exploded in a tiny red meat rose spotted with tiny shards of bone.

Daniel shook his head violently to erase the pain and the image from his head as the debris settled away from the hole he'd knocked in HousMom's control panel, and staggered back.

"Oh God, oh my God, oh GOD!!" he screamed and screamed and screamed, his face distorted with shock and horror.

His hands flew, unconsciously, one each to each side of his face, palms against his cheeks. He felt the cool, smooth metal surface of the recoilless sledgehammer strapped to his left hand, and recognized it, flat against his unshaven left cheek.

He pressed the button.

THE END

Under Wraps

U nmistakably, the wisps of grey hair in its irregular teeth came from a human head, but surely not from his nearly bald pate. Reluctantly, Schlomo Nantier resigned himself to the truth, took his comb, and ran it through the memory of his hair.

Nantier stood on the street corner by a black, cast-iron lamp post. The rusting, weather-beaten sign on it read: "T e Best Li tle Town Aro nd." The old man squinted up into the sun at the hotel before him that, corpulent and feminine, rose like a huge, three-layered cherry cake. The sun hung low on the edges of its roof as Nantier imagined gumdrop houses, naughty German children and cannibalistic witches. Above the roof, a dirty splatter of gulls hung and then swirled and hung again in restless search of a roost.

The massive hotel rose in sedate, ethereal, Victorian beauty. The Crawford was the most famous building in Light's End, Maine, and the residence of Jake Horne, The Fat Man, the infamous head of the Azrealite cult and the Tenebrae Church. It was rectangular, symmetrical, and alive with static movement. A round turret capped with an inverted, sky-blue cone faced the street and Nantier. On the ground floor, a door with a burgundy cloth awning opened onto the restaurant where Nantier had met Horne on numerous occasions.

He walked across August Street to the old servant's entrance, a set of weather-beaten double doors in the hotel's west face. Nantier raised a mottled, bony hand, and knocked. The door swung partially open onto a small vestibule, a door to his right, and almost vertical stairs in front of him bathed by somber light. Nantier wrinkled his nose and the thick glasses on it at a subtle but foul smell.

A smear of black with white paws and luminous yellow eyes crouched on the foot of the stairs. The cat looked at the old man with the utter disdain of complete ownership and unequivocal, occult power.

182

"That's Oreo," said a disembodied voice to Nantier's right. "She actually owns the Crawford, so I guess I rent from her."

In one silent, graceful movement, Oreo swept fearlessly, a whisper of cool air, up the narrow stairs, pausing once to glance suspiciously over her midnight black shoulder at Nantier before she finished her ascent and was gone.

"I don't mean to be rude," said Nantier to the hulking bag of wet flour in a stained, full length apron that was Jake Horne, "but, that stench? Did something die in here?"

"Wouldn't be the first time," replied Jake Horne. He ran a beefy hand over the anomaly under the thick fringe of red hair at the back of his otherwise bald head. "You just missed corned beef and cabbage. Come on in."

Horne sloshed ahead, his shifting internal organs seemingly disconnected from his skin. Nantier stood behind him in the doorway to a cramped, dark kitchen puckered by shadows. Dust motes hung, somber and timeless, in diffused shafts of pale, yellow sunlight seeping through the partially opened curtains of one tiny window. An oversized butcher block and two chairs gobbled up space in the middle of the room. In an iron ring in the ceiling over the block hung a suspended spew of butcher knives.

"Take a load off," said Horne. He waved a flabby invitation at the old poet to sit as he eyed a framed doily on the wall next to a refrigerator that read: You Are What You Eat. He pushed its left corner up in a reflexive and useless effort to straighten it.

Nantier sat in a chair sideways to the butcher block and looked at the moist flour that was Horne's forearms. "If you don't mind my saying so, you look like hell, Jake."

"It's hereditary."

Horne picked up a cheap cigar on the Formica counter top next to the refrigerator and stuck it into the cut of his mouth.

"Didn't we get together for our first philosophical argument down at the bus station about twenty, twenty-five years ago?"

"Park's Drug, thirty years ago. Does it seem chilly in here?"

Nantier glanced up at the ominous knives above him. He ruunked his chair back and from beneath the raw blade directly over his head. One drip of cold sweat crawled down his wrinkled forehead over his right eye.

"Really. Thirty years. I've been lousy with dates since Adam wore pants, Nantier. You should know that. Time is meaningless to me."

"I wish I could say the same. I'm seventy this year."

"Well, then, let's make this an anniversary celebration, shall we?" Horne smiled like a cat with an unhinged mouthful of canary. "Would you like me to beat up some eggs?"

"Couldn't you just reason with them instead?"

"Ha ha ha. No eggs. So here's what we'll do. I always tell the truth when it serves my purposes. So, you may ask me anything you'd just die to know, and I'll spill my guts. "

"All right, then. Who are you, Jake Horne?"

"Again?! Boy, you really must want to die." Horne's eyes burned with unnatural light as he opened the refrigerator and the freezer door inside. "Who do you think I am?"

"Well, some people say you're Eliphas Levi reincarnated. Some say you're Alester Crowley, but that doesn't work. Some even say you're Satan."

"Ah, always keep 'em guessing," said Horne as his fat hands came out of the freezer with a thick, malformed triangle of something wrapped in brown butcher paper. The Fat Man moved to the butcher block and gently laid the stained, freezer-burned bundle in front of Nantier.

"What's this?"

"Some things are best kept under wraps," said Horne, "but, since you've asked, it's the proof that you won't accept of the nasty little story that will answer your question, you old fool. You still like stories, don't you? You've certainly told enough of them over the last three decades. And no one knows better than you that Light's End is chock full of horror stories.

"Some are even true."

"**Y**our kitchen smells like blood," complained Nantier as he looked down at the thick, disjointed triangle wrapped in freezer-burned paper lying on Horne's butcher block. Tiny beads of sweat were gathering around the edges of the paper tape that sealed it.

"Is there some reason it's cold as a tomb in here, Jake? I've got goose-flesh."

"Tea?" The Fat Man set a small pot on the stove and turned on a burner. "I'll need to cut our little chat short, Nantier. I'm expecting company. Cynthia Wells, my hotel manager, and Archie Killingsworth from the convenience store. Linda Richards from *The Citadel* newspaper. I'm sorta playing matchmaker with Archie and Linda. Archie is a real up-and-comer, and I think they'd make a cute couple."

"No tea, thank you." Nantier pushed at the sweat on his left temple with an arthritic hand and looked up at the utensil ring in the ceiling and the serrated blade of the fish-gutting knife hanging directly over his head. "Aren't they all members of your sham Tenebrae 'church,' Jake?"

"Yessss. As for the smell, I didn't really just cook corned beef, and this isn't really a kitchen. It's a secluded little closet where I butcher meat; cold-storage where I can come and spend quiet time, strangling and slaughtering animals that my guests and I will sacrifice later to the profane and nascent Lord of Flies. I'm beginning to sound like you."

"Very funny. At least that explains the crown of metal thorns."

"Crown of...the knives? You really do have the sensibility of a poet. Completely out of touch with reality. By the way, those little stories you write about me and everybody else in 'Light's End.' You know, the one's where you change the names of everyone? I know 'Jake Horne' is me. Do you actually believe that stuff?"

"Me?" replied Nantier as he cringed his chair back from beneath a knife. "I write poetry, not short stories. I thought you wrote them."

"Not a chance. But that doesn't change the question. Do you believe the stuff in them? Like the one about the giant maggot buried under Elliot's Head? That Caleb fathered a monster on a naiad?"

"Of course not. It's difficult to know the truth, but the supernatural stuff is symbolic. The maggot represents the consequences of Caleb's sin."

"Really." Horne smiled with a mouth full of yellow teeth, and lumbered to the chair opposite Nantier.

"And the old lighthouse really is an inverted well into Hell, and Issac Azreal shot an angel?"

"As you already know, the lighthouse story is an urban myth that sells candy at your Feasting carnival, and the angel is symbolic of manic hallucination brought on by Isaac's obsession with his sin. The crazy old coot liked to shoot at birds."

"Then I'd guess you believe the same about all the 'living, rotting Lost City corpses underneath Block Lake,' too. And what about the invisible boy?"

"Saw right through it." Nantier squinted and snuffed his disbelief.

"Ha ha again. After all these years, you still intrigue me. For someone who believes in 'God' and devils, you sure are coldly logical about everything else."

"Quit changing the subject, Jake. Logically, the other old coot in this claustrophobic little ice box was going to explain a Jake Horne who's been hanging around Light's End since the 1600's."

"Lots of red meat and exercise," Horne replied around his bobbing cigar. "The exercise is when I chew asafoetida while I cut up verbose old fools and drooling babies with a cleaver. The red meat is the verbose old fools and babies."

"I am an old man, now, Jake, but I'm still not frightened by your veiled threats."

"Really." Horne lit his cigar. "Then let's take off the veils."

The tea pot burbled on the stove.

Nantier fidgeted in his chair and looked at the disarming triangle on the butcher block, and then at the unnatural light burning in Jake's slitted eyes. In the eerie silence of the squeezed kitchen, a bead of sweat crawled down his cheek as, somber and timeless, dust motes hung and swirled in the mute light seeping through the window curtains.

"I'll tell my lurid little secret first," said Horne and reached up and flicked a knife that swayed back and forth on the utensil ring on the ceiling over Nantier's head.

"I intend to wipe you and every last one of you constipated, uptight Christians off the face of the earth, beginning here in Light's End. Why? Because you cramp my style. I'd say I've done a pretty thorough job already. You're almost the last Christian left in town. Now, how will I get rid of you, you ask?

"I've been watching you pretend to ignore my tantalizing little freezer-burned package. I've kept the secret inside it all these grueling years as a reminder of why I hate your 'just and holy god.' Typical of you to act like you aren't eaten up with curiosity." Horne wiped a hand on his filthy apron, removed his cigar, and blew a smoke ring over the blade of a dangling knife. "That intellectual petulance, your inability to believe what is right before your hooked nose, is what I will use to destroy you, Nantier.

"Now, you, Schlomo. Who do you really think I am?"

"I don't know where you came from, but I think your father named you after himself, and his father did so before him, and his father before that," replied Nantier. "You're probably Jake Horne the Sixth or something. A nasty, profane enigma full of suppressed rage and pain who takes great, sadistic pleasure in scaring people.

"I don't know why you do it, but most people hurt themselves or others out of guilt or shame as a sort of self-punishment. Some push their pain down inside themselves and leave repressed scars. Some people actually 'talk it out.' Word scars. Some just draw or write what eats at them. Documented scars. Some people drown their pain in alcohol or drugs or sex and cover themselves with invisible scars. That's not you. And some even release it and beat up people – transferred scars– or mutilate themselves. Visible scars. But everyone cries out, Jake, even if it's hidden, even you, even the high priest of the Tenebrae Church. They just do it in different ways.

"Who is Jake Horne? You're a lying, manipulative monster who sows corruption, lust and fear in everyone he knows. You are a desperately lonely, horribly scarred old man who disfigures everyone he meets. There, it took ten years, but I've finally said it."

"Aaaaah," sneered Horne. "Surprisingly perceptive of someone nearly senile, Schlomo. And, in a nutshell, I guess that means I am a chip off the old block."

"Block?" Nantier ruunked his chair back and from beneath a knife dangling over his head. "Is this more of your smoke and mirrors? What is this 'block'?"

"The one buried beneath the ocean at the edge of Eden."

The tea pot whistled on the stove.

"More chicanery?" Asked Nantier as he squirmed in the close, chilled air of the kitchen and stared at Horne's package on the butcher block. "So, who is this 'chip' off of what block? Who is 'buried beneath the ocean at the edge of Eden'? And what does that have to do with who you are?"

The Fat Man removed the smoldering cigar from the cut of his mouth and laid it on the edge of the makeshift table.

"Call this a parable, Nantier, or a riddle. If Adam was the father of mankind, you'd agree that the man who brought sin down on all our heads was a 'man horribly scarred who disfigured everyone alive'? Wouldn't that make me a chip off of Adam?"

"Well..." Nantier took his comb from his shirt pocket and touched it to the wisp of hair on the side of his head. The touch brought awareness and embarrassment, and Nantier replaced it.

"As I'm sure you know, there are those who believe human life began in the Euphrates-Tigris Valley in Eridu, the 'Garden of Eden'. Some even believe that Eridu lies at the bottom of the Persian Gulf today."

Horne rose with effort and took the serrated fish gutting knife from its ring on the ceiling and ran a cautious thumb down its blade. He laid the knife on the block.

"Have you ever wondered if Adam's children buried him at the edge of Eden, in the mud of his own bitter tears?"

"I admit I'd never even thought of Adam dying." Nantier adjusted the pinching glasses on his owlish nose as Horne shambled to the stove.

"Your trashy book says Adam was 930 years old when he died. Hard to believe. But if it's true, Adam must have been alive to the eighth generation of his offspring, his great-great-great-great-great grandchildren. There couldn't have been more than a few thousand people alive."

His back to Nantier, The Fat Man opened a cabinet door above the sink.

"They all lived within a hundred miles or so of Eden. But it must have taken weeks for the news of Adam's death to spread. Imagine Seth, Enosh, Enoch, Methuselah, Lamech and the rest dragging their exhausted families for days to weep at a stone cairn that was weeks old, crying into hands cracked and calloused from toil, some already facing old age and death themselves.

"Do you think they hated him, Nantier?" Horne's flabby right arm shook as he poured something into his left hand.

"You think they despised the man who brought death, sin, disease and hardship into the world? Or did they honor him as the father of everyone there?"

"A little of both," replied Nantier, looking at the knife on the table.

Horne closed the cupboard, then turned and faced his old adversary, his eyes smoldering, his left fist clinched. "Do you think that Cain came from Nod, his town east of Eden, and hid in the bushes around that pitiful mound of dust and stone until his brothers and sisters and cousins lost interest and drifted away?"

The Fat Man lumbered to the butcher block and sat, his breathing labored, his balled left ham of a hand on his thigh. He picked up the knife and rolled the haft back and forth in his flabby hand.

"He was 129 years old when he had his little run-in with Abel, you know. Eve's fair-haired suck-up. He'd spent more than a hundred years listening to them grovel, endlessly bickering and passing blame back and forth; of listening about 'the glory days' when they'd walked with 'god,' of watching Abel kiss their asses. All this while they were scratching, tooth and nail, just to eat, trying not to freeze to death every winter or die of thirst and exposure every rotten summer. A hundred years.

"Small wonder that when Cain's offering was rejected..."

Horne thuk stabbed the block with the knife. His cigar jumped.

"And Abel's stinking, burning slabs of fat wasn't that Cain snatched the smoldering skull of a goat from Abel's altar and stomped away. He had killed his fair-haired brother already, in his mind. He waited to do it for real."

Breathing heavily, Horne wrenched the knife free.

"Cain waited until Abel came to the field where he crouched in the deep stalks, the goat's skull clutched in his fist, his face white with rage, his eyes burning with hatred. And when the sun fell on Abel's yellow-haired head, Cain rose from the field...

"And struck!"

Horne thuk stabbed the block. His cigar jumped. Nantier winced back and from beneath the chaos of knives dangling over his head.

Face flushed and hot, Horne wrenched the knife free.

"The goat's skull ate yellow hair and blood and skin! Cain swung the bloody skull high above his head and struck a second time!!"

Horne thuk stabbed the block. His cigar jumped.

"The skull shattered. Cain swung the bloody jaw that was left over his head and struck...again!!!"

The tea pot on the stove rose to a shrill piping.

His hand on the knife, Horne glared at Nantier who sat in the thunderous silence that staggered the room. His eyes still on Nantier, he let his flabby hand on the haft of the knife fall away.

"I-I'm sorry," he wheezed, his chest rising and falling. "That was uncharacteristically naked of me. Give me a minute, will you."

Nantier said nothing, his face closed. Horne inhaled and exhaled slowly and deeply, the muscles in his jaw relaxing and the blood draining from his face. He picked up his cigar from the edge of the block and stuck it in his mouth.

"Surely," he began slowly, "Surely, Cain must have ground his teeth as he looked beyond Adam's grave into Eden, forbidden to him forever through no fault of his. For if Adam hadn't sinned, Nantier, would Cain have killed Abel? For 700 years, his hatred festered and became a living cancer until Adam died."

Horne stood laboriously up.

"As he stood there, did Cain think he'd be reviled forever as the first murderer, Nantier, or that every trace of his legacy, his family, his city, would be destroyed in a flood dumped on his children by your great, good, murdering 'god'?

"How does this answer who I am, you inept old fool? Give me your hand. Give me your god damned hand!!!"

Horne grabbed Nantier's extended arm, jerked it over the sweating package on the block, and twisted it, trembling palm up.

"I don't need to ask you who you are, Nantier, because I've always known. I know why you harp incessantly about Jesus and God and eternal life."

His slitted eyes pierced Nantier's as he dribbled a dry, yellow stream into Schlomo's hand.

"It's to convince yourself, not me, you narrow-minded, self-righteous old fraud."

Schlomo looked down at the mound of tiny, yellow mustard seeds in his palm.

"Because, if you had faith the size of a chit, you could move mountains."

Horne bent low next to Nantier and blew the seeds off and down and across the sweating package like a dry shower that jumped and skipped across the butcher block like drops of water on a hot stove and spewed out onto the floor and lay still in yellow shame.

"But you can barely move your bowels."

Nantier looked at his empty palm. Horne straightened and glared at his package and his fish gutting knife stuck in the block next to it.

"The proof of who I am sits in front you, Nantier, right under your nose. The truth is this: of all who came that day six thousand years ago..."

The Fat Man sloshed to the kitchen door, his internal organs shifting under his skin. He removed his cigar and opened the door. His mouth split into a yellow grin.

"I was the one who peed on Adam's grave."

The Fat Man stepped outside. The kitchen door closed behind him.

The tea pot screamed on the stove.

The tea pot screamed.

Nantier's forehead was beaded with cold sweat. His vellum hands trembled as he stared at the closed kitchen door, and then at the package sealed with paper tape next to the fish-gutting knife embedded in the block. He glanced up at the snarl of butcher knives hanging from the ceiling over his head.

"I-I b-believe," he shivered. "I believe. Lord, God, help...my unbelief."

Schlomo put both of his hands on the package and broke the paper tape.

He peeled back a chilled, triangular flap of paper, then a second and third. Beneath these lay a sheet of yellowed parchment with the smeared, blood-red mark that Schlomo knew also lay in flesh on the back of Horne's head beneath his hair. Nantier pealed back the last flap. He jerked away the parchment.

And cried out, and cringed back, and flailed out, and ruunked back, and toppled out, and fell thud hard, man and chair, to the floor.

His eyes darted as he fell to see if anyone saw him fall.

Then shock burned away into rage at Horne's transparent attempt to beguile and hoodwink him again with such a cheap trick, and then rage charred into anger and physical pain, and that into humiliation at being shocked at all. Then Nantier twitched twice and lay still, embarrassed, hamstrung with pain, his stick legs clinched to his heaving chest, his worn face hot with blood, his eyes dilated and pooled with tears. He rasped "oh god oh god," to the rhythm of the erratic pounding of his heart. His tongue found the thick and nasty taste of blood in his mouth as electric pain pulsed through raw nerve and arthritic muscle and brittle bone. He put a trembling finger to his lips and came away with blood.

And as he lay on the cold, mustard-seed floor in the diffused shaft of light seeping through the curtains of the room's only window, the tea pot screamed itself dry.

"Ooooh," he moaned.

The alarm clock clattered itself hot.

In his otherwise silent, close bedroom, Schlomo slapped it off with a wobbly hand that he let fall on the letter and the comb that lay by it on the nightstand. The blood-red seal on the envelope promised that a member of Horne's cult would confront Schlomo as an acolyte and leave as a Tenebrae priest today. Staring off into eternity, Nantier lay on his rumpled bed sheets and took inventory of his preparations.

He had posted two envelopes.

The first was a letter to his lawyer in Bangor, Maine, that put his meager estate in order. The largest envelope would travel to Israel, and contained a disc and hardcopy of his exhaustive research into the Azrealite cult, his final work on the Genesis Project, and a warning of the terrifying danger it held even if its hypothesis proved wrong. The third lay next to the computer for Jake Horne's flabby hand.

Nantier pictured The Fat Man ripping it open, reading the letter and tearing it to shreds as he coldly ground its tiny packet of mustard seeds beneath his heel.

"Ninety-two years," Schlomo whispered, not recognizing the cracked voice as his voice. "Ninety-two." And as he lay, he silently thanked God for loving him, for magnificent sunrises and sunsets, for books and babies, for cool quiet spring rains, the startling beauty of star splashed nights, for music, for flowers, for a woman's touch, and for the gifts of salvation and the miracle and mystery of his life.

Then Schlomo began the painful, daily ritual of sitting up, and did so, took his thick glasses from his nightstand and put them on, and slipped his blue-veined feet into house shoes. He took the comb and ran it through the memory of his hair.

The mathematician shuffled into his living room to the blank eye of his computer on a desk stacked with his precious books and manuscripts. He pulled out a chair cushioned with a feather pillow and sat. From the books, he pulled out a journal with Genesis Project scrawled on its spine in his own shaky hand, and laid it by the keyboard.

It was a discipline practiced nearly every day of the twenty years since Jake Horne had filled his palm with shame. He had perfected it in the decade since he had resigned his university chair and moved back into his home in Stonebreaker Heights to pretend that this morning would never arrive.

It was a failed discipline. It was here. He sighed in surrender, turned on his computer, and opened the journal.

And twitched on the cold, mustard-seed floor in the diffused light of Horne's unventilated kitchen, the tea pot screaming itself dry.

Nantier shook the memory out of his head and typed his password: Adam.

And lay embarrassed and angry, his legs clinched to his heaving chest, his eyes pooled with hot tears, his heart pounding wildly. His tongue found blood in his teeth as pain shot through every nerve and muscle and bone. Nantier pushed himself up from the floor and staggered from the kitchen.

The computer blinked awake. Nantier opened the Genesis Project file. The screen filled with unbroken vertical and horizontal rows of Hebrew letters. He typed in Schlomo Nantier and Herbert Wells.

And, outside Horne's kitchen, he leaned against a wall and fought down

the sour bile rising in his throat with a hand over his mouth. Something unseen brushed against his leg, and Oreo swept, cat fearlessly, a whisper, up the stairs, pausing once to glare over her midnight black shoulder as Nantier watched.

On the landing above, Oreo purred by the shoes of The Fat Man who bent with a grunt and clumsily stroked her head. His eyes never left Nantier as the poet removed his hand from his mouth, disgusted by the sudden awareness of blood there.

"Well, old man," Horne sneered, "Did I finally get your goat?" and began to laugh a painful laughter of yellow teeth, a laughter that twisted his stubbled face and slitted his eyes and convulsed his flour-sack stomach.

Nantier turned and put his hand on the glass onion knob of the out door behind him. And the epiphany came.

And Schlomo jerked his hand off the computer keyboard. He shuddered. There was a faint and distant knock on his front door.

Nantier crossed his gnarled hands on his chest, his old eyes clear and calm, and embraced the sweet irony that God had finally erased his nagging doubt twenty years ago through Horne's savage attack on his faith. He relished the thought of Jake's rage when he read Schlomo's letter and learned that the horror that had first shaken Nantier like a limp doll had unintentionally given him the proof for which his soul had so long hungered.

For the bloody thing that lay under wraps on Horne's butcher block, which knocked Schlomo to the kitchen floor, was the leering jaw of a goat.

And, unmistakably, the fair hair in its irregular teeth was not his.

Coin of the Realm

Its bell jingled as Schlomo Nantier opened the glass door of the Bus Station Cafe. The mathematician was met by the anticipated and familiar smells of bacon, eggs, hash browns, and buttered toast that were being overwhelmed by the aromas of lunch: hamburgers, French fries, dynamite sandwiches, tuna melts, and meatloaf. It was Wednesday, meatloaf day, and Schlomo always arrived before the noon crowd.

The cafe was longer than it was wide, with a ten-stool lunch counter ending in six free-standing, scuffed tables with faux marble tops, and several booths around the outer wall showing the wear of more than thirty years of use by hungry Light's Enders and bus passengers. Schlomo took inventory of the five customers in the diner, all in the shirt sleeves of summer then walked to his usual cracked, red vinyl stool, one seat removed from an old acquaintance, Heike Otter, who, indifferent to the fashion and conventions of 1959, wore a loose, white blouse and beige dungarees. She was sitting and chatting with waitress Lucy Wallis who, dressed in the thigh-length off-white dress typical of her trade, stood behind the lunch counter with her left hand on her left hip like a fashion model.

"Hi, Mr. Nantier," greeted Lucy with an additional wave, then turned to the counter behind her. Heike glanced at and recognized Schlomo with an affirmative nod that did nothing to disturb her close-cropped, reddish-blonde hair or change the expression of mild boredom she wore to mask a life marred by tragedy and betrayal. Lucy was no stranger to betrayal herself.

"Be right back, Heike," the waitress added, picked up a clean glass, filled it with water from a spigot mounted in the service counter, and

195

moved to meet Nantier.

"The usual today, Mr. Nantier?" the waitress asked, sitting the glass of water on the lunch counter next to a rolled paper napkin holding a knife, fork, and spoon, and removing a stubby pencil from behind her ear as Schlomo sat down.

"The usual, Lucy."

The waitress scribbled Nantier's order on her order pad, tore it off, then impaled it on a vertical nail next to a worn punch bell in a window cut out of the wall and opening onto the kitchen.

"Be right back, Mr. Nantier; gotta make the coffee rounds," Lucy said, and moving to three coffee pots steaming on burners on the service counter, took one and walked briskly to a distant table. Nantier smiled when he heard her laughter diminished by distance.

"Good morning, Heike," said Nantier. "I couldn't help but overhearing a bit of your animated conversation. Mind if I ask, about what?"

"Oh, she's on the 'life is but a dream' kick again, Schlomo," Heike answered with a weak attempt at a smile. You know, 'everyone is just my dream like the ancient mystics have been telling us' business."

"Really," said Schlomo. "Since they've been saying that for just a few centuries short of two thousand years, have you asked her who was dreaming 'the mystics' before she was born? Or, for that matter, who was dreaming the universe before there was anything alive to dream since man was sort of late on the scene?"

"Nope, but I'll sure bring it up if she ever lets me get a word in edgewise, Schlomo. Thanks."

"On second thought, I think I'd like to do it," added Schlomo, and took a twenty dollar bill from his shirt pocket and handed it to Heike as the waitress approached. "And give this to her after I leave. I think you'll know when."

Puzzled but willing, Heike folded the bill and placed in under her plate.

"So, where were we, sweetie?" asked Lucy as she stopped behind the lunch counter in front of her friend and began to refill Heike's cup with coffee.

"You were saying that you can't know anything," summarized Heike, "except what your five senses tell you, and because you can't know everything, you can't really know anything. That's silly, Lucy, and I'm betting big time that you don't really believe that. That would mean that I'm a figment of your imagination, and you're just talking to yourself."

"Pretty much. If the 'world' is my creation, then everyone I talk to is just my creation also. You gotta admit," Lucy opined, "it is possible that you aren't 'real.' I believe I'm talking to a woman named Heike, but I can't prove it. Get it? At no time can I go outside of my senses..."

A hand slapped the punch bell in the window behind the waitress. She turned, picked up a plate of steaming food, and carried it to Nantier.

"Enjoy," she said as she sat the plate of meatloaf, green beans, and brown beans in front of Schlomo. "Need anything else, honey? Ketchup?"

"No thanks, Lucy," Nantier responded and picked up and unrolled his paper napkin, took the fork, and watched Lucy as she returned to Heike.

"Like I was saying, I can't go outside of my senses to verify in any other way that what I am thinking or seeing is 'real'."

Schlomo took a pen from his shirt pocket and, as he ate with his left hand, began to doodle with his right on his paper napkin.

"We are only small lenses," continued Lucy, running the fingers of her left hand through her shoulder-length brown hair. "We see small amounts of the world, and this 'world' exists only as thoughts, a kind of dream, and yes, you are part of that dream. In dreams, you talk with people, you act out things...you live an entire life in dreams."

"I couldn't help but overhear your conversation with Heike, Lucy," Schlomo interrupted, and took a bite of meatloaf. "Do you really think that reality is only what you make it, dear?

"You betcha, Mr. Nantier."

"Are you open to another opinion?"

"Well, I'm working..."

"I'll keep it short. One of the ways we all know reality with certainty is by repetition and cause and effect. If A plus B always equals C, and if we do something over and over again and always get the same result, we are confident of the process and the result." Schlomo ate a forkful of green beans.

"As an example, you've never questioned for a second if there will be air for you to breathe in the next minute, or whether you'll float off into space because gravity no longer exists. Those two events–breathing and staying 'stuck' on the earth– have been repeated so many times, that, frankly, Lucy, you never even think about them." A large section of meatloaf found a new home in Schlomo's mouth.

"And your senses are not the only set, my dear," he continued while he chewed. "Take sight. There are billions and billions of sets of eyes, human and non-human, and they all see the same things. If I hold up a sketch of a circle here, or in India, or in China, everyone will see a circle. No one will see a giraffe, or an airplane, or a gnat."

Schlomo held up a dollop of mashed potatoes.

"They'd all see mashed potatoes, dear. Not a unicorn, or a space satellite or a 1959 Chevrolet." He ate the dollop.

"The same thing is true for all of our senses, for there are trillions and trillions of pieces of evidence of this sort." Another large part of the meatloaf became a part of Schlomo. He chewed for a moment for effect, and spoke again.

"Now, where is your evidence that our senses can't be trusted, Lucy?"

"Well, you know dogs can hear high pitches that we can't hear, Mr. Nantier."

"But we both hear many of the same pitches, dear. Because we don't know everything doesn't mean we can't know anything.

"And frankly, Lucy, as for me being your dream, there is no proof that you or anyone else can sustain even one dream for more than a few minutes, much less fifty years. The old man that I am – the thoughts in my head, the clothes on my back, the furniture in the room in which I stand, and the room itself – and the billions of people alive today who have already lived for many years, each in their own environments, and the billions of people who lived before you were even born, and their circumstances, could not have been dreamed by little, old, limited, you."

"Well..."

"Or the staggeringly complex and incredibly old material universe that existed long before you or any other living thing saw the light of day. Does that make sense?"

Lucy looked at Heike, at the other customers in the cafe, at her order pad, and then at Nantier, the irritation obvious on her face.

"You eat like you're going to a twelve-alarm fire, Mr. Nantier," she said in the scolding tone of a mock mother, and tore a sheet from her order pad. "You should slow down when you eat, honey, or you'll get heartburn."

Lucy handed him the scrap of paper, and Schlomo looked down at his bill of $7.79; there was a greasy partial thumbprint on the right corner. He looked up and smiled at Lucy.

"Come back next Wednesday, and we'll talk again," said the waitress in a more than welcome and familiar, decade-old ritual. "Was everything okay, today?"

"Just a little more, and we'll talk again if you want. Science and history cannot find a single instance when something came from nothing, Lucy. I

agree with science and history. Something has never come from nothing. In fact, nothing has never 'existed,' an oxymoron if ever I heard one. There has never been nothing. There has always been God."

"If you pardon my saying so, it all sounds like doubletalk to me, Mr. Nantier," said Lucy as she wiped the inside of a glass with a little towel.

"And last, but not least, there are other ways we know reality besides our senses, dear. Next time we'll talk about how we knew the world was round long before we saw it was a ball. We knew it with a thing called math.

"We'll talk another time," said Schlomo, and handed her his paper napkin. "Keep the change."

Her stunned and questioning expression was not unexpected by the Schlomo as he rose from his stool, turned, and began to walk to the exit. He knew what she must be thinking: should I say it and insult a regular (after all he is getting old and forgetful) and maybe lose him as a customer, or do I say nothing and end up paying for his meal which I really can't afford to do?

He tapped his finger on the 1959 Double Cola colander than hung on the wall next to the entrance.

"See ya next Wednesday," he added, grinning. The shop bell jingled as he opened the door.

"But, Mr. Nantier?!?" said Lucy, looking at the doodled $20 on each corner of the napkin, and the crudely drawn image of U.S. President Andrew Jackson in its center. "You gave me your napkin by mistake!"

"It's a twenty in my dream world, 'dream boat'," said Schlomo as he glanced back and grinned. The shop bell jingled as the door sighed closed behind him.

Lucy stood behind the lunch counter, her left hand on her hip, as her look of consternation slowly dissolved into epiphany.

THE END

OUR CREATORS

MICHAEL VANCE (WRITER) –

Born in Oklahoma City in 1950, Vance became a professional writer in 1977 and has been published in dozens of magazines and as a syndicated columnist in more than 500 newspapers. His history book, *Forbidden Adventures:The History of the American Comic Group,* was called a "benchmark in comics history." One of his Light's End short stories, *"The Lighter Side,"* was nominated for an international 2004 SLF Fountain Award for Best Short Story. He has worked as an editor, writer, advertising manager, copy writer, journalist, novelist, graphic designer and grant writer, among many things.

Vance also created the new Oklahoma Cartoonists Collection housed in the Toy and Action Figure Museum in Pauls Valley, Oklahoma. He is currently communications director of the Tulsa Boys' Home, a nonprofit agency located in Tulsa, Oklahoma. He is a Christian.

EARL GEIER (INTERIOR ARTIST)–

Admitting he was "born, raised and died in Chicago," where he lives today with some cats and dogs, he is best known for his horror, fantasy and science fiction artwork. In the role playing game industry, his work includes art for Battletech, Mechwarrior, Shadowrun, Earthdawn, Call of Cthulhu, Elric and many others. He has illustrated books for *Cemetary Dance* magazine and in the comix field he has done work for Dark Horse, Now, Innovation and DC Comix Paradox.

CHRISTOPHE DESSAIGNE (COVER ARTIST)–

Born in 1973, Christophe Dessaigne lives in the south of France near Spain. After being a journalist and a scenarist for role playing games, he began to work in photography in late 2007. He is primarily influenced by the sci-fi, horror, fantastic genres of cinema and comics. His creations combine digital photography and manipulation. Most of his work is atmospheric and mysterious, taking place in impossible and surreal landscapes in dark and post-apocalyptic futures.

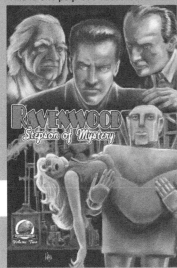

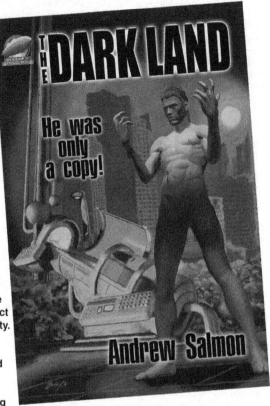

Made in the USA
Middletown, DE
15 March 2020